ABOVE & BEYOND

CHAPTER 1: DEPARTURE

Earth – Aug 30, 2011

For Jack Richman, it is just another day. Waking up on an airplane and hobbling through an airport is like going to the gym—a necessary evil. After a thirty-hour trip in coach, his old knee injury is inflamed.

Maybe a third scoping would help. He thinks. *Or at least wearing that knee brace, again*

Limping through the O.R. Tambo International Airport in Johannesburg, South Africa after the long plane trip was like a surreal dream. With a country so diversely mixed and poor, the high tech European ambience is very deceiving. He could be in Germany; it's pure gravity that guides him toward customs. He's done this many times, in many airports during his career as a journalist. But this time he feels like he was bringing the story to the location instead of discovering it once he's there.

Feeling like a stranger in a strange land, he forks to the right at customs, where aliens are processed. A very distinguished speaking black man opens his suitcases. The inspector carefully looks at the framed photograph, which is lying on top.

"I always travel with our most recent Christmas card portrait," Jack says.

"You're a lucky man."

Jack smiles and says to himself, "I think so."

Last year's Christmas photo op had been a nightmare. His three kids had been tag-teaming colds since Thanksgiving. Getting them dressed like they were going to church took a lot of coaxing. His wife, Christina, had been just about ready to give up. Jack was struggling to set the timer on his new digital camera. He was juggling between the manual and the camera that was barely on the tripod. The kids were insisting that the alley cat, Leo, and their white fluff ball dog, Roxy, both be in the photo. The shot was only as good as it was because he took three versions and photoshopped them together. Next year, he thought, I've got to photoshop my hairline.

"You may proceed." The inspector stamps Jack's passport and points him ahead.

He heads down a bank of post-modern, glass-enclosed escalators towards baggage claim. He feels like he's standing still, and the airport is moving past him. Coming up in the opposite direction, he notices three young, veiled women three steps behind an older man. They are covered from head to toe, wrapped like cocoons in purple and white fabric. Their hats look Egyptian in shape, like something the legendary Nefertiti would wear.

Waiting at the bottom escalator there's a welcoming person holding a sign for the Alzheimer's Association's International Conference attendees. She asks, "And you are, sir?"

"Jack Richman from Chicago, via London and Frankfurt... two days ago."

With no response and after a minute of searching, she checks his name off a list on her clipboard. Jack can see that this conference would be well attended by his colleagues. Some he looks forward to seeing, others, not so much.

Upon arrival, the hotel reception area was packed—too crowded for Jack. Now, an hour later, the crowd is overflowing into the bar lounge. Jack couldn't believe there was a corner barstool waiting for him just on the outskirts of the congested party. Perfect. He is equally comforted by how soft it is. He sighs, exhausted. The trip to Johannesburg was long of course, but more unnerving was how lonely it was to make the trip by himself.

As Jack sits there listening to people mingle, he motions to the bartender for a glass of wine.

"Merlot, please," he asks the bartender.

Jack begins to check the program he'd been handed at check-in. He notices the red headed woman next to him is wearing a badge that says, "Dr. Begley, Brussels, Belgium." He heard her speak in Rome last year, but she was blond then. Good thing she was wearing a nametag. At last year's conference, he had really gotten into it with her during her Q & A period, but they had both enjoyed the verbal sparring. Jack had loved her ideas, but questioned her methodology. She was amused by his rigidity. He truly wanted to speak with her this year to see if she had made any improvements. He puts his nametag on so she could see his name.

"Jack, good to see you again," she said insincerely. Maybe she wasn't looking forward to a repeat of last year. "You're here early?"

"Yes, I had a last minute change in plans. My son, Brian, was supposed to have accompanied me. We were going to make a trip of it, and see a bit of South Africa before the conference started. But you know, things never go as planned so...I'm here alone."

Jack and Brian are sitting at the kitchen table. It isn't the kind of kitchen you'd expect from a published author; it isn't that kind of house either. It is a typical suburban home, outside Chicago, with one exception. Catering to Jack's claustrophobia, there are no window treatments; Jack always has to see the way outside. The kitchen still has the leftover brown nineteen eighties cabinets and spotted white Formica countertops that it had when he and Christina first moved in. They had talked about renovating it many times, but could never come to an agreement on what they liked. Twice they had each made compromises and gone to the store, only to find out that the catalog they were looking at was old and what they wanted had been discontinued. So, they found a way to love what they had; after all, the layout was perfect, with plenty of room for a nice table right by a window that looks out at the backyard. Most meals and homework happen right there. A photo of the entire family, taken in Paris right after Christmas, was proudly displayed in a frame. That had been the family trip of a lifetime! All of the Richman's shared a love of travel, even tiny Matilda.

Buried in piles of travel brochures, Jack and Brian review their planned excursions on his laptop. When they'd planned the trip months ago, Brian had been so excited. Every chance he could, he would Google "things to do in South Africa." But, now that the trip was finally approaching, Brian just sits quietly as they review each part. Jack knows there is something bothering him.

"OK. What's wrong?" Jack asks. "Did something happen today while you were out playing?"

"No," Brian whispers.

"You know, if you don't tell me what it is, there's no way I can help you fix it."

"Well... I don't think you're going to be very happy with me."

"Brian, whatever it is that you did, I promise I won't get upset."

Brian sits for a minute staring at the ground. And then slowly says, "It's just that I'm gonna miss the end of the summer with all my friends. I don't want tomorrow to be the last day I get to play with them." Suddenly Brian starts to ramble. The floodgates were opened. "AND I'm gonna miss the first few days at school AND I won't have all the right notebooks and pencils AND I'm gonna get a crappy seat in class next to some weird kid AND I won't get on a good gym team AND —"

Jack thinks to himself, "Boy, can this kid ramble just like me." He interrupts Brian, "OK, OK. I get the point. So you don't want to go. You'd rather stay here and play video games with your friends than ride horses and elephants and see an amazing part of the world with ME?"

"Well I want to do both, but I can't be in two places at once,

Daddy."

"True. Well, if that's your decision. If you want to stay here, then you can stay here. No point in you being miserable the whole trip."

Brian is silent. Jack shuts his laptop and walks out of the kitchen, leaving Brian sitting there alone, watching his Dad walk away.

Heartbroken, Jack finds Christina, cleaning up in the living room.

"So, Brian just informed me he doesn't want to come to South Africa anymore, that he'd rather stay here to play with his friends."

Christina looks at her crushed husband. She wants to ask him if he thought the plane ticket could be refunded, but she doesn't have the heart to be "practical".

Instead, she gives him a hug. "I'm sorry, honey, I know how much you were looking forward to it."

Jack didn't think the loss of quality time with his son would come at 10! "I thought I had a few more years before his friends were a better option than good old Dad. I thought he loved to travel—he had such a great time in Paris."

"I know," Christina says. "He's about to learn a very hard lesson. You make sure you tell him all the fun stuff you did when you get back. He'll be sorry. Ten's a tough age. His whole world is here, you know?"

Jack had really been looking forward to showing his son that the world had so much more to offer than their little town. Hell, his trip was booked for three extra days so they could go on a REAL safari. He wonders if he should still try and go alone; he certainly wasn't going to get his money back.

"Let's set aside time this week to discuss whatever is on your mind," Dr. Begley finishes. Jack is so tired, for a moment he's not sure if she's coming on to him, or being strictly professional. "I look forward to it."

"Great. I'll catch up with you later."

Dr. Begley turns and starts to work the rest of the room.

Jack's observation as a journalist is that everyone is over-dressed. His relaxed tennis shoes, jeans and a turtleneck make him the Steve Jobs oddball (without the billions in the bank). He wonders if somewhere, in the piles of handouts he received, there is a book about proper attire to attend the Alzheimer's Association's International Conference. Jack believes that there are instructional brochures for everything in life. At one time, when he was starting out, he wrote a ton of them himself, so he was painfully aware of how true this theory actually was.

Hit by a moment of panic, he wonders what time it is. He's supposed to call home to tell them he arrived there safely. Instead of focusing on the call home, he was remembering Dr. Begley in Rome talking about the sense of "now" while in a dementia state.

Dr. Begley had made her theories sound so good with her attractive Belgian accent, but she lacked the research to support them. As his mind drifted he wondered if his lack of focus was something more than jet lag. Jack had been disconnected since he sat down.

People shuffled in the middle of the room near a karaoke machine, which was his cue to get out of Dodge. After an initial blast of screeching feedback, Dr. Begley starting singing "My Heart Will Go On" from *Titanic*. It evoked enough laughter and applause for Jack to throw a bill on the bar and slip out.

Unfortunately, the sound carried out into the lobby. Dr. Begley continued to belt out "once more you open the door..."

No wonder she's devoted so much of her life to studying delusions and dementia, Jack thought, shaking his head. Slipping out of the room, he almost bumped into the AAIC's chairman, Dr. Herman.

"Richman, did I see you having a serious conversation over there with Celine Dion?"

Jack strains to hear him over the embarrassing singing. "I'm hoping the boat sinks sooner rather than later."

"Not soon enough, I think. She's a better talker than singer?"

"Yes, at last year's conference, I was quite impressed with her ideas. She was working on transferring the thought moment to other parts of the memory process before it slipped away. She said her team was 'so close, but so very far away, like the difference of remembering you had a dream last night compared to remembering what the dream was about.' I was hoping to put a chapter in my new book questioning if dementia patients are just always in a dream world. Remember how I confronted her about how she ran her experiment? Her associates were totally defending her, even though they didn't understand? She has good ideas, but her research is suspect."

With no direct flights to Johannesburg from Chicago, Jack's trip takes him a total of 30 hours. He makes sure that he's booked into an aisle seats as close to the exit doors as possible, so he never feels that trapped.) Now that Brian wasn't coming, he will have a full day to recover from the jet lag. However, Jack wanted to be able to take advantage of the extra time to sleep; so he takes an ambient that he was given by a buddy.. He is able to get a solid seven hours of sleep in during the flight from Chicago to London, which was more than he got most normal nights. But he really should've listened when his mother told him not to take other people's prescription drugs... the Ambien gives him a whopper of a dream.

This dream feels like more of a memory than a dream, so the way in which Dr. Begley had described her theory last year, made perfect sense. What's to say there is a difference?

The dream starts at his grandfather's nursing home. Jack is back there, watching the old man slip away to Alzheimer's, breathing that heavy air that is cool and humid at the same time, smelling the smell of the old folks home—antiseptic cleaners and tapioca pudding mingled together. Jack is back there, at the Kennedy-era old folks home, walking down the corridor like he always did, except this time his mother isn't at his side and he is an adult. He comes to his grandfather's room, 1841, and takes a deep breath, afraid of what is behind the door. Then, he walks in, and there is Grandpa Joe lying in bed with his back turned towards him. He rolls over and smiles when he sees Jack. But this time, the look doesn't vanish.

"Hi, Jack." Jack stands there, stunned.

Grandpa Joe sits up and says, "Now don't be making me come all the way over there, I'm an old man... But I am still up to my old tricks."

Just then, Jack notices the live white rabbit on Grandpa Joe's lap.

"Come and sit down."

Jack pulls over a chair from the corner, the same one he always used to sit in. It used to seem so much bigger... He finally says, "Hi. How are you today?"

"Oh, I'm just great. It's good to see you." Jack has never seen his grandfather this lucid for this long. His grandfather continues, "Your kids are getting so big so fast. And Brian, gosh, he reminds me so much of you back in the days when you used to come visit me."

"I know." Jack knows he is dreaming, but his inner mind increasingly questions, how is this possible? On the other hand, he's comforted by the fact that he is sharing this experience with his deceased grandfather. So, he responds with a smile, "It's scary isn't it? God help him."

And with that, his Grandpa Joe reaches over, pats his hand and says with a smile, "No. And as we always say, nothing is an accident."

The next thing Jack knows, he is being asked to put his seat back in its upright position. He has never remembered a dream so vividly. Jack thinks to himself, That Ambien-tini cocktail really is screwing with my head.

Jack snaps back to hear Dr. Herman ask, "And what did she say?"

"Ah, we're going to get together later this week." Jack had already begun thinking of all the questions he wanted to ask Dr. Begley later. He is hoping she will finally get into the nitty gritty details of her research. As always, Jack has a thousand questions. He needs to know how she intends to proceed and if her experiments had finally begun. What were the results? Were they close? Or was this just a nice theory she had yet to prove?

"And what do you think she can add that you haven't already discussed in your other books?"

"Well, let's just say I have a personal interest in the matter."

"Make sure it's a karaoke free zone my friend. How was your trip here?"

"Not too bad. I think I finally figured out the perfect blend of Ambien and gin—an Ambien-tini."

As they laugh, another badge carrier member/drinker, "Rick from Colorado," walks up to them.

"Richman you gonna attack Begley again this year? 'Cause you should ask her if she's done any experiments about self-delusion." The three men cringe as they glance over their shoulders to watch her reach for the "big finish."

Jack laughs, "All I want to see from her is data."

Dr. Herman, "To deal with a personal matter?"

"Exactly."

"Well, from what I understand, this year she's going to be addressing the concept of having less access to short term memories as opposed to having total recall of long term memories," says Dr. Herman.

Jack, still beating the same drum, says, "Oh great, I'd love to see the data collected on that."

"It's in her study results, right next to déjà vu," adds Rick from Colorado.

Jack looks over at the next karaoke singer grabbing the mike from Dr. Begley. She counts off the tune like an old pro. Obviously, this is not her first karaoke rodeo. She sounds every bit as good as she looks with her bluesy rendition of The Lion King's "Circle of Life." How appropriate, now that Jack is actually in Africa.

The completely enamored Rick says, "Oh God, I must have died and gone to Heaven."

Dr. Herman jokes, "Well, I guess that completes the circle of life."

"If this is Heaven, then where did Dr. Begley's number come

from?" Jack retorts.

"Ha ha. I don't know. Why don't you go collect some data and then come to a conclusion Richman?" jokes Rick.

With that, Jack shakes their hands and walks off. The song reminds him how disappointed he is that he wouldn't be taking Brian to see a pack of real lions. Right then he makes the decision that if he can't bring his family to South Africa, he'll bring South Africa home to them.

Nothing could substitute having his son with him, but shopping for Brian and the rest of his family would fill some of the void for Jack. He scoots through the modern mall connecting the conference center to his hotel. He now has enough time to shop for gifts for the family before the opening session. Through the tall glass doors, he exits the back of the conference center and enters an outdoor shopping mall. He alternates from side-to-side, window-shopping in the African-themed center. Even so, he has a feeling that everything here is not authentic, local African goods. This time, he wants real mementos. Ironically, gifts bought from here will be an improvement over the airport variety that he's famous for. But, Jack wants to be more thoughtful this trip, and he knows this store is not where he should be.

He stops for a second in front of a beautiful statue of Nelson Mandela, then glides up a huge staircase to the hotel lobby. He spins through the revolving door and receives a "welcome back" from a security guard. The misting air conditioning, jungle motif, and piped in bird chirping in the vast lobby confirms it —nothing here is handmade. At the concierge desk, he inquires about authentic, African-made gifts.

"It's a fifteen minute trip by cab, sir. We can arrange a car to take you there and back if you wish." The concierge says smoothly.

Jack automatically waves him off and says no thank you out of habit, but then reconsiders. "Will they take credit cards?"

"It's preferable that you bargain in cash. As a matter of course, while you're here, try not to flash any signs of wealth. You should leave your valuables in your safe. So you want a car?"

"Why not? I'll be back down in ten minutes and ready for an adventure." Jack agrees.

Upstairs in his room Jack stares out the window through the smog and dust, wondering which direction the market is. He notices cranes and construction everywhere. He then stashes his wallet, watch and computer in his open safe, then carefully sets the code: 1-8-4-1, his lucky numbers. They always seem to pop up everywhere from airplane flight numbers to dry cleaning receipts.

Jack glances at his suitcase on the floor and how neatly it is packed. Not his doing by any means, Brian had helped him pack. Jack wasn't quite as precise when he packed for himself, but he had his own way of maximizing space.

Brian is trying to make up for backing out of the trip at the last minute. He doesn't want Daddy to forget something or not have enough room for everything. Jack has no idea Brian can fold so precisely – it's taking him forever! Jack can't take the silence anymore.

"You know you'd better watch out—if Mom finds out how good a folder you are, you're going to be helping her with laundry every week."

All he receives back is a faint smile.

Brian can tell his Dad is disappointed in him. He doesn't know how to say he is sorry. He hopes that if he can do everything possible to help his Dad, he can make up for it. But deep down he knows folding a little laundry won't help. So when his Dad isn't looking he buries a small note that says, "I love you. I'm sorry," at the bottom of the suitcase, hoping his father will find it when he unpacked.

Jack appreciates the help, but he is doing it all wrong, and Brian is folding as slow as humanly possible.

"It's OK. Really. I understand. Believe it or not, I was a kid once too. Now, if you really don't want to lose any summer time, get out

there and go play. You're wasting the day in here. I can finish up."

Brian tucks down the socks he has in his hand into the empty corner of the suitcase and smiles.

"Thanks, Dad. You are the best. I'm gonna go call Matt and see what he's doing." The two exchange their secret handshake—they put their index and middle fingers just in front of their eyes. Then they point them to each other and touch them together for a moment.

"See ya."

"Not if I see ya first," Jack adds, completing the ritual. And just like that, Brian runs out the room. Within seconds, Jack hears him Skyping Matt. So much for the telephone.

Just then, his hotel telephone rings, "Your car is ready and waiting for you sir."

Anthony, a scraggily 60-year-old with a gray complexion, stands guard next to his 10-year-old sedan. He is eager to inform Jack that he is a former radio actor.

"I was a star really." He says.

The blue suit he is wearing might have fit him 20 years ago, but now it comically hangs over his limbs, as he lets Jack in the back seat. Anthony and his car smell like an ashtray. As they drive away Anthony coughs repeatedly and apologizes in between each cough. It is very annoying for Jack, who is now gasping for air.

Jack opens a back window just to mask the smell and drown out the hacking and "so sorry" chorus. Unexpectedly, Anthony apologizes with, "Lung cancer's a bitch, but it's not slowing me down." This makes Jack more tolerant of the smell and cacophony of sounds.

As if Jack needs another reminder of why he isolates himself from strangers, Anthony clears the phlegm from his throat.

"First time in Johannesburg?" Anthony asks.

Jack acknowledges it is with a nod.

"What brings you to South Africa, may I ask?" His English

accent sounds like it is coming from a seventeenth century royal, or an unemployed former radio actor.

Jack politely says, "I am writing a book on the international differences concerning Alzheimer's progression. The world symposium is being held at the conference center."

The car nose dives through a ditch and bounces back up on the gravel-surfaced road. "How interesting," the unperturbed driver says between another cough. Jack figures that at least Anthony's chatter will be short because of his bad lungs, which is also probably the reason that driving like a bat out of Hell is not a worry.

"The Rosebank Flea Market is over that mountain." Anthony says, after coughing some more. "Pardon me, the villagers have to be licensed to sell their wares you know?" Jack realizes that everything the driver says is in question form.

"Is it safe?" Jack asks a question of his own.

Anthony retorts, "During the daytime, is the safest, wouldn't you agree?"

Not the answer (or question) Jack wants to hear. Jack notices the oncoming traffic is so backed up that people are getting out of their vehicles to evaluate the wait.

Anthony whispers, "Road construction on the M1 to reach some of the new neighborhoods, is really a problem out here. Right?"

"Right."

Jack is assured that Anthony will be able to circumnavigate the congestion on the return, if he doesn't mind a bumpy ride. Like this isn't the bumpiest drive Jack has ever been on.

Jack reluctantly questions, "There's nothing you can do for your cough?"

"You know here in South Africa some people see Sangomas, or what you would call a witch doctor." (Cough.) "I went and he started coughing right back at me. Then he burped, then he farted. I couldn't get out of there fast enough." (Cough.) "Before I left, he gave me something to drink. Half Bloody Mary, half petrol." (Cough.) "It burnt a hole right through me. It stopped my coughing for about a day, and then I sobered up." (Cough.) "I don't think I'm ready for any more treatments. Right?"

"You know, you could go to a real doctor, right?" Jack can't believe he's talking like Anthony now, nor can he believe that Sangomas are still the primary physicians for some people in this country.

At this time in the afternoon, the sun is relentlessly bright. The car pulls through a manned gate into a huge paved parking lot that is surrounded by a barbed wire fence. The market itself is under a complex of thatched roofs that is centered in the lot. Jack notes that even though he's been let on the property through security, he'll still have to pass through a row of uniformed guards carrying pistols, who are lined up almost shoulder-to-shoulder like a human fence. Before one breaks formation to let Jack through, he looks over his shoulder to see Anthony leaning against the hood of his car. He is already lighting a cigarette off of one he hasn't quite finished. Anthony zigzags both butts in the air to acknowledge Jack's look.

The alarm goes off and Jack rolls over to look at his beautiful wife. Jack always likes to say something positive about the day ahead first thing; this drives Christina insane, because half the time, his positive is her negative. Since they'd met in college, his half-full mentality versus her half-empty attitude has worked for them, even when she used to edit his manuscripts. They can finish each other's sentences, literally.

"Well, today I go to South Africa." Jack says.

"What? Oh crap. I totally forgot. Damn that means..." She stutters sleepily.

He knows she finished the sentence in her head going over each thing she now has to try and finagle because she is going to be two hands short for the next twelve days. Jack hates doing that to her, but he knows that she always makes a bigger deal of it than it really is. Other women wouldn't be able to handle it, but she thrived. The more Christina has to juggle, the better she gets at it. It is simply amazing to watch. She makes the cutest face whenever she worries. He can tell her mind is going a mile a minute when her right eyebrow crinkles.

Jack smiles at her, "It'll all be fine." She is already up and running around the room and barely hears him.

Jack purposefully booked his flight at 11 a.m., which means that he'll be able to have breakfast with his family, and see the morning rush out the door as they go off to camp. He'll have to drive through rush hour traffic to get to the airport, but whenever Jack travels he makes sure he can spend as many final moments with them as possible.

He comes down the stairs and the kids are running around (big surprise.)

"Guys, I'm leaving soon. Come give me a hug." Nothing.

Matilda, his four-year-old "baby girl," tugs at his pant leg after a minute or so and asks him if he can sew Moosey's shirt button back on before he leaves. He tells her he doesn't have time. She frowns and walks away with her little stuffed reindeer in tow.

Jack eats breakfast with the kids and it's normal. Completely. No one seems to care he is leaving for twelve days. Although this upsets him, it is a perfect little snapshot of his life. Christina toasting the pop-tarts; Kimberly, their seven-year-old daughter, hitting Brian; Matilda sitting quietly, attempting to feed Moosey part of her poptart.

As he loads his suitcases into his Volkswagen, Christina loads the kids into her minivan. Jack leans his head into her minivan, like he does every morning, and kisses everyone on their foreheads. He expects a reaction from Brian at least, an extra effort to say, "I'll miss you" perhaps? "See you later."

Christina gives him a quick hug before she gets in the van and tells him to be careful.

He waves goodbye to his family as he watches them back out of the driveway. He realizes, that even when they don't give him what he wanted, they always give him more than what he needed.

Presents galore! The tribal doll outfits will fit Matilda's

dolls and even Moosey. Assorted statuettes representing warriors carrying spears, knives and shields all have protruding points facing upwards so they can really hold candles—Christina will love them. A plethora of thin paper satchels are stuffed with fabric table covers. There are amazing patchwork quilts with colors that shouldn't go together, but not only do they, they work together intensely well and will look great in his living room.

Laid out on many fabric-covered tables are very intricate bracelets woven from telephone wire and slid over crude rolling pins. Each bracelet is more beautiful then the next, so Jack buys 20 of them for his two daughters and wife.

Something comes to life in Jack. Instantly, he becomes an amazing shopper eventually securing scads of bracelets and necklaces at five times less the asking price. His bargaining prowess peaks when he sees the drums, because he knows that Brian will love to drive the house crazy with native percussion instruments. He sees hundreds of them lining a top shelf that wrapped around the entire hut. Bells, shakers, sticks, hand drums, etc... Jack has to have as many as he can carry. He insists that he won't buy any of this collection unless they throw the goat bells in for free. The boisterous craft people show great respect for his confidence. Whatever they are screaming, Jack can tell it is with approval.

Jack looks over and sees another tourist buying goods; he would have sworn it is his wife, Christina. He starts to walk towards her, but when she turns a bit more towards him he realizes it isn't her. Is it so silly of him to think Brian backing out was just part of a ploy for everyone to come and surprise him? He would have noticed the crippling balance on the credit card by now if that were the case. But this woman reminds him so much of her that he glances over at her again. On the second glance, he realizes she looks like the Christina he'd met his first year at SIU, their alma mater Southern Illinois University.

"Mista... are you gonna buy that?" Jack snaps out of his favorite memory (meeting his wife) and looks down at the things he picked out for everyone.

Not to diminish the moment, Jack goes into his pocket and peels off a wad of bills. He hands an artisan, who seems to be in charge, more money than is required by at least twenty percent.

"Here's something extra for your family." He says to the man as he pays in cash. "I know my own family will love these gifts."

With his bags in front of him, Jack spins around walking between two of the guards in the human chain facing the parking lot.

He catches Anthony in mid-motion, trying to keep his chain of smokes going. Flustered, Anthony starts to put the lit cigarette back in the pack instead of the unlit one. He awkwardly smiles at Jack as he tosses the burning butt to the ground, pausing to look at it longingly. He gets back to business and relieves Jack of his purchases.

"A success," Anthony claims. Jack can't tell if that is a question or a statement. Either way they approach the trunk of the sedan that Anthony proudly has opened with his remote. The trunk is filled with opened and overstuffed suitcases; it's apparent that this radio star lives out of his car.

Jack is in the back seat of the car surrounded by his bags of souvenirs. "Shall we go?" Anthony coughs.

"Shall we?" Jack answers.

Anthony has the news blasting on the radio. The opposition to the annexing of the housing projects has come to a boiling point. The announcer states the protestors have been organized and aided by anti-government opposition, making them a quantifiable threat to public safety. These extremists are threatening to blow up the construction in an effort to stop it. Protesting is taking place right outside Mandela Square where the conference is taking place.

"This is nothing unusual. Don't worry about this, OK?" (Cough.) "I'll get you back safe and sound." But Jack is unnerved.

Anthony takes off in the same course they arrived on. "Why don't we circle back right through the projects' work roads instead of the jammed highway? What do you think?"

"Think? Think what?" asked Jack curtly. This 15-minute "shortcut" takes three times as long, but finally, the conference center is in full view; they are only blocks away. The demonstrations have gotten louder and more violent, while Anthony's coughing has reached a crescendo as well.

The mob chants, "Freedom means Freedom!" and alternates with, "Equality Now!" The extremists look angrier by the minute. One signs reads, "Apartheid Dead?" Up ahead, Jack can see that the crowd is now hurling stones and holding up bottles that might be homemade grenades.

Threatened by the advance, Anthony makes a beeline for the conference center parking garage. A few protestors have to jump out of the way. A policeman wearing riot gear blows a whistle and motions for Anthony to slow down. The angry marchers start to come around the corner. Jack panics. He can't take it anymore. He has to get out.

"I'm gonna make a run for it. Bring my packages to the concierge desk." Jack says to Anthony as he opens the car door and gets out of the car. He pushes through the crowd and looks up to see the Nelson Mandela statue again and wonders what he would think of all this.

Just then Jack hears a loud bang; feels a concussive blow; sees plumes of smoke; closes his eyes and then experiences being lifted.

Beep.
Beep.
Beep.

As he slowly focuses his eyes, Jack hears a beeping, which sounds like a heart monitor. There is a team of medical technicians hunched over him. He closes his eyes.

"Where am I?"

He opens his eyes for another try but everything is so cloudy.

"Welcome." He hears, a very distinctive English accent. He closes and opens his eyes again, and observes that the lead doctor is now in an elaborate, corseted, Victorian dress.

He closes his eyes once more mumbling, "Where am I?"

When he opens them again, he sees five smiling doctors in scrubs looking down at him. The lead doctor, who had been dressed in the Victorian gown is now in a lab coat

She looks at him with a smile and says in her beautiful English accent, "I guess some might refer to this as Heaven, love."

CHAPTER 2: ARRIVALS

Jack's World

Jack opens his eyes. He's excited to wake up from this hospital dream, but he realizes that he is still there. He hears all of the regular sounds of a hospital, but somehow the feelings and smells are contradictory.

He looks for the call button to alert the staff that he is awake. He wants to ask about his family. There is no button. The old fashioned rotary phone sitting on the end table next to him has his favorite numbers on top 1-8-4-1. He remembered seeing doctors standing around him earlier and one seemed to speak about Heaven when he asked where he was.

Where are the doctors and nurses now? He wonders. Jack senses activity in the hall, but he cannot see beyond the curtain that is pulled around his bed. Maybe the doctor called this Heaven because it was a state-of-the-art facility and he should be glad they brought him here and not to a Sangoma in Joburg.

Not clear how much time has passed, dazed, confused, and afraid to make any sudden moves in case he was in an accident, Jack's vision blurs a little. The sounds and smells are quite sharp in detail and he thinks that maybe he was given some type of narcotic to suppress physical pain. Actually, he doesn't feel anything physically. Instinctively, Jack knows this *place* is different. Feeling a bit like one of the characters from *LOST, like he's* crash landed on a mysterious island, Jack recognizes a glow, hum, and vibration around everything he looks at. The visual resonance of the objects just affirms that everything seems amplified. All his senses are heightened. With his newfound sensory awareness, he is hesitant to attempt walking yet. If he was in an accident, there could be injuries.

Jack quickly picks up the bed sheet and assesses his body. No bandages, no tubes, nothing! More curiously he is in his old track team workout pants—the very same ones Christina had thrown out right after their honeymoon. He had loved these sweats. He wore them like a second skin even though the elasticity was gone, and the emblem of the wolves was worn off from years of washings. Christina had deemed them the *least sexy sleepwear ever*. Jack didn't care.

It amused him that when he slept in them, they would ride up his legs, like they were now. He notices the wolf emblem, which had been faded, now looked brand new. "How is this possible?" he mumbles out loud. Beyond the old sweats that are new again, he has the body of an 18-year-old athlete. This is a better body than the one he actually had when he was running track. Now he is clear that he is dreaming. Not fearing injury anymore, he sits up quickly and lifts his plain black tee shirt and sees that his abs look airbrushed, sculpted.

There is an odd quality to the light, but Jack cannot pinpoint exactly what it is.

As he looks around the room he notices things he remembers writing about in past articles. "*Symbolic representations of my life and work, all being put on the dream screen of my mind. Dream interpretation 101.*" He remembered interviewing a specialist once, on the interpretation of dreams, comparing Freudian and Jungian techniques with a metaphysical approach. Her name escapes him. As he looks on the end table next to his bed, for a brief second, he thinks he see her book, *Dream Power*, by Cynthia Richmond. He blinks and it is gone. *WOW! This beats Google*, he thinks with a small smile.

The hypothesis of this experience being a dream is a much better alternative than something like, a hallucination from narcotics, or waking up in recovery as the anesthesia wears off. Enamored by his new physique, he pulls up the sweats a bit higher and is surprised to see his surgical scars are much more faded than ever, as if they were being erased. The conscious thought of moving his head makes him dizzy and feel cloudy. When he stops trying to actually move his head and just allows his thoughts to guide him, he has a feeling of clarity.

"You're not dreaming Jack," says Grandpa Joe's voice. But Jack cannot see him.

Questions formulate robotically, in Jack's mind, like a reflex, and anything illogical stands out, like, *Why I can hear Grandpa Joe and not see him?* or *Why was the female doctor in my mind wearing a corseted dress out of history? Maybe there's a sexual fantasy coming up and the female doc is really Christina, who will get to experience my new god-like body.*

"She is not Christina, Jack!" the voice of Grandpa Joe boldly states as fact.

Nothing can kill a sexual thought faster than your own mind.

If that was not Christina, and I am not dreaming, then why am I here and why was she dressed like that? And why would she say that I'm in Heaven?

He certainly didn't feel dead, but then again, neither did Bruce Willis in the movie *The Sixth Sense.* It had to be a dream. It was the only logical conclusion for all of the sensory experiences he was having. Beside the Ambien-assisted dream on the flight over, his dreams were normally not this vivid.

"Remember, Jack... Remember..." Grandpa Joe patiently replies.

Remember what? Why is the symbolic depiction of my dead grandfather interrupting my sexual fantasies and asking me to remember? Jack automatically finds his thoughts jumping, *What was my last memory? What was I thinking?* Jack ponders the final moments right before the explosion he had experienced. The answer comes to him like an image from a movie scene.

There had been violence, anxiety, a coughing infused cab ride, protesters screaming in the streets and a feeling of claustrophobia.

"Go over it again. Nothing happens by accident," whispered the voice of his dead Grandpa Joe.

Thoughts of the vehicle loomed. *Maybe I was in a car wreck. Head trauma? Concussion? Coma?* His next thought is of jumping out of the car, running up, pushing through an angry mob of people and seeing the giant Nelson Mandela statue in the square. Then everything goes black.

The energy of the people running and seeing smoke in the distance brought back images of September 11th, and that exacerbated his feeling of being closed in. Jack didn't like this, as he knows this is real on some level. He is indeed remembering. There was a distant hiss, pop, and a feeling of an impact. Maybe he was attacked by one of the rioters? The smell of something burning is bombarding him, actually invading him, and as a result it triggered a feeling of terror.

"Remember Jack, choices are a funny thing, nobody else can make them for you," Grandpa Joe recites from his lessons on life.

Jack remembers making the choice to get out of the car and walk into the dark angry energy of the crowd, in the same way he succumbed to peer pressure at the age of eleven. With that, he experiences a rush of frightful images, thoughts, sounds and scents, which act as a catalyst and suddenly he is eleven years old again.

Jack is standing in front of a local historic mansion, nicknamed HELLHOUSE, which is decorated each year by a local Academy Award-winning set designer. Each year this neighborhood manor gets magically transformed into a fundraiser for the local hospital.

He knows he is forbidden to do anything but trick-or-treat on Halloween, and is not allowed to be out with the big kids, who were egging and spraying shaving cream on cars. "Bunch of hoodlums!" Grandpa Joe called them. Jack's parents said that HELLHOUSE attracts the "wrong type of crowd" and a "bad element."

It was an autumn tradition and a rite of passage for many. During the early evening, families came together to take photos, but the hardcore scare tactics happened once the sun was down completely. HELLHOUSE was a place for guys to take their girls to hold and protect them. Many first kisses happened as a result.

The choice Little Jack Richman makes that night is to follow his best friend, Richie, and his older brother and friends to the annual "Care & Scare."

He tries to assuage his guilt for going by telling his parents it is for charity, how bad could it be? Deep down he knows that they are more concerned about the underage drinking, drugs and fighting that would often occur. Jack learns firsthand about the dangers of peer pressure on this night. Richie challenges him to make a choice that goes against his better judgment and desire. If he had not been seeking Richie's approval, he would never have disobeyed his parents.

"Come on, Jack. Don't wimp out now!" Richie yells at Jack, as he enters Hellhouse.

For a brief moment, Jack stares up at the house that looks haunted in the brightest sunlight of summer; he thinks it is an evil dwelling and very intimidating under the starry nighttime sky. Then the creaky wrought ironed gates clang behind him, sealing his fate. The rustling of the freshly fallen leaves and the chill in the air create the perfect backdrop for a child's imagination to run rampant.

Jack is scared and standing at the base of the porch steps of HELLHOUSE worrying about remembering what's to occur. He agrees with what Grandpa Joe had just said before taking this trip down horror lane: "Choices are a funny thing, nobody can make them for you, you have to decide for yourself." He remembers wishing his parents would drive by and stop him, but instead the darkness beckons him to enter its evil lair. His Grandma always told him to listen to his heart, and if it was singing off key—something was wrong. Well, something is definitely off, but he still succumbs to the darkness.

The moment he enters, he knows instinctively that it is a mistake. He turns to walk out, but he is pushed into the house by a hairy-armed beast. Jack immediately calls out to Richie, "Hey wait up!" but only hears giggles in response. The images flash like a montage in his

25

mind with a sound, smell and feeling that intensifies the actual mem-
ory. A sound of glass breaking and a cat screeching sets the mood. In
the distance he can make out a slow and deliberate squeaky rocking
chair beginning to move.

Like a black canvas for his imagination to paint upon, the
ruby-lit ghostly images, Halloween Hollywood special effects and
soundtrack elevates Jack's heart rate and blood pressure. As the sweat
starts to pour down his neck, he yell-whispers, "Rich!" into the abyss.
No audible response is returned.

He brushes up against the furry beast once again and this time
it groans a deep evil sound. Desperate and feeling isolated he begins to
cry. At that moment, he casts aside his need to be cool and belong and
just wants to feel safe. The walls are closing in on Jack and he cries
out for help from anyone who will assist him. For a moment, he is
paralyzed in the darkness. Afraid to move, the hairy beast guides his
journey by pushing him in the grand foyer. A concurrent werewolf
howling and crackles of thunder and lightning show Jack that he is
not alone. Instead, there are monsters at every twist and turn.

The experience is proving to be too much for Jack... then he
feels the hairy hand descend on the base of his neck. With the next
crackle of thunder and lightning, the hairy beast steps up behind
him and holds him. He tries to run as the claps of thunder progress.
Wicked laughs from ghouls and patrons alike fuel his fear. Jack
wants to run across the room as quickly as he can, but is frozen in
panic. It is seconds later, during a flash of the lightning and choral
movement of the wolves howling, that a ghoulishly made up zom-
bie growls and pulls him into a dark space. Little Jack Richman feels
sheer terror as this beer-smelling phantom drags him into an up-
right makeshift casket and tells him to "Stay here and don't move!"
Everyone there knows the routine and prank. Jack later learns the gag
was to lure a friend into various rooms, or traps that were set up,
and scare him. For people who knew the joke, it was funny to watch
others go through it. Every year a new person was brought to the
"party" to be the star of the show. Jack is the reluctant "star" of the
story this time.

In this room, one guy hides in the casket ahead of his friends and then someone else tangles the newbie in a web of death, as the first guy jumps out and scares him, pulling or pushing him into the casket. The scream then fuels the sound effects for the rest of the guests in the haunted house.

Jack is not let in on the joke. The specter leaves him there, trembling and standing in his own urine-stained pants, wanting to scream, but not finding his voice.

Jack's claustrophobia is born.

It must have been an hour before the bright lights of the room are turned on and light pours in through the grid in the casket. Jack responds to a familiar feeling and voice—Grandpa Joe who is a local town policeman. Seething in anger towards the perpetrators of this inhumane act, he looks right at Richie and his brother and tells them that he will personally be calling their parents. If looks could kill, there would have been real *dead bodies in that haunted house that night and Jack wouldn't have minded.*

The smell of Grandpa Joe's Canoe cologne and his touch will forever stay with him... Grandpa Joe is his savior, his Superman. Jack remembers thinking the red blanket he swaddles him with is an extension of his red cape. He later overheard Grandpa Joe tell his parents that he only wrapped him up to cover his wet, pee stained-pants and prevent further embarrassment with some of the other onlookers. As Grandpa Joe carries him out he speaks in his ear, "You're safe, Jackie... I'm here, and I've got you!"

"You're safe, Jack... I'm here!" Grandpa Joe whispers standing in front of his grandson, smiling. Jack is amazed at how youthful and energized Grandpa Joe looks. Better than ever, actually. Grandpa Joe was the type of person who looked old even when he was young. And with a blink... he is gone.

He might be confused, but Jack immediately feels safe in *this* place.

"GRANDPA!" exclaims Jack, "WAIT... COME BACK!"

The connection to him is so clear that Jack doubts his sanity. He had dreamed of Grandpa Joe on the flight over to South

Africa and he was old and sick in *that* dream. *Why all of a sudden did he look and feel so good?* Jack questions if he is remembering Grandpa Joe, or is actually hearing him, *again. If so, how can that be? He's dead! How can I be so awake and yet still so lucid in a dream?*

"Nothing happens here either by accident Jack..." Grandpa Joe stated. Jack is clear that Grandpa Joe is somehow interacting with his thoughts. He just wishes Grandpa Joe would appear and carry him back to safety once again.

In addition to Grandpa Joe knowing his thoughts, when Jack thinks of something it immediately manifests a smell, feeling, touch, and taste *simultaneously* (like he had experienced with the dream lady earlier). Jack is very confused; he cannot discern if he is experiencing something or conjuring it up. He also continues to see flashbacks of his life which are haphazard and all connected to meaningful moments in his life up until... up until what?

"NOW! Jack... NOW!" Grandpa Joe says from wherever he dematerialized from. Jack tries to organize all of these downloaded life experiences by applying his earthly logic, to a place his nineteenth-century doctor referred to as Heaven.

Earth – Present Time

As Matilda is playing with Moosey, Brian and Kimberly are flipping through the TV channels not spending more than three seconds on each. Christina looks over at them and wonders how her children would have survived if they were born in an era where they had to get up to answer a phone because it was on the wall with a cord, change the channel on the TV with their hand, and not ever hear the word Google. Her thought is fleeting and hypocritical, as she is multi-tasking herself—making meals while watching her iPad. She and Jack both love all of the latest technologies, even though she also loved to complain about them. One of their best sparring matches was over the better advances of APPLE vs. the World.

The task at hand for Christina is half listening to the news on CNN.com, while preparing breakfast and bagged lunches.

Brian only likes his bologna sliced thin, it must lay flat on the bread, and not hang over the edges. Kimberly will only eat a sandwich if the crust it cut off. Matilda, she's an angel. She really has no demands—*yet*.

"Last day of summer camp, guys!" Christina sings out from the kitchen as she lays out breakfast and their lunches, too. Her voice is musical, with a hint of the *you're all going back to school sooooon!* excitement.

Kimberly stares her down from across the room and Brian isn't even listening. Matilda exclaims that she can't wait to go to school and that she is going to be a teacher. As Christina moves the iPad from the counter to the table where all the backpacks and lunches are labeled and waiting to be picked up, a scroll of breaking news comes across the screen.

"A LARGE EXPLOSION HAS ROCKED MANDELA SQUARE AND RIPPLED ACROSS CENTRAL JOHANNESBURG, SOUTH AFRICA...CASUALTIES ARE REPORTED TO BE IN THE HUNDREDS..."

Christina's hand covers her mouth to quiet the gasp.

Jack's World

If he is having all these "life moments" flashing so vividly in 4D scratch 'n sniff, maybe he is dead... They say your life flashes before your eyes... *Better to stick with what you know,* he thinks, *stick to logic.*

His thoughts are like lightning. "*Better not to move,*" he remembers the female doctor saying when he saw her dressed in her frock. He hears a *Click! Click! Click!* like horses' hooves on cobblestones. He smells the combination of moisture and moss growing in-between the stones (*How is that possible?*) only to be overpowered by another familiar smell—lavender.

Jack closes his eyes and breathes in deeply, so he doesn't get claustrophobic and anxiety ridden.

"Jack!" Grandpa Joe says with love. Jack remembers him in his younger form with his personal bank of smells: Canoe cologne, tobacco, industrial strength cleaners, death and tapioca.

Jack feels the presence of his Superman. This just confirms that he really is hearing Grandpa Joe.

"Oh my God! How is this happening? What is going on? Grandpa?" Jack calls out.

"Go over the facts, Jack."

Grandpa Joe was right. "Journalist Jack" needs to assess this experience and collect the data. Time to apply investigative logic and scientific measure. Looking around the room, he determines it is definitely a hospital room (no sign of Grandpa Joe). Everything is pristine and clean. The colors are the brightest and purest hues he has ever seen. They all seem to have their own frequency or hum; like looking at an image through a barbecue and seeing the heated wavy lines alter its appearance.

It must be daytime, because the sunlight is lighting up the room. He pulls the curtain surrounding his bed back quickly to see if there is anyone sharing this room with him, but is blinded by the actual brightness of the white light pouring in through the windows. The light is hypnotic, loving, calming and serene. Light is good. Darkness is bad. Jack is OK as long as he is in the light, and this light is mesmerizing.

He feels spiritual. *Spiritual?* Jack has never used that word in definition of his self before. He actually admired people who are able to define themselves as spiritual. Sure, Jack felt religious when in church; he was searching and logical when he was learning, but never, *ever,* spiritual. Maybe this is what he was always supposed to get from the proper combination of God and life?

Jack's thoughts manifest another scene. He feels a sort of golden haze come over his consciousness as the scene becomes clear.

He is sitting in the auditorium of the Tilles Center in New York listening to Dr. Oren Smith speak on the phenomena of synesthesia. With that image is the complete remembrance of what synesthesia means—when a person's sensory experiences become a hybrid of all of them. He isn't aware that it could just get turned on, or that it could happen in a dream state. From what he knows, it is an experience that is applied to the moment, not past memories. How could he know what something smelled, tasted or felt like from a past memory and a different person's perspective?

Jack continues to assess his new found "feelings," in a logical, scientific way, with no success. His sideline diagnosis is that whatever is occurring, he is somehow starring in, directing, writing and producing it. Only if he were in charge, right about now he would cue Grandpa Joe to swoop him up again, take him out of this place and wake him up on a South African Airways flight home.

"I am still with you, Jack," Grandpa Joe says calmly.

His thoughts jump to his previous medical history. There were the childhood fevers and chicken pox—no exaggerated feelings with those thoughts. Water on the knee after a bad fall off his bike only weakened his knee, allowing the damage he later did to it running track. All-star or not, he had multiple surgeries as a result, and even with the scars disappearing, he knows he had them. But no freaky feelings or sensory overload in his past. Jack is perplexed. Logic and normal analysis isn't helping.

"Let go, Jack," Grandpa Joe whispers.

Jack is going over his facts like he is formulating a theory. He recaps once again: He is in some sort of hospital, either in a dream, or after an accident—thoughts of Anthony the driver are prevailing—so it had to be the vehicle accident. If it is a dream, there will be a lot of major symbolism to address when he wakes up. He doesn't believe he had surgery... unless he is having it now and this delusion is the result of the anesthesia, which might explain the heightened senses.

He is going over what makes sense but: *Why would a doctor in South Africa look like she stepped out of the 19th century? Why did he hear horses' hooves on cobblestones and smell the moss in between? Why is "why" the first word of all his questions?*

Jack realizes in a heart-sinking moment that he didn't take any identification with him when he went shopping. As advised by the concierge desk, he'd left all valuables in the hotel safe. He only took some RAND, the currency used in South Africa.

"Dear God, NURSE... NURSE!" Jack is screaming as loud as he can. "You need to let my family know I'm OK! You need to call my wife!"

Earth – Hours After the Explosion

Every news website is covering the story of the blast, all stating the same thing: MANY MISSING PRESUMED DEAD... PROTESTORS AND TOURISTS. One reporter goes on to say that at first, it was being presumed as an anti-government terrorist attack, but new information reveals that the explosion was caused by a ruptured gas pipe. A meteorologist say that if the blast had been an earthquake in the ocean, it would have been twice as bad as the tsunami that affected Thailand during the holidays a few years back.

Christina regains her composure, and quickly closes the cover to her iPad as the kids settle on *Sponge Bob Square Pants* in the other room.

"Hey GUYS... SHUT THAT OFF!" Christina doesn't mean to yell, but her fear of them seeing this on television is overwhelming her. *"Cereal and Pop tarts are on the table. Go eat,"* she barks, as she runs past them to her desk to check Jack's itinerary. The soundtrack of her life is playing in the background: animated music, a pirate yelling he can't hear you, kids laughing, maybe bickering, and Kimberly announcing that she is not eating carbs anymore because they make you fat...

Her worst fears are confirmed. Jack is at ground zero of the South African explosion. That is his hotel.

Running on pure adrenaline, she calls her neighbor Mrs. Literia, explains what happened and asks her to stay with Matilda while she takes Brian and Kimberly to camp. Christina is now on a mission, a quest for information. She will not get emotional, she cannot. She must stay strong until she has all the facts. She knows that her first stop after dropping the kids off will be Jack's office to see if they heard anything from him, any good news. But on the way, she will be calling her cousin Bobby, who works for the FBI, to beg him for any information she can get from him.

Jack's World

Jack's cries for a nurse to help him call home are not immediately answered, not even from Grandpa Joe. He is easily distracted by his new sensory skills. Suddenly he detects the very same "minty freshness" that Shrek's Donkey had appreciated, and he feels a lead blanket of despair wash up on him. The faces of Christina, Brian, Kimberly and Matilda are now his focal point, and he is feeling wistful and blissful—what a mixture of thoughts, feelings and emotions. Everything starts to swirl together in a dizzying manner and his vision starts to stretch and elongate into a fluffy, white-lit hollow tunnel that is pulling him in.

Getting carried out of HELLHOUSE
Mom and Dad scolding him for going with Richie and not asking them
Meeting Christina... watching his children being born... Brian's disappointment
Landing in South Africa and seeing a billboard for the Big Five
Doctors milling around the hotel lobby, hearing karaoke in background
Seeing Dr. Begley's drink, knowing it was white zinfandel, being able to taste the drink while feeling her thoughts
Getting into a claustrophobic car with Anthony the driver who was dying from cancer
Feeling like everyone turned on him... being angry at his family... Wanting to avenge himself and his reputation
Horses and an apothecary... people being fearful of death
Choking, feeling claustrophobic, not being able to breathe
Hearing Anthony coughing and speaking in his South African accent
Jumping out of Anthony's car... an awareness of "falling" combined

with it...

The circular tunnel of cloudy light, illuminated with shades of purple, blue and orange, swirl with the minty fresh taste... and he is seeing screens of his life playing simultaneously like family home movies.

His thoughts create a rush of energy that is both overwhelming, exhilarating, and out of control. The centrifugal force of his entire life starts swirling faster and faster and he feels that he is no longer flying, but falling. The speed of the descent can only be described as a nose dive, and once again Jack is plunged into a place of feeling claustrophobic and out of control. He closes his eyes, as he is fearful of what he is going to see, hear, and feel next. He knows it will be unpleasant, as everything inside him tells him so. At that moment his energetic and earthly worlds collide.

Grandpa Joe wraps his loving embrace around his grandson and they descend together. "I got you, Jackie. It's OK. I am here with you... Just remember everything happens for a reason my boy."

With that Jack faces the harsh reality that life has to offer every living creature, their own demise.

"Look at me, Jack." Grandpa is now standing directly in front of him as the lights and colors are flying past them. The elevator of energy is crashing and with one look in Grandpa Joe's eyes, Jack knows all is well. And then it stops. It all stops.

Jack is standing in a familiar place, one that he has been too so many times before. Like a helium balloon past its prime, Jack and Grandpa Joe descend onto the congregation of people there to mourn the life of Jack Richman.

He looks down the aisle of the St. Hyacinth's Church for the casket, the tell-tale sign of a burial, but it is not there. He overhears the priest say that Jack was returned to the Earth... ashes to ashes... Jack is moved by the thoughts and outpouring of love directed to him in that moment. He is able to feel in unison the love and in turn, the loss they all now feel.

"Grandpa, how do I help them?" Jack pleads to his elder. "They are all in so much turmoil!"

"Jackie, do you want me to tell you what transpired? Do you know what is actually happening here?" Grandpa Joe's voice questions him, talking to him like he is a five year old, not an adult.

Jack is drawn to his family in the front row. Matilda just puts her head on her Mommy's shoulder, and doesn't seem to even care. They all have the same look of emptiness.

Jack starts to hear the *Click, Click, Click* of the horses on cobblestone... and like Christopher Reeve in *Somewhere in Time*, feels pulled away from the one place he wants to be more than anywhere else—his family. He looks at Grandpa Joe, who is looking up. Jack doesn't want to look up at the lights that are falling around him like sparks from a welder. He knows he is being called to his heavenly home. His love for his family is so strong; he has to let them know he is there. With great pride in his voice, while looking up at the sparkling lights getting more pronounced, Grandpa Joe says two words, "Tell them!"

Jack channels all his love for his family into one thought and feeling, *"I'm here!"*

In that moment, Matilda popped up quickly and questioned, "Daddy?" for she not only heard him, she felt him. Jack knows he has broken through whatever veil existed between their worlds, and that is all he needs to see to know that he will find a way to do it again. As the lights pull him and Grandpa Joe up, like being beamed up to the *Enterprise*, a light bulb explodes in the same place they are standing.

Kimberly, Brian, and Christina, as well as the rest of the congregation, know something weird just happened. But only two people in that church know for sure that Jack is acknowledging his presence—the medium sitting in the back of the room, and Matilda.

"I love you, Daddy," Matilda squeaks out, looking in the

direction of the still sparkling bulb. The rest of the congrega-tion looks down as the priest struggles to help them find peace.

Jack feels lifted and pulled once again, this time not fall-ing, but ascending. Realizing he has somehow left the physical world does not concern Jack Richman. He doesn't care that he has discarded his physical vehicle. The only thing he cares about is letting his family know that he is OK and will still be with them. He knows that if it happened once, he can find a way to make it happen again. He is soaring and flying into the colors, still feeling safe in the light and loving touch of Grandpa Joe. They are flying like supermen.

Jack's journey is just beginning to take flight.

CHAPTER 3:
ADMISSION

Jack's World – The Hospital

The Director of Admissions telepathically senses interference with one of her new arrivals. Like Darth Vader, she feels a shift in the energy of her world. This feeling, an uneasy, energetic break in the divine force that governs this realm, indicates she will need to micromanage the latest admission, Jack Richman.

OH NO! Not again. I will not let this happen again, she thinks to herself. After doing this job as long as she has, she no longer questions her feelings. Her feelings are more like knowings... facts in the Earth realm.

"The man who just arrived under Dr. Brooks' team—watch him closely," the Director said to Anthea, her assistant.

"Yes, TD," Anthea says without hesitating.

Cool, calculated and with the beauty of a Greek goddess, The Director, who prefers to be called simply TD, thinks she might have had a name once, *I think it was Lemuria,* she once mused to herself, *or maybe that was just where I'm from...* It didn't matter now. She looks at souls in the same way Galileo looked at the celestial universe—with one glance she can assess "all" that was, is, and will be for any patient (soul) entering her hospital realm (or as Dr. Brooks and others refer to it, "TD's domain").

If Heaven were a dramatic series or stage play, she would be the vixen. Sexy and smart, The Director could tell that Jack Richman was going to be a problem—she knew immediately that she needed to block him in any way possible. If what she sees by looking at his chart, test results and karmic path is correct, Jack could be the one soul to expose her secret, one that she has been keeping successfully up until his arrival. This is no small matter. The "unexpected" can wreak havoc throughout the realms of Heaven and Earth.

It would remain vitally important that she control her thoughts and not let the enemy—who is out there, she is certain—inside her head, even if she has to "fake" it to distract him.

"Anthea, I need you to transfer Jack Richman out of Dr. Brooks' care immediately and—"

Anthea interrupts her in a passionate plea for understanding, "But Madame Director, TD, there is *the* protocol that must be followed with all new arrivals, that is set by the *Council* and Jack Richman needs to—"

The Director cuts her off, incensed at being questioned by her assistant. "You *will* do as I ask and you will *do so* now, or you and I both will not be able to move beyond the energy of this hospital! Do I make myself clear?"

The Director is not about to allow her secret to be exposed. *Jack Richman's soul might have to be collateral damage if he continues down this path. He will have to pay the price for keeping her secret...*

The Director knows that being the head of this place has its consequences. She's been placed here to be a leader, not to be loved. She is the Warden of Souls in many ways, not the nursery teacher. She uses her guidance, as she knows she should, and that makes her wildly unpopular with many of her staff. Dr. Annie Brooks and the Director are going to have an apocalyptic showdown—but Jack Richman's soul—and her own secret—are both at stake.

The Council of Elders

The men and women wear iridescent robes, mainly of white, with little substance to them, as if they are a trick of the eye. The garments cling to them and follow their movements, which are slow and stately. They take their places at a long, curving table in the Council chamber.

There are no sudden movements or thoughts in this assembly of beings known as the Council of Elders, the senior governing body of twelve in this realm of existence that their earthly counterparts call the Other Side. Their rule, such as it is, consists of powerful intellectual and spiritual projections of ideas and suggestions. They are not gods but merely somewhat godlike in the minds of newcomers from the earthly plane who first encounter them.

As time goes on, the members of this Council come to be understood by those who cross over as less than superhuman but very much human—having accepted their own humanity, and that of others, in its fullest implications.

The Council monitors the flux of life between Earth and "Heaven" (a word often used and almost always misunderstood) and tries to achieve some balance in the forces that flow back and forth between the realms. They know better than anyone how humans fight the very idea of balance and attempt to upset the forces of nature put in place by the Creator countless ages ago.

The hospital is an adjunct facility that the Elders do not directly control. The Director, their chosen executive authority and future member of the Council, if she is successful, runs the operation with their blessing.

The Elders gather periodically, as needed, when something good—or ill—requires their attention. Their leadership, which emerges naturally to fit the situation at hand, is based solely on wisdom and compassion, though intelligence and long experience play a part for those senior Council members, too. It is a sort of natural democracy and benign monarchy combined with a "system" that works.

The Director has reached out to the Council to tell them about the latest wrinkle in the fabric of their world: Jack Richman.

Newcomers to the Other Side are often surprised when they encounter the Council of Elders—if they are privileged to encounter it at all—because there is no apparent conflict or politics in what they do, but a deliberative adherence to the truth and to universal principles of justice.

At this moment, though, there is some agitation in the Council, there is a keen awareness that something is awry in the normal balance between the worlds. And they know it is caused, as usual, by the forces that oppose the light and truth the Council represents.

Word has been dispatched to the Council of Elders from the hospital: The Director is seeking some guidance and wants the Elders to know that the bombing in Johannesburg has unleashed chaos that now threatens to ripple through the finely tuned "system" for receiving those who pass over... The forces of darkness have succeeded in another disruption—which happens every now and then. Far too often for the Elders.

The Elders' concern, now and always, is that there be a balance of energies and that light prevails in the end.

"We know this Jack Richman has an interesting history, to say the least," one of the most senior members of the Council states aloud. "And we did not expect him on this side so soon. Is it *safe*?"

Another Elder, one of the female representatives on the Council known for her wisdom born of deep experience as a leader on Earth, spoke up: "Of course, it is not safe if it allows entry to our realm by one of the enemies of peace."

"This Jack Richman is no such enemy."

"No, but there is one who has been very close to him on the Earth plane who has much influence over him—one who actively opposes our purpose."

"Is it even his time?"

"We cannot say. The Director and the hospital staff will discern the answer to that question and put this man on the right path—if he cooperates with them."

"And if he fulfills *his* true purpose here, as well as on

Earth."

"The unknown factor is always the most—interesting—one might say."

What passed as a smile on the side of the divide between the worlds shines on their faces. Yet they are genuinely concerned about the potential disruption to their plan for ultimate redemption for this soul.

As they observe with ease through the veils that mere humans cannot penetrate, Jack can have no clue that he is the subject of such solemn conversation.

CHAPTER 4: EARTHLY MEMORIAL

Earth – 24 Hours After the Explosion

After picking Matilda up from the neighbors', Christina is sitting in her minivan in the circular driveway of the Rosemont Junior High School, which hosts the summer camp program. Christina reflects on how all Jack's colleagues reacted to her; they clearly have no hope. If one more person says, "I am so sorry," she is going to scream. A few people treat her like she had leprosy, or has contracted some weird contagious disease called grief. When she adds all the looks, mumbles, and sympathetic stares, it all confirms what she knows to be true in her heart. She just can't bear to hear anyone utter it.

Even though she fights the feeling that a family member should do more, she appreciates that Bobby Anderson, her cousin who works for the FBI, returned her call so quickly. Realistically, she knows that all he will do is register Jack's name with the American embassy as one of the hundreds lost in the explosion.

Bobby Anderson is a celebrity agent of sorts and is always being called in on unusual cases: This time it's a ritualistic, zodiac serial killer wannabe that took his investigation to Ireland.

"It's a macabre crime scene, Chrissie, I can't and won't go into gruesome detail, but some sick demented people are at work here. I even put a call into my friend Dawson, to weigh in."

Christina doesn't mind hearing the name Chrissie from certain members of her family. They all called her that growing up. Ordinarily, she'd be interested in his case, and news of Dawson, as well, but now she just wants to find Jack.

"That's cool, you keep in touch with your friend, Dawson. He is so famous now. You must be really proud of him. I've read all of his books."

The thought quickly turns to how Dawson lost his fiancé in the 9/11 attacks on the World Trade Center—in that moment, she feels more related to Dawson Rask than to Bobby.

"Um, Bobby, I am so sorry to bother you, but there's been an accident? Incident? It's Jack... He's missing."

After he listens to what Christina has to say, he explains that communications in that area are not the best with the United States, but he will call in every favor he can to find out as much information as possible.

"Maybe he was hurt or injured and has amnesia?" Christina laughs out loud, a little bitterly when she says it. She knows she's grasping at straws.

Bobby is direct with her. He tries to be supportive without giving false hope. He sees too many grim things in his job every day to lie to her.

"If there is information to be found, you know I will find it." Bobby hangs up, without leaving her much hope at all.

Christina thanks him, feeling like she has wasted his time, but glad she has explored all her options. *How is this happening?* If she could just rewind a few days—she would take more time to appreciate the life she was living, and most of all Jack. As she reflects on the subtle ebb and flow of relationships in general, she finds herself staring at her iPhone every thirty seconds, eager for a text or an email from Jack letting her know that he is OK.

It never comes.

CHAPTER 5: BACK-TO-BACK VISITS

Jack's World

Jack is back in his hospital bed... His *Christmas Carol* voyage with Grandpa Joe had been remarkable, painful and about a hundred other adjectives, tastes, smells and visions all wrapped into one. He quickly looks all around for his childhood hero, but Grandpa Joe is nowhere to be seen. Uncertain as to why he is in the hospital, not a scar on him, with a revitalized energy, he is forced to question, *Was that a dream? For that matter, is this all a dream?* Jack flashes back to the hotel bar scene and in that moment, he is almost positive that someone slipped him something in one of his drinks. This hallucinogenic sojourn will eventually end—Jack is ready to have it end. He is starting to feel too much out of control and doesn't like it.

Jack feels like Keanu Reeves' character Neo in the movie the *Matrix,* having a difficult time understanding what is real and what is fantasy. He had watched the movie so many times and knew that Neo, the main character, had to come to terms with the understanding that the life he was leading was not real, albeit, a real and vivid experience. Jack wants out.

Time to wake up. Time to connect with his family. Time to get back to work. This *Matrix*-type experience is only missing the Jedi knight training of Morpheus, although he would prefer Yoda as his teacher, truth be told. Logic is second nature; analysis and scientific explanations are the landscape of Jack Richman. In his mind, he knew the kids had been dramatically on his mind since he landed in Johannesburg, so that must be why he was seeing and dreaming so vividly of them mourning his absence. He quickly goes over the imagery, visions and "soul trip" Grandpa Joe accompanied him on; he can't shake the scene in the church. It was so overwhelming to feel what his family was feeling and to want to let them know he was right there, and OK.

A memorial means he is gone—gone he clearly is not. And the reality for Jack that he was dreaming comes in the symbolic form that he couldn't be dead—there was no casket! This whole thing is some elusive code for him to crack. He could hear his colleagues kidding him about Dr. Begley's lack of conclusive evidence and data. Maybe that is what this dream is all about: how something can actually happen and yet not have conclusive data. How would he be able to rectify, scientifically, his experience? He can't. He can only relate it.

Jack is anchored to that church scene. The feeling is weighted and heavy. He just knows that all the people in that church were there to celebrate and mourn his life.

"Go over it again, Jackie," he hears Grandpa Joe whisper in his mind.

His dream analysis kicks in. He attempts to logically and rationally define his experience. He goes over the entire experience, again. He remembers the sparkling lights falling from above Grandpa Joe and pulling them both upward into that bright light, the same light that is pouring into the hospital room he is now occupying.

Jack is questioning his sanity, in addition to his new super senses, when he realizes that he is not alone. No, not Grandpa Joe, but familiar strangers are in the room. It is as if they materialized from nowhere. Four doctors wearing lab coats are standing in front of him.

At first glance, they all look and more importantly *feel* familiar. He remembered them. They had all been there before, but one woman was missing, the one who told him he was in Heaven. *HEAVEN?* Wait... Jack's thoughts come to a screeching halt as he remembers the British woman welcoming him to Heaven.

CHAPTER 6: SIX SOUL DEGREES OF SEPARATION

Earth – 1 Day after the Explosion

Matilda is anxiously waiting for Kimberly and Brian to come out from their last day of what she calls *summer school*. Being straight-A students, it irks both of them when she refers to camp as summer school.

Christina has a million thoughts springing through her mind, and a strong desire for a cigarette has taken hold of her brain. It's been almost ten years since she quit smoking. She gave up the nasty habit when she found out she was pregnant with Brian. Crying and visibly upset, she is trying to keep herself together. She looks up at the clear blue sky and thinks to herself and God, *How do you tell your children that their Dad is never coming home again?* Her feeble attempt to suppress her emotions is only exacerbating the intensity of this cold, harsh reality. The DJ's voice is heard in-between songs with updates on the latest news of the day. Christina switches the radio to iPod mode.

"Wiggles! Wiggles!" Matilda chants from her car seat.

But before Christina can select the Matilda playlist of songs, the iPod shuffles its playlist and the song that starts to play is Bon Jovi's "Never Say Goodbye." Christina breaks down.

As she exhales slowly, wringing her hands together in her lap and twisting her engagement ring and wedding band, Matilda asks, "Mommy, are you upset and crying because Daddy is never coming home, because he was blown to kingdom come?"

"Matilda!" Christina exclaims, losing her cool, "Why would you say such a thing?"

Matilda innocently explains, "Mrs. Literia told Mister Literia that on the phone when she had to watch me while you ran errands... Mommy, if daddy went to kingdom come, is that also in South Africa? Will he be away longer now?"

The words hit Christina hard and fast, and the normally in-control mother just sits in the driver's seat with her head pressed upon the steering wheel thinking, *This can't possibly be my life. Someone needs to wake me up from this nightmare!*

CHAPTER 7:
DIAGNOSIS DEATH

Jack's World

Jack looks up at the medical professionals desiring answers and assistance. He looks at all four faces, distinctly different in nationalities, but they offer nothing in return except silent stares. Jack is feeling a bit like Richard Dreyfuss in the final scene of the movie *Close Encounters of The Third Kind*.

I'm not dead. I can't be, Jack thinks. He is feeling lost and his thoughts are happening two at a time. Like kryptonite to Superman, he is that to himself, especially for the regularly in-control, articulate, science journalist. Gone is the vast understanding of things that most people take for granted. Now he is left feeling like a frustrated amnesiac struggling to come up with his past and present. He would rather this be a complicated dream within a dream—simultaneously he thinks, *What would Freud or Cynthia Richmond have to say about that?*

Waiting for Jack to come to the understanding and acceptance of where he is, the four doctors are omnipresent. They have been standing with him the whole time. His consciousness has not allowed him to see them. Now, they are ready to help him take on his Life Review and make his transition to the afterlife by walking him through the last life that he led—the process. These "Doctors of the Soul" have been rescuing and attending to those who crossover since their last lifetime.

"Jack... Just so you know it's different for everyone."

Jack is still just sitting there in disbelief, looking at the doctor who just spoke to him so quietly.

Jack senses their energy becoming clearer now as he focuses. He is able to read their names on their badges and the hospital's name on their lab coats. *The name of the hospital in South Africa they took me to is JACK RICHMAN MEMORIAL HOSPITAL?*

"How is that possible?" Jack thinks out loud.

The doctors are just staring at him—giving Jack the feeling that he is expected to say something profound. "Are you waiting for me to talk about my death? Or what about my magic memory journey with my dead grandfather?"

The first of two male doctors speaks, "Hey, buddy, I'm Dr. Gareth Roberts. How are you feeling?" His voice is strong and affirming.

"Ayudame Mama!" a young girl cries from outside of Jack's hospital room. The sound is overwhelmingly loud to him—as if a speaker into his ear is amplifying it. Jack is distracted and pulled towards the painful request for help. He quickly turns in the direction of the voice calling out for her mother. It beckons him.

The residents do not hear the young girls repeated cries for help. The cries are distracting and hurt Jack on some familial level. He looks back at the same male doctor with disbelief. He makes a gesture of inquiry.

"What is it?" Dr. Roberts replies.

"No, not what is it? Who is it? Aren't you going to help that crying child?" His paternal instincts are ignited and fueled each time he hears the girl cry.

"Mama… por favor… ayudame!" this voice erupts.

Jack is now vibrating from the inside out and drawn towards the voice. He's haunted by the images of his family in the church, empathically feeling their pain as they mourn and Grandpa Joe telling him to remember… and Jack does. He remembers the feeling of wanting to get back to his family, to let them know he is OK. This disconnect from his family and Grandpa Joe has made him irritable and in that very moment, he wants to see, hear and feel his family, but isn't sure how it happened in the first place. Jack is starting to fall apart like an over-tired child. "Are you guys going to help her?" Jack demands.

The cries get louder, "Mama... por favor... ayudame!"

A female Asian doctor, labeled Dr. Susan Chin, standing at his bedside is the first to speak to Jack compassionately, "Help whom, Jack?"

"Whomever that girl is. The one who is calling out for help?" He says angrily.

She stares at him blankly.

"Really? We are in a hospital right? Why are you not helping her or at least getting her mother for her?" Jack is clearly agitated. The combination of feeling his family in despair and hearing this anguished girl's cry for help is almost too much for him to handle. *His* parental instincts are kicking in and he wonders why *their* medical urges to assist aren't. He thinks of Christina. He knows that she would be rushing towards the cries if she were here.

The residents look at each confused—they clearly hear nothing.

CHAPTER 8:
PHONING HOME

Earth – 1 Day After the Explosion

Matilda, holding her stuffed best friend, spots her siblings walking out from the school, "There they are, Mommy! Moosey spotted them."

Looking out of the minivan's front window, Christina doesn't see them because she is watching a biker-looking man drag and reprimand a helpless girl. Christina instinctively knows she is not his daughter. He doesn't have the protective energy of a parent, the energy that they have even when they are upset or scolding their child for a wrongdoing. Plus, this girl's tanned skin is a major contrast to his shaved head and ghostly white skin. If it was not for the camp counselor running up to hand her the iCarly lunch bag she forgot, Christina might have called the authorities, which is still an option by the way he is directing his aggression and anger at this poor girl.

"Mommy! Hit the button! Hit the button!" Matilda exclaims so that the automatic door to the minivan would glide open, letting her siblings in to tell her of the adventures they had that day.

Christina did it without thinking. She locks eyes with the girl and they make a connection as she approaches the street in front of Christina's minivan. The little girl is no more than eight years old.

Jack's World

"Ayudame Mama!"

Jack continues to watch the doctors stare at him like he is crazy. The fact that they are completely OK with letting this little girl cry hysterically, has him seething. Hospitals are supposed to *help and heal* people. *Can they not hear her?*

"Mama... por favor!"

Earth

Brian is patiently waiting for Kimberly to say goodbye to one of her friends, while Christina is completely concerned and absorbed with this girl's well-being. As they approach, she really feels the abusive energy the man has, and the girl's eyes are always looking down when not on Christina. She is in despair. The man is saying something to her in a language Christina doesn't understand completely, or the music on the iPod is too loud for her to make out what it is. Clearly from his tone, and her expression of fear, she is most definitely an abused young girl. The scars and black and blues on her sleeveless arm reveal the truth.

Why doesn't the school or camp do something about things like this? Christina thinks in frustration. This girl is an immediate distraction from her own pain and Hell, worrying about Jack, consuming her from the moment she laid eyes on her.

When the girl and the man are directly in front of Christina's minivan, she notices that the girl has black and blue bruises up and down her arms. In a macabre way, her skin matches her eyes and black hair. She has the most beautiful blue eyes and has a blue butterfly hair clip on each side that matches. She would be a beautiful little girl if she didn't look terrified.

The man's face is arrogant and gnarled. He raises his voice and hand simultaneously as if to hit her in the space between the black Escalade and Christina's minivan. Christina's rage and bottled up emotion boils over. She slams on her horn.

"WHAT THE... HEEEEEEEEY!" Christina yells out her window, so loud that it startles Matilda, who drops Moosey to cover her ears.

The beep of concern and parental passion alerts the

shaved monster with the teardrop tattoo by his eye, that some-one is there and watching his actions. The little girl looks at her with appreciation and terror. Christina thinks she sees a glimmer of a smile.

Christina is almost out of the car to confront the man when Brian and Kimberly approach the minivan with a ridiculous tornado of excitement and frenetic energy. Christina is under so much pressure already that when she turns to greet Brian and Kimberly, it momentarily distracts her from the direction the blue butterfly clip girl walked in. She quickly looks in her rear view mirror and alternates side mirrors to see if she can see where they went, what car they got into.

At least the make, model and maybe part of a license plate, she thinks, since she wants to report this man anyway. But, she failed that girl and she knew it. The child is going to be abused the moment they get into the car—Christina could see it in his eyes—he is in a rage and whatever his issue, that little girl will be to blame.

All of this is now contributing to the overwhelming feeling that Christina is trying to suppress. As they put their seat-belts on, a barrage of questions comes hurling from behind her. For the moment, she forgets about the girl with the blue butter-flies in her hair. Her hands are shaking—she's shaking.

Brian's first question is, of course, about his dad. "Mom, you heard from Daddy? Is the hotel nice? Is he going to call us soon? Did he text you? Did he say he got my note? I am gonna so make his day when he reads it. That's right—I'm working it!" He bops his head up and down to the rap music playing in his mind.

Christina puts her sunglasses on to cover her blood-shot red eyes and calmly says, "I got an email from him once he landed. He still had to go through customs, immigration, get his bags... don't forget there's a..." Christina's voice cracked as she attempts to remind them that there is a time change. Jack is now hours into the future. The thought morphs into him being caught up in the explosion, and actually hearing her daughter say the words "blown to kingdom come"—it is the final thing that makes her break emotionally.

She clears her throat and finishes her thought, "There's, um, something that I need to tell you guys..."

"What is it, Mommy?" Kimberly said.

Christina answers, "Um...uh... Yes, honey?" Tears start to leak down her cheek. She grips the steering wheel to stop her hands from shaking.

Kimberly picks up Moosey, who was on the floor, and makes him dangle in front of Matilda, while asking, "Do you think that Daddy will get to ride an elephant?"

"Well, I don't know." She grabs the steering wheel so tight her knuckles turn white. "I guess we'll just have to wait and see..." Christina just looks straight ahead out the windshield at the black Escalade in front of them, blocking her from moving forward. She identifies with this as a metaphor for her life.

Brian suddenly starts to regret not going on the trip with Jack. He knows that's exactly what his dad is going to do, it had been in the brochure! He couldn't wait to talk to his Dad soon. Now that camp was over and he had experienced it, South Africa would have been the better choice.

"You know, I should've gone with Dad," Brian began, "Camp wasn't that much fun and Matt chose to go away with the Petersons to Miami this week..."

"I can hear Daddy's 'I told you so' from across the Pacific!" Kimberly says with sarcasm.

"Atlantic! It's the AT-LAN-TIC idiot!" Brian snaps.

"What-evah!" Kimberly says as she rolls her eyes and reaches for her iPod to scan through the songs.

"Hey, Mom... Smartarella back here has a crush on Mr. Togneri, the camp counselor," Brian blabs.

Kimberly punches Brian in embarrassment. Christina isn't even listening.

"Mommy, can I send Daddy a picture of me and Moosey eating dinner later?"

"Yes, Matilda."

Matilda hugs Moosey tightly in excitement. Christina has

to smile when she thinks of how many Matilda and Moosey (whom Dad had nicknamed his "M&Ms") pictures she had sent to Jack. Her smile quickly fades as she realizes that he would never see her and Moosey, or any of them, grow up.

Matilda smiles in satisfaction with her Mom's answer. Jack always sent pictures of his adventures while he was traveling, and if he never saw anything more than a conference room? He'd take pictures of his dinner or make silly faces. He always wanted his family to feel included in his day-to-day activities. They in turn did the same.

Christina finds herself thinking hopelessly that Jack probably didn't even get a chance to send photos, as he was only there less than 24 hours before the disaster. She doesn't even have all the details of what exactly happened, nor does she know when the appropriate time would be to explain to their children that Daddy is not coming home.

Does she sit them down as a family? Does she tell them one by one? And her anger is now being directed at that bald man for almost striking his child like that and at Mrs. Literia for being so senseless in speaking in front of Mattie. *What if she was older and found out THAT way?*

The kids are talking louder and louder over each other —getting ready to bicker over something else. Christina thinks the last thing she heard Brian say to Kimberly was that he wanted to hear *his* song play through the car's iPod dock and not hers. Christina can't hold it in any longer and erupts, "GUYS! Guys! I need to tell you something important!" The energy in the car turns quiet, calm and intense. The kids know that something bad is going to be said by their mom's demeanor.

"Mom... what's wrong?" Brian asks.

Christina starts to well up, because Brian *is* his father's son. He sounds just like him. This ten-year-old boy is now using Jack's voice and words in such a way it makes his mom feel like she is speaking to her husband, and not her own child.

Christina explains to her children that Daddy may not be coming home. She finds their shock and silence at the news deafening—she wants them to yell, cry and scream. But they don't. Kimberly plugs her ear buds into her iPod and puts her head back... Matilda clutches onto Moosey with her large, almond eyes full of tears ready to spill out... Brian just breaks her heart as he turns and stares at the sky through the passenger window, pinned under an avalanche of guilt and grief.

The silence is as loud as the explosion that took Jack away from them. The Escalade pulls away, signaling to Christina that whether she wants it to or not, life is moving forward.

CHAPTER 9: THE NINE LIVES OF JACK RICHMAN'S WORLD

Jack's World

After not answering any of his questions regarding the other patient in the hospital crying for her mother, Jack only semi-pays attention to the doctors standing in front of him.

"Where's my grandfather?" Jack asks.

The second male doctor, whose nametag reads, Dr. Umberto Avanti, questions in perfect Italian, "Your dead grandfather?"

Jack completely understands him, though he's never studied Italian...

"I had this dream, for lack of a better word, or whatever this place does to you, and my Grandpa Joe was in it... and in my dream... I was flying, so, yes I am asking about my dead Grandpa Joe!"

Jack stops speaking. The doctor looks at him with concern, and Jack realizes that he just admitted that he was not only seeing, but flying, with his dead grandpa.

In reality, the doctors feel it is a good indicator that he is aware of why he is there and that he'll be ready to be reunited in some way with his grandfather, but they know he is not ready for any visitors, yet. They have a lot of work to do with Jack Richman.

The doctors are about to update Jack Richman on his condition and explain a bit more about what is happening to him, when the loud *click, click, click* of footsteps approaching is heard. It reminds him of the click of the horses' hooves on the cobblestones, that he had heard earlier.

This is the only thing that distracts Jack from the anguish and torment of his soul noise—the young girl's cries and his flight with Grandpa Joe. The sounds blend into an image of horses' hooves on cobblestone. He simultaneously smells damp moss and lavender. These feelings fade as the *clicks* approach, turning into the sound of the heels on a very attractive female physician with a gregarious energy and sexy voice—the original doctor who announced to him he had safely arrived in Heaven.

The glass doors automatically open, with the same precision as the doors on the Starship *Enterprise*, same noise too. (The TV and movie soundtrack that Jack is adding to this dream just keeps getting more and more retro. He is waiting to hear the *chh-chhh-chhhh chhhh* of the *Six Million Dollar Man* next.)

"Hello, luvs!" The woman proclaims in her melodic British accent, as a wave of intoxicating energy rushes into the room. "Glad to see you are up and awake!"

When she speaks, she commands Jack's attention. He has to admit that he is somehow really attracted to this woman.

"Jack? Are you OK?" She asks. Something about her voice validates that she knows he finds her interesting. Jack realizes that she is beautiful that doesn't take away from his feelings for Christina, but he has to look at her. She is wearing casual clothes covered by her lab coat, not like the first time when opened his eyes and she was donning a nineteenth century frock.

Jack is confused, "Why were you wearing that Victorian dress before?" With this question, the residents survey each other to see who knows what he is talking about.

Dr. Annie answers, "What do you mean, wearing a dress? We're always dressed in medical attire."

The dress question snaps Annie into an altered mindset. She can't explain it, but she knows *he* is different. There's something about this one...

Initially, Jack had thought maybe this doctor was just his sexual "It" girl, his type. But right then and there, Jack immediately rules out the sexual fantasy, as he is positive his id and ego would have kept her in the elaborate gown. He always did find it more attractive to leave more to the imagination. He prefers a one-piece bathing suit to a string bikini every time. She smiles at him, almost seeming to accept the compliment that his eyes are certainly communicating. Quiet and pensive, Jack is feeling detained.

"Who are you?" he whispers. No answer.

"Who are you?" he demands to know in a rage.

Dr. Chin speaks up, "Calm down, Mr. Richman... we are here to help you not hurt you."

Jack feels trapped, cornered and erupts, "Why does that door sound as if it's hermetically sealed? It's bad enough I somehow sabotaged what could have been a really great, sexual fantasy, but now I think I am seeing my dead grandfather, possibly witnessing my own funeral and you're indicating to me that I am in some sort of afterlife heavenly hospital that bears my own name!"

"If this is 'Heaven'—" Jack uses his fingers to mark Annie's words, "then why would you make it look like a hospital? No one likes hospitals! They aren't comforting at all!"

The five doctors are standing around him allowing him to come to the conclusions that they are there to help him define. He is indeed in the Afterlife. Jack formulates the only conclusion he can—he's convinced, momentarily, that he is indeed on the Other Side. But he doesn't even believe there is an afterlife. He is a card-carrying member of a few skeptic societies and now here he is coming face-to-face with a realm that is more real than the world he lived in. Jack has the wind removed from his sails.

Then his thoughts begin to race again. *The memorial vision... Implying my death... Oh and the flashes of my life that are not so heart-warming... Am I really locked in here? Is this like purgatory or limbo?* The thought of leaving behind his family hits him and makes him highly emotional.

"Wait so you're telling me, I'm dead? And my family never gets to see me? That my children will grow up without me? How is that fair? This is insane. You can't just do that to little kids. They'll never be the same again."

There is a moment where silence is the star, as the doctors closely watch Jack. Annie locks eyes with him for a second and senses what he needs.

Jack takes a breath and sits back to watch how this all is going to play out. *It is clear that this Dr. Brooks means business. She is in control and evidently is somehow in charge.*

Dr. Annie Brooks scans the room, glides to the right of Jack's bed and draws back the curtain, allowing more of the melodic light into the room. Bright, white light encompasses all of him—smelling like vanilla, tasting like chocolate and feeling like illuminated silk—he is blissfully sedated by it. It calms Jack for a moment.

At times the light seems to flood in through the tall windows that are, for the most part, higher than he is tall. It is a right light of white-gold and at times possesses a density close to liquid.

"OK. Let's do this properly from the top, shall we? Welcome, Mr. Richman. How are you feeling?"

Jack becomes un-stunned for a moment, re-embraces his earthly personality, feeling that finally he is going to get the answers and assistance he requires from this woman and like Brian bombarding Christina, he unleashes a litany of his own.

"How am I feeling? Who the hell are you? And where exactly am I? Can you explain why I am wearing pants that are over 15 years old and why I don't have any of my stuff... my ring is gone... my wallet? Cell phone?" Jack is annoyed. He is asking earthly defined questions in a place that had its own set of rules. His energy is really more like a child's than of a successful writer, husband and father of three.

The woman in the lab coat smiles and it seems to instinctively calm him. She feels and looks like the perfect blend of lavender, tea, and Xanax. As tough as Jack is attempting to be, he is absolutely intoxicated by this woman.

"My name is Dr. Annie Brooks. Today begins a process of transition, which is highly individualized," Dr. Brooks says with a loving yet forceful smile. "There is much to be done, Jack, and we want this process to happen as swiftly and efficiently as possible. Most people are here for a brief moment and others, depending on what we need to work through, a wee bit longer."

Still feeling calm, he manages to blurt out, "Where the hell am I?"

Dr. Brooks raises her eyebrow and looks at her residents with an amused expression. She ignores his question and glances over to the other residents. When Dr. Brooks does not officially recognize Jack's question, he hears the cries of the young girl yet again.

"Help me, Mommy... please help me.... Mama! Ayudame Mama!"

Being ignored in this foreign healthcare facility is annoying, but hearing the cries of a child go unanswered angers him. Realizing that she is choosing not to answer him directly, Jack reaches over to grab Dr. Brooks' arm. When he touches her they both get more than expected.

Jack links to Annie, and for the second time, a kaleidoscope of imagery is dancing in front of him. Annie, mutually stunned, looks at Jack and without hesitation joins him in watching the scenes unfold.

Whooosh.

An engaging young lady, who looks like Annie, steps out with laced boots from a handsome carriage onto a cobblestone street. She looks at him and opens her white, fringed parasol. Behind her he sees the Tower Bridge in London off in the distance.

Whooosh.

A slightly older embodiment of the same lady is kneeling in church, to the left and right are her children, also deep in prayer.

Whooosh.

The woman, now wearing a flowing white nightdress, sits in front of a Victorian-era vanity. In her left hand is an ornately decorated silver hand mirror that she's intently staring into. In her right hand, she holds the matching silver brush... she strokes her hair. A man in a nightshirt and sleeping cap appears from the shadows undetected. He walks behind her, leans down, takes the brush out of her hand, and slowly brings her hand to his lips for a gentle kiss. She smiles. She stands up, and he embraces her from behind as he unties the front string that keeps her neckline taut, then his right hand caresses her bosom.

CHAPTER 10: ALTERING LIFETIMES OF THOUGHT

Jack's World

Dr. Annie Brooks and Jack look at each other in astonishment, uncomfortable and speechless about what just happened. He is clear that whatever it just was, she was not expecting it either. Their chemistry seems to be quite volatile, or maybe compatible would be a better way of explaining it. The two of them had witnessed vignettes of Annie's life that were personal and fragmented, full of emotion, laughter, sorrow and history. Jack stops analyzing and just becomes one with the moment.

The four doctors look at each other to see if anyone can explain what just happened between Dr. Brooks and the patient. Noticing her residents' looks, Dr. Brooks tries to sound even more professional and proper than her normal lilting, British-accented speaking voice, as she regains her composure. The other doctors look at each other in shock.

Jack knows in that moment that they are *all* connected in some way, but can't explain how. Or why.

Snapping back to the situation at hand, Jack begs, "Can you please tell me if my family has been notified?"

"Yes, your family has been notified... But apparently you already know that?" Dr. Brooks is now trying to pull Jack onto the program of thought *she* needed him on. Jack looks down at the emblem on his pants, still trying to figure out how and why?

Deep down he knows the answer—but he doesn't want anyone to say it.

Dr. Brooks continues, "Jack, we will be working through and analyzing what just happened to you, and its implications."

"Lady, I just had some serious flashbacks about my life, I might have watched my funeral, then I touched you and felt like I time-travelled like Doctor Who in his Tardis to nineteenth-century England, and now I am supposed to unpack the lessons learned in my most recent lifetime?" Jack glares at Annie.

Annie Brooks smiles at her newly admitted patient and simply says, "Yes, and that last part about the lessons, that was all you, luvs. I didn't mention that part yet."

Jack thought with clarity, that he knew she did not say it verbally, but she did impart it to him when he touched her. His thoughts immediately go to a place of what it would be like to make love to someone with whom he had such a visceral connection, to be of one body and one mind.

The one male doctor, Dr. Roberts, looks up and laughs out loud, commenting under his breath, "Good luck with the ice queen, Jack."

Really? Where is your professionalism Dr. Roberts? Dr. Brooks reprimands him. But Jack is looking at her perfectly sculpted face and her lips do not move. This place *is* "different." He's reading their thoughts.

Dr. Brooks regains her composure and looks at Jack's face. He looks like he is entranced with her. "The energy of the Universe is not accidental and all of us are working here today towards a successful discharge. So listen and learn, and we will move through this process as quickly as you possibly can."

Dr. Chin speaks out, "As we make the rounds your karma and its evolution will be evaluated on a spiritual scale." Annie puts both hands out to her sides, palms up, and tips her body to the left like she's a scale. "On this side we measure the Love in your soul now as compared to when you started this last incarnation, life or as we put it, journey." She alternates sides. "And over here we weigh the Fear, then and now. To progress of course, the Love will have to far outweigh the Fear."

To Jack's right, there is a familiar smell of Grandpa Joe again, as if he is a cologne, lingering to remind him who just walked by. Jack is drawn to the smell. He looks down on the floor and sees the white rabbit his Grandpa Joe was holding on his lap in the dream on the flight over. He laughs out loud and questions if he is about to go down the rabbit hole or through the looking glass. *In dream symbols what would this mean?* The rabbit hops out of the room and Jack tries to move in its direction. He feels thrust backwards like he has vertigo and his vision becomes a kaleidoscope of images, again.

Suddenly 'Super Jack' is flying through the moments of his life like people fast forward through commercials on their DVR. He enjoys his own version of *This Is Your Life*, and stops to relive subtle moments—from his first day of school, to smelling cookies, to the day Brian was delivered.

"JACKIE! Go to them." Grandpa Joe's voice echoes.

Unbeknownst to the doctors, a part of Jack has joined Grandpa Joe on a second Peter Pan ride through his memories. This amazing, mind-expanding trip down memory lane puzzles him as he sees images of a horse drawn carriage, cobble stone streets, eclectic tea pots, herbs, and the beautiful image of the corseted doctor stepping out of the coach and smiling at him.

Dr. Annie Brooks yells to the team, "We are losing him! Quick! Energize his etheric double, and anchor him to his thoughts here. *I cannot lose another one.*"

The doctors spring to action, making changes to the monitors next to Jack's bed.

The familiar memories warm him, and he is flying faster again through the tunnels of colors, he looks for London's Big Ben because, *What Peter Pan flight would be complete without a flyby of London's famous clock tower?* But it's not there. This thought jumps and morphs quickly into the Sears Tower in Chicago.

Along the journey songs are whisking by as quickly as a radio on scan. Pieces of the soundtrack of his life are being dropped in and he is enjoying every aspect of this magic carpet ride.

Just like Superman flying through deep space and hearing a cry for help, Jack is pulled to his left where he sees an image of his kids dancing in the living room to *Shrek's* remake of "I'm A Believer." He smiles at the image. This journey is quite awesome. He continues to soar and explore all the while thinking, *I had a great life.*

The good vibrations of his flight cease when he finds himself staring at his family from the outside looking in. He had been to this place before. It was the Junior High School in Rosemont where the kids got dropped off and picked up for camp. He had done this a million times before, but this time, it's different. This time it's the exact moment Christina informs the kids that he might be dead.

Jack is unable to hear what she says that puts the energy of his family into such a dark place. It feels like the lowest key on a piano is being pressed down haphazardly and held for no good reason... The pain is felt in seven different places on his body. Jack has no idea what the origin or cause of this pain and toxicity is, but he is eager to stop and fix it. He knows what they are feeling—despair—one look at Brian's countenance makes Jack burn at the center of his being. Jack feels poisoned with information, and it is slowing him down and making his flight nosedive.

"Jackie! Go to them," Grandpa Joe's voice echoes, again.

Jack feels helpless. He hates the way it washes over him, filing him with despair and yet, he's unable to help them. This is why Jack didn't watch certain movies that forced you to feel. He didn't like other people telling him how to feel. After witnessing this dark and intense scene, he recognizes *everything* he just experienced was a montage of earthly moments that had *already taken place.*

Earth – 3 Days After the Explosion

"Answer the phone, Daddy... please... answer the phone." Brian is standing in the kitchen, with Christina's cell phone pressed up against his ear. It's ringing and ringing. Tears are running down his cheeks.

Christina walks in, sees Brian from behind, and tiredly asks, "Brian, honey, what are you doing with my phone? I've been looking everywhere for that."
Brian turns around, knowing he's been caught. Christina's heart melts as she sees the tears streaming down his face. With an innocence she's used to hearing from Matilda, "I'm sorry, I just wanted to hear Daddy's voice."

Crushed, Christina can do nothing but scoop him up into her arms. The phone continues to ring.

Jack's World

The flight is over. The scenes are complete. Jack's back in the hospital bed. All the doctors are hovered over him, letting out sighs of relief. He knows something went wrong; he's completely weakened.

The phone next to Jack's bed begins to ring...

Always on top of all situations, The Director sees this unfolding, presses a button, then gets up to attend to the matter herself. She will not risk her secret being revealed.

Jack looks at the phone next to his bed. It should sound like the old fashioned rotary phone that it is, but instead its ring is loud and reminiscent of a regular modern household phone. Unsure, but comforted by the 1-8-4-1 on it, he slowly reaches out to answer it.

Dr. Roberts sees Jack's arm move and attempts to help him, just as the Director storms in, "Do not answer that phone!"

CHAPTER 11: DECEIT

Jack's World

"Do not answer that phone!"

It is a command, not a request.

All the doctors stand in astonishment as The Director looks at each of them in Jack's room. Her fury is commanding, and she becomes the alpha—the leader and the boss. Jack observes the dynamics of his medical team shift immediately upon her arrival.

Dr. Annie Brooks looks at The Director with annoyance that her authority is being undermined in such a blatant manner. Her statistics for soul retention (that is, "saves") is extremely low, so she knows she is being watched and now, apparently, micromanaged. Understanding her weaknesses, she recently finished putting together an integrated team of professionals. Together, they are just the right blend of personalities, past life experiences, and needed lessons learned to help guide patients on to the next level.

Dr. Gareth Roberts had been a womanizer in his past life, so now he would learn his lessons by helping patients assess the relationships in their lives. Dr. Susan Chin's karmic rehab is to temper her own overinflated, self-destructive image of herself. It's like looking in a mirror as she helps patients deal with their own egos.

Dr. Lesley White was picked to evaluate generosity, making sure that over-compensation for guilt is not mistaken for kindness. Finally, Dr. Brooks' latest addition was Dr. Roberto Avanti, who was brought on to assess the truthfulness of the patients in order to understand the slippery slope from fibbing to downright fabrication.

On one level, with the creation of this team, the souls to be admitted to Dr. Brooks' floor of the hospital would be successfully triaged and discharged to their next energetic existence. On another level, by successfully processing them, she should be pleasing The Director, and the Council of Elders. However, on her deepest level, she's still scanning each soul and investigating clues for the current whereabouts of her own long lost children.

Dr. Brooks knows the process of crossing over from the physical world to their world is an individual's very unique journey, and like an earthly fingerprint or a snowflake, no two will ever be exactly the same. As a team, the doctors have to manage each soul or patient's case with meticulous detail.

Towering over all, though small in stature, is The Director.

Again, Jack notices a point being made without a word having been uttered, but somehow the intention is understood. And this time, he can't hear it.

The Director looks as if she has walked out of a Chanel catalog. She is wearing a classic two-piece black suit that is made up of fabric that seems to move and capture light variously. Her regal brown hair has the same rhythmic shimmer as her ensemble. Jack's thoughts about this place are still developing rapidly. The colors, smells and sounds all tell the same story: This is The Director's domain.

She oozes control. She is exercising her power now. In this brief, timeless moment, The Director is the quintessential and consummate chess player—as yet undefeated. But with all that power, something about Jack challenges her title and position. Jack does not yield to her power, and he is compelled to defy her.

Jack hesitates as the ringing phone rocks the depths of his soul. It creates a stirring, an urge that only the worst of addicts could identify. It is a need that has a mission all its own. The desire to connect with whoever is on the other side of the receiver overpowers Jack. His intention is to ignore this alpha female's demand. His confidence in reaching for the receiver is bolstered by the overpowering clairalience (a psychic smelling) of Grandpa Joe. Jack's beliefs are being challenged right there and then. Jack continues to wonder, *How can my Grandpa Joe communicate through his own scent?*

Jack notices a direct correlation between Grandpa Joe's ability to materialize and the doctors' lack of presence. There is a distinctive pattern; he can only feel and smell him when they are *not* there. Jack trusts that Grandpa Joe, his savior and hero, would guide him toward the light once again. Now, with The Director in the room, he feels an added distance between himself and his guardian. He discovers a useful weapon—if he blocks the doctors out of his present energy, he can embrace Grandpa Joe.

"Do not trust her Jack. Answer it! Answer the phone!" Grandpa Joe urges him directly into his consciousness.

Jack defiantly reaches for the receiver to answer the call, unaware that Brian's desire, intention, and love are crossing energetic worlds to make this call possible.

CHAPTER 12: DEARLY DIS-CONNECTED

Earth – 3 Days After the Explosion

Brian hugs his mom in a way that makes Christina actually feel appreciated. She feels guilty for experiencing happiness under such extreme circumstances. But the connection with her son is too sweet, and they both need each other.

She pulls away from her embrace with Brian to offer an idea, "Maybe we can watch some old family videos tonight? I know it might be hard, but it's important for Matilda . . ." Christina tries to sound positive. "She might not remember Daddy like you and Kimberly will. OK? Please?"

"Sure, Mom. Sounds great."

"Go into the den and look at some of the DVD titles, Bri, and we can discuss which ones to watch later. OK, honey?"

Brian is very much a mixture of his mother and father at this moment, full of determination. He continues to hold the ringing phone out of her eyeshot. He fakes a smile.

She begins to sniffle and tear up, but she doesn't want Brian to see. She forces a smile and turns back towards the dining room, where Jack's office files wait to be addressed. She's trying to shield him from the waterfall of emotion that is about to burst through her calm, maternal front.

The table looks daunting, so she heads up to her bedroom where the journal she just started lies open. Three days ago, when she found out Jack had been in an explosion, after she finally got the kids down, she needed someone to talk to. She needed her best friend. She needed Jack.

So she went down into the basement office and found one of Jack's composition notebooks. (He always kept a stack of them in there for when he was writing a story.) She took it to her bedroom and stayed up all night "talking" to him. Tears constantly blurred the writing, but it didn't matter. She just had to get her thoughts out while she could. If she kept them bottled up, sooner or later she'd lose it.

Brian quickly heads into the den before his mom can remember to ask for the phone back. He'll be out of sight and can continue to make his call.

Christina writes:

It's now been 3 days since the explosion. You can come home now, you know. The joke's on us. Good one. I need you home now, OK? Everyone—and I do mean everyone —thinks they are being helpful when they tell me to prepare for the worst . . . that you're not going to come home. I know there's no sign of you at the hotel, hundreds of people have been pronounced dead. I have been, and will continue to contact the Red Cross. You can't be gone. How do I deal with this? Your son just tried to phone you. I look into his eyes and completely understand. For Christ's sake, I'm writing to you, and you could be dead. And then I turn around and there's this pile of your stuff . . . all your writing drafts and bills, stock information. I just can't deal with this. I don't know how to help them Jack. You're the one who always levels with them. How can I try to help our kids when I am in denial myself? You always laughed when I read those self-help books, claimed that I was the most "together" person you knew. What do you think now? I can quote some of those books, but now they are just other people's words on a page, devoid of feeling. I guess the best I can do is hope that they are helping me on an unconscious level. I mean half the time when I speak these days I don't even know what I'm saying. Maybe I am saying something right? Who knows?

I'm trying to do the best I can. You know my lists that I can't live without? Well, I mean, how do I make a list for this stuff when I can't think straight? I'm calling FBI Bobby constantly. I tried to call the hotel, but that's a pile of dust now. All I can get at the hospital is a busy signal. Earlier today, I got through and the woman went to check a list, but I got disconnected. I just don't know what to do. Neither do the kids. Are you alive, or not? This limbo may be worse than knowing you're actually dead.

I've been trying to go through the things from your filing cabinet to keep myself busy. I don't want anything important to slip through the cracks. Boy, do I wish I'd tried harder to understand your thought process behind organization instead of suggesting we keep our things separate and each do it our own way. Sure it saved us fighting over dumb stuff, but now I don't know where to begin. Your stuff is in piles all over the dining room table. YOU KNOW HOW I HATE A MESS! I'm reorganizing my way, but it's taking forever.

I guess I don't have to do this now, but I feel like a) it's something to do, and b) when you're back home, then I'll stand by and laugh as you try to make sense of my system! I mean, I totally understand now how you always complained there isn't enough room in that office to "spread out." Ugh, that's why it's all up in the dining room now— taunting me. But I've made some progress. Bills are blue; bank info, yellow; car insurance, orange; research, green; book drafts, pink. I'm going to run out of colors soon . . . Gotta go to Staples.

You see this "mess" is why MY "system" starts out in the kitchen with an expanding pocket folder, with each bill type having its own section. Why couldn't you just do it MY way!

Sorry, don't mean to lash out at you. It's not your fault

people suck and don't know how to fix a gas leak or keep a person on hold. I just can't control my emotions. Jack, I need to hear you tell me to breathe. That's what you always do. You focus me and I'm OK.

As her stream of consciousness runs faster than she can write, Brian compulsively continues hitting redial on the phone. He feigns searching for a family DVD knowing he's safe for a bit because his mom is "processing." His dad was always saying, "Your mom's 'processing.' Give her space."

Brian is in a better place than Christina. He knows it, and she knows it too, but there is no app, no tool, no book, nothing to organize her emotions or feelings . . . She needs Dad. He needs Dad. They all do. He just *has* to be all right.

Christina scribbles:

I hear your voice telling me to just analyze the situation. Here's the analysis Jack: We're broken without you. We're a puzzle that is missing the biggest, most important piece. Analysis? That won't help me sort out my grief or whatever you want to call this! Nor will it help me control or process the emotions of our three children. I can't get that look on Brian's face as he tried to call you out of my mind. All I could do was hug him. I mean, a hug's nice, but is it enough? I just don't know.

Brian is on a mission. He surreptitiously hits End Call and Redial on her phone. Brian also knows that Christina is so lost in her own thoughts that she is going to forget to ask him for her phone back.

Fortuitously for Brian, his little sister, Kimberly, starts screaming, "MOMMY!" Brian knows that this new uprising will buy him more time.

"What now, guys?" Christina calls out.

Oh great—your children are fighting. AGAIN. I swear,

when I was growing up all I wanted was a sister. But the way these 2 girls fight? Glad I never had one. Jack one of these days I'm going to lose it with them. All this emotion is just going to spring out, and they are going to get the brunt of it. I'm so scared. Do you think if it happened they'd ever forgive me? God, and here I thought I was a good mom. What kind of mother lashes out at her kids? How could I play the role of perfect mother and wife if I no longer have the perfect father and husband to work off of?

She pauses and the answer pops into her mind.

Time? Time. I don't know if it's you that just answered . . . I hope not, because that means you're dead. But I don't want time. I want you, Jack. That is what the self-help books always say: "Things will get better. Time is the best medicine in life."

This morning I looked up a number of grief support groups online and was shocked at how many there actually were.

> *Missing a child? Check!*
> *Missing a parent? Check!*
> *Suicide support? Check!*
> *Parents of murdered family? Check!*
> *Lost a spouse? Check!*
> *Lost a pet? Check!*

HUSBAND POSSIBLY BLOWN UP IN FOREIGN LAND ON ASSIGNMENT? No check. ☹ Maybe I should look up September 11 groups. A lot of those people would know about this limbo feeling—or disaster relief. Perhaps I was just looking in the wrong places. I don't know . . . why isn't there one for us? Don't you think our kids are more of the private one-on-one type of kids? I do. I am for sure. Grief is like sex—it is something that you handle on a personal and private basis. Why would I want to go to a therapy petri dish? Ugh, I can't bear the thought of walking into a

*group and having to share what happened to you and dis-
cuss our feelings. What if people had conflicting religious
views or thoughts about parenting in general? Would I
want to listen to them on how to parent a child who is dealing with the loss of one of the parents? Maybe I should go
to a divorce support group?*

Christina's rapid-fire stream of consciousness thoughts
are firing six times the normal speed. But she realizes she can't
continue right now. She has to get the house ready for their
dinner guest. She needs to clean up and stop World War III
from happening between Matilda and Kimberly. As she is picking up Brian's socks and sneakers from the hallway, she cannot
understand for the life of her why Kimberly, as mature and well
spoken as she is, is so unkind to her younger sibling.

She heads toward the escalating crying of Matilda, who
wants to know where Moosey is.

Kimberly is arguing her case. "ONE, I would not touch
your dirty little toy, and, TWO, why do you need to walk around
carrying that smelly thing everywhere?"

Christina's thoughts start splitting into why therapy
might really not just be an option, but a necessity. She tells herself that she has to switch into mother-mediator mode. She'd
have to continue these thoughts for later tonight, with Jack. *But
do I believe in therapy? Yes, I do. Therapy is good . . . on paper and
in theory but so much depends on the actual therapist. Where to go
first?*

Brian, completely out of sight from the three women in
his family, knows that his mom will be overwhelmed by the
fighting and continue to forget all about her mobile phone. He
will continue to hit redial until someone answers. For once his
annoying sisters come in handy. He does, however, agree with
his mom that watching a family movie with Dad in it, is a really
good idea.

*Maybe the last Disney World vacation would be the best one.
Matilda will remember being dressed up like Princess Jasmine and*

Daddy allowing his face to be painted. Yeah, that's the one. Brian smiles as he remembers about better times.

Christina trudges down the hall towards her fighting "princesses." For the third time in an hour she feels like she is going to lose it. *Maybe I should call the insurance company and see what, if any, type of therapy is covered.*

She pauses just before Kimberly's bedroom. *I wonder if there is time where Jack is?*

Brian, refusing to believe that he will never see, touch, feel, or hear from his father ever again, pulls the receiver up to his ear as it rings endlessly. Now his face is solid, serious, and more determined than ever.

"Answer the phone, Daddy." The phone goes to a steady busy...busy...busy...

Brian's arms drop to his sides, his head falls forward and his shoulders start to move quickly up and down. His guilt, grief and reality become a silent wailing for his father. Brian hangs up and hits Redial on the phone for what feels like the hundredth time.

"Why hasn't it gone to voice mail?" He sighs in disgust.

Busy.

He would have to find another way to connect with his Daddy. He stops dialing and, out of frustration, goes down the basement stairs to his dad's man cave, a.k.a. the office. While booting up the family iMac, Brian looks around the room. Side by side with Jack's journalism awards are his and Kimberly's spelling bee, science fair, chess, and debate trophies. Never to be left out, last June Matilda had prominently added her pre-school diploma to their "Smart Wall." Brian is sitting in the very same swivel chair where he once sat on his daddy's lap, dazzling everybody with his computer prowess even before he could walk.

When the computer finally boots up, Brian notices the blue and white "S" icon in the Mac dock. Oh, how he wishes he could Skype his father! His curiosity takes over as he Googles "explosion in Johannesburg."

He looks at the thumbnail photographs and reads the search results: "Everyone in Immediate Area Assumed Dead," "Death Toll Rises," and "Foreign Death Toll Higher Than Expected Due to AAIC—Some of the World's Greatest Thinkers Gone." Brian reacts to these headlines with horror.

"Why couldn't you just answer the phone, Daddy? Why didn't you make me come with you? We could've been together! And now I'm never going to see you again."

He pulls himself together. An image of a book cover he'd seen on Matt's kitchen counter flashes in his mind. *Questions from Earth, Answers from Heaven,* written by a psychic. He made note of the title because it was something he was planning on talking to his parents about. He was going to talk to them separately knowing his mom would be more sympathetic than his scientifically minded father.

Since that wasn't happening now, he googles "psychic". He is a bit overwhelmed by how many millions of sites the search engine yields with one small word. So he decides to narrow the search and types in the phrase "talk to the dead." If his dad is in fact dead, then this will be the only way to talk to him. Ten-year-old Brian's world is about to get infinitely bigger and more complex.

Just then Kimberly sneaks up behind him. "Whatcha you doin'?"

"Research," he says, in a tone that Jack would answer in when Christina would come down to the basement ready to ask Jack to do something for her upstairs.

"Research? Well, you're not gonna like what mom has in store for us tonight. You might want to pay attention to your sister." She continues in a singsong voice, "You know they didn't let me skip a grade for no reason. *Brian!*"

Brian is ignoring her. If there's one thing Kimberly likes —and needs—it's attention. Brian is not interested in feeding Kimberly's ego. He wants information and knows that if he ignores her long enough she will walk away.

"Yeah . . . research. I don't think Mom would like whatever it is you're doing."

Annoyed at the exchange, he watches Kimberly run out. He wonders if she is going to alert his mother to him being up to something. He hates the fact that she is so good with words and so manipulative. *And* he hates that his dad doesn't see how smooth she is; he thinks Kimberly is funny.

Realizing she can't get a rise from Brian, Kimberly decides to try and scare him by shutting the lights off at the bottom of the stairs. Sitting in the dark, with only the glow of the iMac screen lighting up the room, he remembers his dad telling him that you only need a little bit of light to alleviate the darkness. Brian feels they are all living in darkness, what they need is way to find that light.

Kimberly continues upstairs, laughing.

Brian shakes it off and goes back to reading. Google pulls up a metaphysical bookstore five minutes from his house called Moonbeam. The store is hosting a Psychic Fair this Sunday, from 11 a.m. to 5 p.m., featuring the return of world-renowned and local psychic medium Shelley Southport. She'll be signing her book, <u>The Dead Can Speak</u>.

"I am absolutely going!" Brian decides. He just needs to figure out how he can get there.

CHAPTER 13: RINGTONES FROM HOME

Jack's World

The Director moves in front of Jack's bed in less than a nanosecond of Earth time, astonishing Jack with her speed. He never imagined movement could be so swift. With her simple and powerful energy, she spoke to him with her eyes, "You cannot answer that call, Jack. I am sorry."

Jack can feel that she is only partially remorseful. He reaches for the phone as quickly as he can, but it seems that his arm is "heavier" in some way. He questions his reflexes. Jack's delay is The Director's gain.

"In due time, Jack, in due time," Grandpa Joe whispers as his Canoe cologne lingers.

The Director knows that she has averted one disaster, but that the case of Jack Richman is going to prove difficult. In order for her to protect her secret from being revealed, a transfer would be necessary—and STAT. Jack Richman's status as an L1, or Level 1, needed to be changed immediately. The Director motions to her staff to meet her outside so she can have a word with them. They walk out into the hallway. Inexplicably, she is already waiting for them. This time, her movement is not storm-like; she only pulls that string for effect. Her evolved vibration at its higher frequency transports her as fast and as silently as she pleases.

The Director demands they not let Jack answer his phone. She knows that Jack is still tethered to his Earth life.

"A call will establish a link to the physical world. That was his son Brian trying to make a connection. We cannot afford for that to happen."

The doctors are embarrassed for their lack of foresight. The Director worries that the call could ruin everything. She especially needs to make sure that the transition he is making is going to be the *right* one. *Jack's energy is unusual, his case is unusual, and it needs to be handled with care.*

The Director reappears at Jack's bedside in another flash. "Mr. Richman, you and I need to have a talk." The Director states matter-of-factly, as the four residents stand silently behind her.

Dr. Brooks remains in the hallway to review Jack's chart. Surely she hasn't missed anything? What caused TD's reaction?

Jack hopes he can finally get some answers, but remains skeptical.

"Well, that's great. I can add you to the list of orderlies or wannabe doctors that seem to be dictating and narrating my afterlife journey. Everyone is completely keeping me in the dark! I have tons of questions, but nobody seems to desire to give me any answers. So, in this cast of characters, who might you be?" Jack asks sarcastically.

"I am the person who is in charge of this hospital and—"

"This hospital. The one that bears my name? I don't remember making a huge donation to any church for an afterlife hospital!"

"Are you finished now?" The Director's patience is gone. "I honestly don't do the whole 'Heavenly afterlife protocol' BS. The 'Are you OK with being dead?' routine. That's not my job. You are one of the millions of souls who transition all the time. You're not special. So, I am having you moved to a different floor —Level 5. I will be assigning you to a different team of doctors, and let's just say they are more equipped to deal with your type."

Jack is taken aback by her rudeness. His type? For the first time ever he feels victimized by racial bias, ethnic profiling and religious prejudice. But it doesn't have to do with being black, white, Muslim or Christian . . . it is dead or alive.

"Well, you know Ms.—I am sorry, you didn't mention your name. But actually, I don't care what it is. What *does* matter to me is that you are being so rude. Let me tell you, I am not going to any other level, floor or wherever, until Dr. Brooks comes back. And I want to see my grandfather. How can I be in heaven or the hereafter and he's not right here like he was earlier?"

Jack is assertive, but emotional at the same time. "For heaven's sake, I am a reporter. My nature is to ask questions and get answers, but no one will tell it to me straight."

Jack is feeling defeated. The Director, raises her eyebrows. "Here's what happened. You were walking through Mandela Square in Johannesburg, South Africa after finishing your family shopping spree. The smell of the driver's smoke-polluted car, coupled with the break out of protestors blocking your way, caused the panic attack which made you need to get out of the car and run. You never made it back to the hotel. There was an explosion. A huge gas leak blew and left a crater, where you were standing, that is the size of a man-made lake. So now you know."

The Director is staring at him with the energy of defiance. She knows that she should not have blurted out all of these facts, as Jack needs to realize them on his own. But he is gnawing away on her last afterlife nerve.

"Your being *here*, and your refusal to follow our protocol, is upsetting the balance in my hospital and—"

Jack cuts her off, "Right. So, you're Obi-Wan, and there's a break in the force, and it's my freaking fault!"

The Director is showing her impatience and annoyance on her face, like she would with a pebble stuck in her shoe on a hike.

"Who or what is an OB1?" She looks at the other medical staff for assistance.

Dr. Chin pipes up quickly with confidence, "Obi-Wan is short for Obi-Wan Kenobi or Ben Kenobi, who was a Jedi knight. He was trained to be a master under the Jedi Council and Master Yoda. He's an iconic character from a series of inspired writings from our world. The story has been attributed to a gentleman named George Lucas. There were movies, books, TV shows, and merchandise during the last half century of Earth time. The Council of Elders, helped to bring it to fruition for teaching purposes, for the younger generation." She smiles at The Director, happy to bring her this information.

The other doctors see this pop culture definition as Dr. Chin's way of sucking up to the Big Cheese. Her instant recall pisses them off frequently.

Dr. Brooks is visibly appalled at the impolite style of The Director's interference.

"*Star Wars*, ah yes, I remember now." The Director flashes a smile. She looks at Jack., "Here's the deal, as they say in your part of the universe: I am in charge here, and things happen here in the way I say, when I say, how I say, as I say. Got it?"

"Yes, Darth Vader." Jack suppresses his desire to attempt to use his new old physique to take her down. Giggles erupt from all, including Dr. Brooks.

"Prepare to be transferred, Mr. Richman."

Dr. Brooks quickly asks, "TD, may I ask what this is all about? What has brought you here? All protocols are being followed and I know that our, er, *my* statistics for saves and transitions are lower than the joint commission would want for our compliance but I—"

TD raises her hand for Dr. Brooks to stop speaking and "expressing" in front of Jack. She motions for the team to walk outside again so she can have a moment with Jack alone.

As she begins to walk out, Dr. Brooks starts to think very loudly, enabling Jack to hear her thoughts clearly. He looks directly at The Director to disguise his focus.

Annie is thinking: *Why on bloody Earth and heaven would The Director herself come down to investigate one of my L1s? Why is he so special? A Level 1 protocol does not ever require administration to get involved. Is it because lately I have been having difficultly doing my job correctly?*

Admittedly, Annie has not been focused. She has been getting more distracted and frustrated with the search for her own family. At this point, her ongoing quest is murky at best and shaking her confidence.

Dr. Lesley White meekly speaks up, "Dr. Brooks, I believe we have done something wrong to offend The Director."

The Director takes her eyes off Jack for a second and has a firm telepathic energy exchange with Dr. Brooks.

Dr. Roberts, who has been uncharacteristically silent, finally lets go: "Again. Wow! Well isn't that a shocker? We did something to go against The Director! We made her peeved . . . yet again. You know what? She's a b—"

"Doctors! Please!" Annie releases an exasperated sigh.

"Enough, all of you!" TD pops back into their conversation. Busted. She's the boss and what she says goes. She will explain her rationalizations on a need-to-know basis and that time is not now. When she feels they are ready, she will enlighten them on why Jack was placed in their care in the first place.

Satisfied she's made her point, she disappears to return to her office and arranges Jack's transfer.

Dr. Brooks looks at her team with an invitation for patience. "Ugh, I hate when she does that."

"It's very Samantha of her," Dr. Chin looks around to see if anyone understands her *Bewitched* reference. She prides herself on keeping pace with Earth Time and is always referencing something that none of the other doctors understand. And as usual, they just stand there with a mix confusion and annoyance.

Dr. Brooks continues, "Look, this too, shall pass. We will deal with TD, Mr. Richman and the rest of our patients in the most professional and uplifting manner we can. Remember, this is not about us. It is about them." The lilting British accent seems to semi-disappear while Jack is feeling Annie's pep talk from afar.

Jack assesses each doctor's reaction to The Director, the relationship they have with Annie, and each other. For a heavenly hospital, this is much more dysfunctional than any heaven scenario he has ever imagined.

"These people seriously do not have their shit together," Jack says under his breath while looking for Grandpa Joe to re-emerge now that they were gone.

Jack makes an attempt to get out of the bed. He desperately needs to look outside the window of the Jack Richman Memorial Hospital and is suddenly startled by a new visitor standing in his doorway. Sitting on the edge of the bed, he is surprised to see a young woman staring past him, looking towards the light flowing in from the window.

This olive-skinned young woman is obviously approachable. Her athletic build and thick, black, curly hair represent strength. He has a sudden intuition that she will become the friend and support that he so desperately needs.

"Hi!" she smiles through her green eyes and amazing energy. "I am Anthea. I'm the assistant to The Director."

Jack has now seen a number of people, souls or whatever you want to call them, flutter in and out of his room. So what is just one more?

"Hello," he says with a laugh and a nonchalant nod.

"Jack, I am going to make a promise to you—one that will sound completely strange and somewhat crazy. I promise to help you. I just need you to listen to me when I say that you can trust no one. Can you do that for me?" Anthea is still smiling, yet conveying a determined stance.

"Sweetheart, that is the easiest thing to ask of me. You got it!" Jack says without hesitation.

Anthea looks away again towards the corner of the room where all the light is pooling on the floor, and she recognizes the darkness in Jack's room. It's why she decided to come visit him now—she's alarmed at the war brewing over his soul.

When she looks back at him, she smiles and says, "We are going to be friends. I am going to show you some amazing things about yourself and this place. But *this place* will ask things of you as well. Are you ready?"

Jack pauses for a second and at the hearing of this question feels what would have been his heart racing. He only has one response. The question is a real one, a powerful one. He knows that when he answers it he is answering a call to action...

He responds in a barely audible sound with a single word: "Yes."

CHAPTER 14: FATHER PATRICK MORAN

Earth – 3 Days After the Explosion

Brian is unsure what to expect from this fair. He had been to a science fair before, but never a *psychic* fair. An hour or so goes by and Brian continues to delve deep into the occult via internet research. He is reading about psychics, mediums, and those who purported to speak with the dead. Tarot, numerology, astrology, mediums . . . *This is some crazy shit,* Brian thinks. A lot of the people, whom Brian is reading about, immediately have credibility and then some are just ridiculous. Their websites have freaky music playing in the background, doves, butterflies, birds and angels plastered all over the place and more adjectives to describe their *gift* than actual demonstration. Brian knows that some of these people are just trying to steal people's hard earned cash.

Dad would be laughing with me right now, he thinks to himself.

Whenever he helped his dad research concepts, the first rule to weed out potential sources to interview would be if the candidates had too many words, specifically adjectives, to describe themselves. Titles like "The Greatest Scientific Mind of the 20th Century" were immediately disregarded. Jack would always say to Brian, "If they can't say it succinctly then they are not well versed enough in their field."

Now Brian is applying that formula to this weird new world he is exploring. He doesn't approach it with cynicism; he approaches it as if he is helping his dad look up the migration of manatees from one part of Tampa Bay to the other and why. He knows nothing about manatees and he knows nothing about mediums.

And apparently a lot of mediums come from Long Island? What the heck is up with that? Brian wonders.

Brian comes across one man from Holland who, when he did a direct translation, came out to being "the greatest instrument of the Spirit World". What Brian really can't understand is why this man would be standing in front of an audience without his shirt on? *Don't they care more about talking to Grandma, than seeing his man boobs?* Brian starts to laugh and then stops when he realizes his dad isn't there to laugh with him.

Another advertisement he sees that he has no clue what it means, is: "If *Good Housekeeping* was to give a seal for predictions." *What does house cleaning have to do with predictions?* Normally, he'd ask his mom about this stuff, but he knows he's not ready to explain this to her.

Brian's personal favorite is the woman who guarantees she can connect with anyone that ever existed for $12.99 a minute. He guesses, *A lot of people must want to connect with Elvis, because his picture is posted next to that blonde lady with the beauty mark on her face, and Michael Jackson.* He begins to talk as if his dad is sitting right next to him, "Is this for real? Puh-lease."

In addition to all the websites that come up in the search about psychic stuff, there is an equal amount of anti-psychic stuff. He discovers that psychics are still persecuted like it is the Inquisition. (He's proud of himself for paying attention that day in history class.) Brian finds information on skeptical societies, magicians, and illusionists, to religious fundamentalists all explaining how a belief in the paranormal made you a "para-MORON" (his word). Jack taught him that when doing any exploration or research into a project he couldn't mistake for fact another person's bias or opinion. Data was to be collected and explored.

If scientists did research, it was up to them to replicate

and extend the data under laboratory rules and regulations using the scientific method. Jack's job as a journalist was to do objective research. But Brian always wanted Jack to have an opinion and when Brian would ask, he would simply say, "I just don't know yet what I think." Brian always replied, "How can you not know what you think?"

Now, Brian completely understood what his father meant. He really does not know yet, what to think, nor is he ready to formulate an opinion. He does, however, know what he desires—these people to be real. He *needs* them to be real. He wants to explore the potential that there is something else out there that his Dad is a part of and, if possible, to connect with him.

Click after click and site after site Brian is bombarded with images and words that are like a different language. Some of it might as well be about vampires, witches, werewolves and the people who hunt them. This is foreign and freaky territory for a ten-year-old kid. He's guarding the computer screen as if he had googled "naked girls" in the search and doesn't want his mom catching him.

"Minister of Death: The Untold Story of Reverend James Joseph Jones." When Brian clicks on this heading, he is freaked out by the look in the reverend's eyes. He looks a touch crazy. This "man of God" conducted séances in the dark and was later exposed as a fraud when all the reported psychic happenings seemed to be explained in a logical and rational way. Brian sadly concludes, *Well, if that's possible, then maybe this is not real.*

But when it came to death, funerals, or heaven, he doesn't know anything about it—not really. He never had a tremendous amount of conversation about death, or heaven for that matter, with his dad or mom. Once or twice, he talked about his dad's Grandpa Joe and how much he missed him, but that was it. Now Brian is trying to find a connection between what he is reading and his real life experience. The only show that he comes up with is Disney's *The Wizards of Waverly Place*. There is the basic battle of good versus evil on the show, but no real conversation about heaven or talking to dead people. Dad had made him read *The Lion, The Witch and the Wardrobe* last year as a punishment for rudeness and *that* talked about another world or dimension, but not the hereafter. Although, Jack had said something about the last book in the series having to do with God and heaven, but that they was not ready for *that* conversation yet. *Sure feel ready now! Maybe I should read that book next,* he thinks.

Just then, Christina yells down into the basement, "Brian, come on up and eat, sweetie!"

He looks up and is shocked to see how much time has actually gone by. He thought he heard the doorbell, he's been transfixed by the screen. He realizes he is actually getting hungry and that he hasn't eaten since lunchtime. Not even a mid-afternoon "snackaroonie," as he and dad called them. The thought of that word anchors him right back to the harsh heavy feeling of loss. Grief is like a panther; it sneaks up on you like a predator and attacks when you are least ready for it . . . when you are defenseless. Brian quells his emotions by telling himself, *Mom didn't use the word "dead." The reports said there were survivors.*

When he turns the corner, he smells pizza. It is an undeniable smell that is a go-to food for the Richman household in a crunch time. Brian loves pizza nights.

What he doesn't love are surprises. *Yup! Doorbell most definitely rang.* Sitting before him at the kitchen table is a priest who Brian has seen before.

"Well hello, son!" Father Patrick Moran says jauntily.

He puts his hand out for Brian to shake. Brian is the second child in the room as Matilda is already eating a breadstick in her booster seat. When Kimberly is walking towards the kitchen, Brian looks at her in that sibling code that something is up, or in this case off. She shrugs and rolls her eyes; she'd had tried to warn him earlier, but he was too busy. Christina is embarrassed by their lack of respect for a man of the cloth. Father Moran is unfazed as he sits with his hands clasped together, his bearded chin resting on them.

Kimberly has the same reaction that Brian does, indifference and slight annoyance. Christina looks at the priest apologetically. He, smiles at her, acknowledging that they have their work cut out for them. He is on a mission and is hoping to make a difference in the lives of four people who just suffered a terrible, tragic loss and need to come to terms with it.

"Nice going, Mom . . . pizza and a priest. That should fix everything!" Brian snaps.

"BRIAN! Apologize to Father Moran right now! I did not raise you to be rude like this. Remember last year when you were rude like that? Your father made you read *The Lion, the Witch and the*—" Christina is completely befuddled and can't remember the title of the first book in the C.S. Lewis series.

"The Wardrobe," Father Moran and Brian say in unison. They both smile like they are in on a private joke.

This exchange throws Christina off even further. She's trying to so hard to do the right thing, to bring someone here so the kids can get some guidance, and nothing's happening like she thought it would. Kimberly and Brian really are cut from the same cloth and they are far more mature than their age. The conversations their parents had with them are now evident. These kids know how to not only communicate, but also navigate an adult conversation.

Kimberly stares at the priest skeptically. Without skipping a beat he returns her gaze and smiles. "Father? Why are you so handsome? You are too good looking to be like a priest and all." She asks, her eyes narrowed suspiciously.

Father Moran bursts out hysterically laughing with a soulful laugh and says, "Thank you."

As if she's on a mission, she continues, "So, it's like all those good looks are wasted on you . . . right? I mean, it's not like, um you can, ya know, use them to have a girlfriend or get married, right?"

Christina is mortified again.

Father Moran puts his pizza down, wipes his lips, takes a sip of the sparkling water on the table and recognizes that this dinner just took an adversarial turn.

"No, I have dedicated my life to God. I am married to the Church—my life is one of service."

Kimberly is a precocious girl fueled by today's modern technological tools. Texts, Facebook and Twitter are all modern-day note-passing, and they've honed her sense of sarcasm. Cyber bullying and mean girl-ness is a reality that adults didn't have to think about as kids, but she does. Survival in this arena is the training ground for her adolescence. As a result, she was used to navigating all the other girls and manipulating a conversation to flow into a direction where she maintains the upper hand. Kimberly was taught to be an empowered girl and she is. She is like her dad, always in control—always.

"So, basically you are a man married to a man . . . I mean Jesus," she says with a smirk, "or the Church, God or whatever." She gives him the good old attitude filled eye roll. "You don't know what it's like to be a husband, or a father. You don't really know what it's like to create and have a family of your own, OR deal with the loss of one of those members? So you're completely in over your head in *this* household." She stares him down. "So, are you just here for the pizza? Or are you thinking about dating my mom cause she might be free now?" She smiles meanly, and twirls her hair for added effect, and then waits for him to tuck his tail between his legs and get out of their house.

Christina is beyond mortified. She is not sure she's actually breathing at this very moment. Kimberly's outburst has pretty much sucked the air out of the room.

Matilda looks at everyone with staccato head turns and Brian is grinning, enjoying Kimberly verbalizing exactly what he was thinking, but was too polite to say. *Better her than me.* He knows the punishment for this will be severe.

Father Moran places his water down, but never once loses his control or waivers in his energy. He doesn't look at anyone but Kimberly, and it feels as if there is going to be a staring competition. Brian would later describe what happens next as a "no-he-*dit-int*" moment . . . Father Moran leans into the table. He is a big man that stands at over six feet tall and is pretty muscular for, well, a priest. He clearly takes good care of himself.

"Wow, you're a little bitch!" He says with a smile. *BOOM! The air is back in the room and this priest just brought it!* Brian is thrilled someone is finally putting his sister in her place. *This outta be really good,* he thinks.

Father Moran continues, "You are really angry, and you have a right to be so. And that is why I am going to tolerate your outburst, and stay here, and help you work through those feelings."

Kimberly turns beet red with embarrassment, pain and anger. Never in her life has she been talked to this way, and certainly not by any stranger.

"Are you sure this kid is only seven?" Father Moran asks Christina. He's used to getting this kind of treatment from the teenagers he counsels.

Trying to find words Christina manages to blurt out, "Seven going on 17, I'm afraid. I am so sorry."

Father Moran redirects his attention to Kimberly, who is looking angrier by the moment.

"You're right on most accounts. I am not married to a woman—technically, I am married to the church, that is, to God. But, my family responsibilities stretch beyond one house and into hundreds of houses and families—moms, dads, children, etc. I am on call seven days a week, twenty-four hours a day for souls like you. I put my own personal life on hold, so that I can help others. And you do need help, Kimberly. Because if you don't get help, you're going to grow from a sarcastic child to a deeply unhappy woman."

Christina stands up and says, "Father, maybe it's too soon."

"Sit down, Christina! I am *not* finished!" Father Moran says firmly, without taking an eye off the little python who is ready for her next attack.

But Kimberly's tough front can only get her so far and her eyes start to well up. Father Moran knows the type well.

"My time is important. I chose to come here tonight because I want you to know that I know that your dad loved you very much. Excuse me . . . LOVES YOU very much. Still does and always will. That is how my God, Father, loves ALL of us. That is why I am here tonight—because He sent me to help all of you. So please, allow me to."

The priest sees and feels that he is starting to get through to them and smiles.

Kimberly wants to hate him and yet, she feels his compassion for her and her family. Realizing she'll soon look like the bad guy, Kimberly softens her face and genuinely begins to listen to what he has to say.

Christina wants to light up three cigarettes and smoke all of them simultaneously with a glass of wine right now and then maybe add a Xanax at bedtime. She is beyond being at a loss for words but tries to find them.

"You know guys, this is not easy for any of us, including me. It's not like on the drive home from the school, I could just be normal again. That conversation can't be followed up with the simple mundane questions like 'what do you want for dinner?' or 'What happened at camp today?'"

She looks at the priest for mature and adult support, hoping he won't reprimand her. Christina needs to remain in charge and in control at all times. But, she is at a loss here and now the person who was going to be her ally, her support, her backbone, was clearly going to be her *mirror*. She knows that if Father Moran has no problem getting direct with her daughter, (who in her defense acts just like an unfiltered adult) she just should shut up and allow the night to flow as best it can. She regains her composure and takes a sip of the Brita purified water in her glass.

She looks at her children and smiles. "Guys, I know this is the worst time of our lives and you don't know what to say and you have to process exactly what you are feeling, or maybe you are processing it just fine and I am . . . well . . . There is no rulebook for parenting. I am doing the best I can. I invited Father

Patrick over tonight for just a talk. I do think he can help."

Father Moran sees this as a place to jump in and take some of the pressure off Christina. He recognizes that she needs him more than the kids do, and that he can talk to her by speaking to the children.

"I am not here for any other reason than to be a sounding board for you to share your feelings and for me to let you know that God has not abandoned you at all through this tough time." Father Moran only looks at the three children during this statement and uses his energy to punctuate his thoughts and feelings.

"I don't believe in God!" Brian blurts out. "God can't exist. God would never take away my father away from his family like this." Angry tears start spilling down his cheeks.

Matilda looks at her brother and can't share his pain. She doesn't feel what he is feeling. She looks at her big brother with confusion and wonder simultaneously. She is feeling happy and doesn't understand fully why everyone has been so sad faced and unpleasant to be around. "MORE PIZZA! MORE PIZZA!" she begins to chant while banging her plastic Elmo fork.

Father Moran serenely smiles at Brian's outburst and acknowledges his feelings, while placing a very healing hand on Matilda's arm that is not airborne. Now knowing what kind of communicators these kids actually are, he doesn't have to gauge them any longer. They are well beyond their years, and clearly their dad spoke to them as mature creatures with opinions and feelings. He did a good job. Christina is continuing to do the best job she can. He directs his positive energy towards Brian.

"OK. Full disclosure. I am not here to tell you what to believe or not. Quite honestly Brian, I don't really care what you believe." Everyone at the table is surprised by this priest's candor. "But my God, and my belief, and my ability is to be a really good friend and listener and to help my God's children, of which you are one of, to think, explore, feel and ultimately heal. So, how can I help you? Tell me how I can help all of you!"

The air in the kitchen gets immediately lighter by the priest's directness and honesty. It disarms all the Richman children and immediately makes him *cool.* Brian is the first one to speak.

"You want to help me? For real?" Brian asks sheepishly.

"Yes, I do." The priest responds.

"Good. Then I need to come to work with you on Sunday. Let's say the 9 o'clock Mass?"

Father Patrick Moran thinks to himself that there's more to this request than meets the eye.

Christina looks at her son as if he is speaking a completely different language. They are not the Sunday Service family. She doesn't want to have to start now either—grief or not.

"Great. Father, can you pick me up at 8:45?" Brian negotiates while the women at the table watch him. He definitely does *not* want Christina on this mission. "Or do you need more time to get into your priest mode?"

"I will pick you up at 8:30 a.m. Brian. You will have to make one concession for me first. Is that all right?"

Uncertain, he answers, "Sure… "

"I need you to pray for your dad tonight, for yourself and family, too. Will you do that?"

"Sure, you got it. Pray it up I will. 'Our Father full of grace, hallowed be thy name…"

Father Moran now pulling a slice of pizza from the box shakes his head because he knows he has his work cut out for him. "Yeah, something like that would work. It's a start!" He laughs out loud.

"Kimberly, will you promise to try it with your brother? Pray for your father?" The priest asks.

"Well, what do I get out of the deal? Brian got something."

"Hmm, how about you get an I.O.U from me that you can cash in anytime?"

"No restrictions? That sounds pretty powerful, Father."

"Well, it can't be anything that goes against my vows *and* your mother will have to approve, of course." He responds.

Kimberly mulls this over for a second and then says, "It's a deal. How about you have to say 'fart' during your next Mass with a straight face? Brian will have to confirm."

"A deals a deal." He says with a chuckle.

The rest of the night consists of light conversation about Jack and how much Christina misses him, with Father Moran assuring her that she is doing a good job. "Day-by-Day" is the message he imparts to her. She wants the quick fix—the pastoral pill of healing—but all he has is the truth. It's bad, and it's going to get a lot worse and more intense, and then it will start to lighten up. First though, she has to allow the belief that God and His love is available. She is standing in darkness and he doesn't want her children to be dragged down into that place.

Brian isn't ready—and doesn't know he isn't ready—for the adventure he is about to embark upon.

CHAPTER 15: THE INTERVIEW

Jack's World

For the first time, Jack has actually been given *permission* to move from the confines of his hospital room. No more is he just trapped in this heavenly cage, but now he is being given the opportunity for some type of afterlife adventure. They head out into the hallway and begin to walk around.

He turns and sees a number on the door of his room: 1841. Coincidence...? He smiles.

"Jack, I am excited to embark on new ground, and I will show you things that will help you understand a lot of what's happening to you," Anthea calmly states.

"Great, because I have so many questions! Why is my Grandpa Joe here, but not here? Why can I see him only when the doctors are not present? Why does everything here have a smell, touch, taste and memory attached to it? Why is everyone speaking English when they are not clearly of an English background, but I hear Annie's English with a British accent? And why am I able to see her in some weird movie in my mind? My body is better than it was when I was 18 years old. What's up with that? And why was I able to attend what looked like my own memorial and connect with my kids? I want to do that again... and why does this hospital bear my name?" Jack takes a breath. "How is that for starters?"

"Whoa, Jack. One at a time." Anthea smiles. "You have your 18-year-old body because that's still how you truly see yourself. As far as Grandpa Joe, generally people are greeted on Level 9, and this is only Level 1, so he really shouldn't be here."

"Anthea, is there Alzheimer's and disease here? And are the people from the conference here as well? Can I see them?"

"Look into the rooms," Anthea says as they glide down the hallway. "As for the rest, I think as you go through the process here, you'll figure out many answers."

Sure enough, as Jack looks into each of the rooms they pass by he sees the people from the hotel and bar. In one room is Dr. Begley, and in the room across from hers is the concierge. He looks for his animated cab driver and before he can even ask...

"No Jack, Anthony is not here. He's still coughing up a storm in his cab. For some people it just wasn't their time."

Jack shakes his head, *"That guy's still alive?* He was a mess and already had two feet in the grave."

Anthea laughs, "Well he still has some things to learn, clearly. His business isn't finished."

Just as Jack is about to ask Anthea about Annie, he hears the young girl once again.

"Ayudame Mama!"

Jack stops, turns towards Anthea and is overwhelmed by the cry. "Please tell me why in a supposed place of healing nobody is attempting to help a crying child who is clearly in distress?"

Anthea stops and stares back at him. She looks through him and recognizes that he is having an experience that the rest of the staff is not able to participate in.

"Jack, I am not really sure exactly what you are experiencing. May I do something? Will you trust me?"

Jack has no logical reason whatever to trust this stranger, but instinctively he knows he can. Anthea puts both of her hands on his etheric chest and closes her eyes. He feels foolish. He's standing in the middle of a hallway in a hospital that has his name everywhere, yet he has no control over what happens here. As she touches him, he looks around the hospital and like an artist painting a portrait things become clearer.

The once-empty hospital hallways start to bustle with activity. Jack is able to see that it is as busy as any modern hospital emergency room. The cacophony becomes overwhelming with all the beeps, yelling, and energetic rumblings of what could be mistaken for thousands of patients being treated. All of this comes to life as Anthea touches him and closes her eyes....

Phhhmnpfh! Thud!

Anthea opens her eyes, and in that moment all the noise and traffic disappear. Jack is standing there alone with her once again in complete silence.

"What?" Anthea asks with a hint of teasing behind her eyes, knowing full well that her hands have power.

"What happened to all the patients and the doctors—all the noise?" Yet again, Jack is perplexed about this mysterious hospital.

"Jack, in your world people bitch, moan, and complain about having a private room. Here you get a whole hospital to yourself! Didn't you notice it was named after you?" She laughs as she says it.

Jack now understands that his experience is just that. It is *his* afterlife experience and he will be allowed to see, hear and feel things that will help him to... get better? Be cured? Move on to a new level? Jack looks at Anthea with gratitude. She is the first person to assist him in seeing this place clearly. "Jack, can you concentrate on the girl you are hearing? I want to tune into her vibration and see if I can locate her. Think like a radio station. I need to find her soul frequency." Anthea means business. Finally! Jack is happy that someone is moving him along and helping this little girl.

Anthea once again touches him and this time, he feels a rush of vibration and frequencies moving through him. He is the conduit and she is the source. It is science, to say the least. Jack feels like he is on a job again, reporting about the latest technology in MRIs or CAT scan science. As soon as he thinks about the girl, he develops more questions. *Why is he the only one who can hear her?*

"Jack, concentrate," Anthea says, reprimanding him. "Anthea continues. This time Jack is able to concentrate and hear the cries clearly. But it is painful for him.

In Jack's mind's eye he is standing outside Christina's minivan once again, watching the expressions on his children's faces. Now, with the energetic assistance of Anthea instead of Grandpa Joe, he knows exactly why his children have that look and feeling. Christina has just told them that he was in an accident and might not be coming home again . . . ever. This is the moment where their lives change.

"Jack, hold on. Don't get stuck here. I am locating the origin of your connection to the cries. Keep moving."

Anthea is leading him like a guide dog leads the blind. She is directing him to locate the source of the energetic connection. Anthea knows that she is in dangerous territory. Her responsibility is to deal with The Director and assist her on all things in the hospital on all after life levels. She is not supposed to take charge and make decisions. But, she is already down this road and knows she will have to deal with the wrath of TD later. She is curious as to what she can do here and now to help.

"Go inside Jack . . . go deeper . . . and allow."

Anthea's energy and voice give Jack the confidence to explore what he's seeing, journalistically. Instinctively, he goes back to just a few minutes earlier, to the origin of the cry.

CHAPTER 16: AM I ALLOWED HERE?

Earth – 3 Days After the Explosion

"Thank you guys for the pizza," Father Moran says as he pats Matilda on the head.

Christina picks Matilda up as Brian reminds the priest, "See you tomorrow morning at 8:30."

"Looking forward to it, buddy." The nickname makes Kimberly roll her eyes.

Can your eyes really get stuck up there? Because she sure does that a lot. Brian wonders.

Kimberly doesn't like the fact that Father Moran has knocked down her walls. The pain she'd been avoiding, now hits her. Yet, at the same time, she's wise enough to know that his presence and help is a good thing for her family. Boy is she jealous and mad that *the priest* and Brian planned this whole thing for tomorrow right in front of her, and didn't even ask her if she wanted to come.

"Thanks for coming, Father. I really appreciate the help." Christina honestly doesn't know what she'd do without him. The evening had a rough start, but she knows how important this first step was for her and her family. Father Moran's degree in psychology perfectly complements his theological studies for situations just like theirs.

Father Moran waves goodbye, shuts the door behind him, and walks to his car. He gets in and takes a deep breath. He knows Brian is going to be a handful. He checks his cell phone and there's a missed call from Advocate Lutheran General Hospital. He sighs, *It never ends.* The voicemail is a nurse requesting his presence to administer last rites, known as the Anointing of the Sick, for a woman in his parish.

He puts the key in the ignition, and turns the engine over reminding himself, *There's a reason for everything. Clearly, you were needed.*

Father Moran pulls up to Advocate Hospital and drives to the clergy spots by the Emergency Room labeled "Pastoral Dept." He takes a deep breath collecting his thoughts and putting the evening's other events out of his mind. Administering last rites always deserve his full attention and energy.

He walks in and takes the elevator up to the oncology ward. Once there, he looks around the waiting area and spots Angie. He locks eyes with the old woman, and he knows that her being out here isn't a good sign. He reassures her as much as he can with his eyes and rushes past her down the hallway.

Angie is isolated at the end of the hallway, sitting in the waiting room feeling alone with CNN blaring in the background. The broadcast is talking about the amount of people who perished recently in Johannesburg. Despite the booming audio of the television, Angie can still hear the medical instruments forming rhythms of disease and sadness. She's glad when she sees Father Moran, knowing that at least someone with a heart will be there for the end.

Her cellphone alarm clock goes off, as it has for many months systematically. This is to alert her that it is time for the hourly dose of pain meds to be given, with a follow up of anti-nausea pills. Angie thinks, *It's so hard to watch my love battle cancer . . . but I suppose that a lifetime of making joyful memories is the trade-off for the pain now.* Angie gets up with a creaky knee. It is difficult for her to fully stand as her own ailments bring their aches and pains—but none like the love of her life.

Might as well sit back down—I'm not needed, she thinks to herself. She's no longer the primary care giver; here, there are nurses for this kind of thing. Plus, even if she could administer them herself, it's not like this family would allow her in the room to do it. The emotional reality Angie is feeling has to be comparable to the physical pain some others are feeling in this hospital.

She knows that she needs to go home and also stop the bedside alarm from going off every four hours all through the night. She mentally notes, *While I'm home I have to remember to feed our dogs and bird, Oscar.* It is just difficult to leave when the end is so near.

Angie always believed in God and Heaven, but was never really convinced there is a place called Hell. She doesn't buy into the guy with horns, she doesn't believe in fire and brimstone. Nah, those stories are all for the kids to learn about right and wrong. It's to show the balance between positive and negative. As a successful designer for years she had known all about balance and symmetry, the Yin and the Yang. Whether it was dresses or negligees, she had to make sure that balance and symmetry was met. She believes God and life are like that, too.

Now, however, she knows Hell exists. It is a phase of life that people can be thrust into, and the Devil is in those closest to us, in some form or another. A few friends who know what she is dealing with want her to hire a lawyer, but most just spoke of how they feel it is all about money. The thought that the end is near and that she might not be allowed to be a part of it breaks her heart.

How is that possible? Hell!

CHAPTER 17:
ROOM 302

Earth – 3 Days After the Explosion

"Angie?" She looks up to see her tatted "nephew," Bradley, and her priest, Father Moran, standing there with looks that tell her the end is here.

"I want you to come and be with us in the room. It's close." Brad says.

Angie wipes her tears once again, getting up. She looks at Bradley with an expression that pleads, *Please don't tease me— I'm fragile and can break.*

Father Moran smiles at her. "It's OK, Angie. God wants you to be in there. He knows how important support from loved ones is. And remember, He's here to help support you too."

She is so glad he is here.

"You should be in the room. I will walk you in." Bradley extends his arm to support her as they begin a slow trudge down the hallway.

His strength and the energy in his words make this almost-75-year-old woman feel like she has an army of support. Angie is escorted out of the waiting room like a prisoner who is just being released after thirty years. She releases Bradley's arm, inked with a curling snake, and freezes. She is paralyzed in front of the antiquated double elevators. Bradley, towering over her with his six-foot frame, places his right hand on her back. He then takes her hand in his left hand and places a single thin gold wedding band on top of the one she is wearing. He continues to escort her past the elevators and through the double fire doors that have a plaque, which reads, "Family Only Beyond This Point."

Angie arrives at room 302 and sees some of "them" hanging outside the room . . . clearly it is too painful to be in there. As Bradley is about to walk her in, his mother, Sue, spots Angie from the window and stands up. She'd been keeping a bedside vigil for two whole days and she doesn't want Angie ruining these last few moments. No words are spoken, but they don't have to be. It is a clear line drawn in the sand. If Bradley walks *that* woman into this room, she will walk out. She eyes her son. *Make a choice.*

Father Moran watches the family dynamics objectively. He knows all the players and their history. If only people would just put aside their differences in these moments, he knows they'd all be happier. But they rarely seem to get the point that it's not about them.

The majority of the family does not recognize Angie as Bradley's aunt. However, the *woman* in the hospital bed, in room 302, is Bradley's father's older sister, Aunt Jersey. His father, Philip, had only passed two years ago. Bradley remembers Lynda, a.k.a. Aunt Jersey, taking her brother's passing extremely hard.

It was a widely understood fact that Angie and Jersey were "friends," but their life partnership was really never discussed until Jersey became sick. When health care, finances, proxies and wills became involved, the labels were brought out and the name-calling began. Philip's wife, Sue, refused along with rest of Lynda's family, to acknowledge their union. There was talk about them being of the devil, diseased, corrupt, and a host of other names to describe their same-sex relationship.

Philip had always accepted Angie as part of his sister's circle of friends, but would never discuss the potential they were more than that. They were just two women who were unlucky to find a husband. That was the world they grew up in—a world of prejudice and bias. "Don't Ask, Don't Tell" was nothing new for anyone in the gay and lesbian community for quite a while. Angie and Lynda would often talk about how lucky some of the youth was today growing up in a world of acceptance and tolerance, in comparison to theirs.

When it is evident that Bradley is bringing Angie to be at the bedside of her life partner, Sue starts to walk out of the room. She looks at them with disgust.

"Know this: She was not accepted in this lifetime, she will not be accepted in God's kingdom. And that is *your* fault. I hope you're happy. I hope you're both happy. Especially you, Brad, with your choice." She walks out into the hall. She would rather be hateful and spiteful than be with her dying sister-in-law.

Father Moran pipes up, "Excuse me, but this was my suggestion. I asked Bradley to get Angie. She was very important to Jersey and should be allowed to say goodbye. At times like these we have to put aside our differences and try to think of what Jersey would have wanted."

"Father, you don't see me physically keeping her out of the room do you? I am, however, entitled not to like it or to participate." Sue responds coldly.

The rest of the assorted family is shocked that Sue said what they were thinking themselves. Father Moran shakes his head in disbelief. He's always amazed at how some people never hear what he's *really* saying.

Sue looks at one of her daughters, Marie, who's been waiting in the hallway. "Let's go. I'm done here." Her daughter does not want to go, but she follows her mom throughout life and does whatever she says, even when she knows it's not right.

Father Moran smiles at Bradley for what he is doing. Bradley is making a huge impact on Angie's life right now. And she will be eternally grateful.

Angie steps into the room ahead of Bradley, and it becomes all too real again. The doctors' appointments, the late night vomiting sessions, the fear of what was going to happen, the medication, the pain, and the memories.

"Has she said anything?" Angie asks Bradley.

"No, she hasn't been communicative in quite a while. Angie, she is very heavily sedated and the doctors don't think she will make it through the night. I needed you to be here. It is like I told my misguided family, it's right."

Angie finally lets go emotionally, grabs onto Bradley, wailing.

"I just love her so much. I would never do anything to hurt her or your family in any way. It's not my way. You don't do that to your family's family." Her tears stream down her face.

Bradley holds her up while motioning for his other sister, Laura, who has been quietly sitting in the corner of the room, to get a chair for Angie. Angie pulls herself together for a moment and sits listening to the machines, the beeps. She looks at the love of her life and doesn't see the 73-year-old balding woman, who is run down, gaunt, and void of color. She sees the beautiful girl with flowing auburn curls, who saved her from making a terrible mistake, 50 years ago.

Fearful of what her life was about to become, one night Angie drove to downtown Chicago to take a walk along Lake Michigan. On this springtime night the moon is full and illuminates the trees that have begun to bud. She tosses pebbles into the water and in the ripples sees her life getting planned out in front of her—marriage, children, death.

Then it happens. Destiny. Lynda comes over and sits next to Angie. She looks at her sitting on the grass by the lake and looks in the direction where Angela, not yet Angie, is gazing. Lynda looks back at her with a fiery gaze and laughs. She picks up a flat rock and skips it perfectly across the moon's reflection.

"What?" is all Angie can think to say as this beautiful stranger sits down next to her. "I don't know but whatever it is you are reaching for out there looks kinda shitty. Don't ya think?" Lynda quips.

"Thanks for the insight. As if thinking about my future is not difficult enough, I now have a complete stranger sitting next to me telling me how shitty it will be. I am really doomed." Angie laughs

bitterly.

"You're right. I'm sorry, what's your name?"

"Angela."

"Right, Angela—no . . . ANGIE. You know you are taking your-self tooooo seriously. I think we need to have some fun before your shitty future starts. How about a chocolate egg cream with extra syrup and some light gossip?"

"Sure," Angie says, knowing that something about this woman projects energy like nothing she has ever felt before.

Later, she will always describe it as gravity. And by the end of that day, Angela knows that she is going to spend the rest of her life with the person she fell into . . . Lynda.

As Angie sits with her head on her partner's hand, she recalls that first meeting with a warm feeling. She feels happy again, just being in the room with Lynda and her energy . . . it just makes everything feel better.

"Anj . . . ANJJJJJJJJ!" Lynda opens her eyes for the first time in days at the mere touch of her other half. Everyone is shocked.

"Hey, you beautiful specimen of a human being." Angie can't help but leak tears from her eyes. She takes deep breaths to try and control them, but they are real, pure and powerful.

Angie doesn't make small talk or waste time; she knows that they don't have a lot of it. She looks at her partner and says, "I just want you to know that it's OK for you to go. Don't worry about me." She smiles through her tears.

"Anj, I want to thank you for everything you have ever done for me and for putting up with my crazy family." She smiles and looks over at Bradley and his sister.

He winks at his godmother getting ready to make her transition. *My mother is an idiot,* is all Bradley can think.

Angie squeezes Lynda's hand, kisses it and pulls it to her face. "I wish I could trade places with you."

Jersey starts coughing, "Me too." She laughs, literally meaning her words. She is miserable and needs to get out of her weakened body. She barely manages to whisper, "Anj, I love you."

Her wheezing becomes heavier. She looks past the family in the room. They turn around to see what she is looking at and they hear her say, "Philip! You came for me."

"Of course. You're my sister."

From a point of view above her body, Jersey is looking at Angie, her niece and nephew looking over their shoulders. When they turn back, she has a more elevated vision of the room as Father Moran walks in. She focuses on her old body as her mind's eye floats upward.

"Let us pray."

Bradley and Laura close their eyes and bow their heads. Angie looks up to the sky knowing that Jersey will be safe and happy in Heaven. This is the moment Angie will cling to. She's relieved that Jersey is whole again. Somewhere . . .

That somewhere for Jersey is a transitional moment she shares with her brother, Philip. Even though it's a moment, it feels like a lifetime of its own. During the prayer Philip tells her that the rest of their loved ones are waiting for her.

"Don't worry about them," he says referring to the prayer circle. "Love is what connects us. We are always just thoughts away. You're going to love it here, it's beautiful."

Jersey still feels a pang for Angie. Before she can even say that to her brother, he acknowledges her feeling by telling her, "You will meet her in five years time, like I am meeting you now. She has work left to do."

Dazed and devastated, Angie stands up. She kisses Jersey on the forehead and lips one last time, and walks out into the hallway. At the stroke of midnight, Father Moran discovers his purpose for being there—to catch Angie as she falls. Everyone else is too absorbed in his or her grief to notice.

He helps Angie over to a chair in the hallway. She looks up at him and asks, "Father, did you get to administer her last rites? You know how important that was to her."

"Yes, Angie, just before we came and got you. I was able to

anoint her and absolve her. God will welcome her. He loves her, as He does all His children."

At these words, Angie experiences a new insight. Her mind is opened in a different way. She thought, *Jersey crossing over is not the* end *of our journey together, because I am at her side, and she is not at mine. I know we will be together again.*

Another thought came into her mind: *There must be more for me to learn before my journey here is over.* And, for the first time in a long time, she says a little prayer.

CHAPTER 18:
ROOM 302A

Jack's World

Anthea continues to touch Jack and search for the source of the little girl's cries. After a few moments, she begins to hear them herself.

"Good Jack, I hear her. Now really concentrate, we're almost there."

Jack becomes relieved that someone can finally hear this little girl. But this moment of relief begins to break his concentration. He looks over to his left, through the glass doors. He can see a soul slowly materializing in the hospital bed, with his same team of doctors standing over her.

Because of his connection with Anthea in this moment, Jack knows this soul's complete back-story by just being there. He sees the spirit of the old Lynda lift out of her worn out body and appear young and revitalized looking as she did that full moon night at Lake Michigan. It's as if the story of this life is a book and Jack and Anthea have just turned a page to the next chapter.

Jersey seems genuinely happy, albeit a bit confused. Jersey looks at her team of doctors—Dr. Annie Brooks and her residents. She asks, "Where has my brother gone? Is this heaven? Have I been accepted?"

"Don't worry. God does not judge our choices." Dr. Annie comforts her, patting Jersey's hand reassuringly. Jack notes that no strange flashbacks occur during this physical exchange.

The doctors file out of the room and notice Anthea and Jack watching. Their knee jerk reaction is that this is not OK. But since Jack is with Anthea, they decide that it must be part of TD's plan. They collectively and telepathically decide not to question it.

It's all Jack can do to wonder, *Why wasn't she scared and confused like I was? And why did it all seem to go so smoothly when my welcome was so chaotic?*

"Jack." Anthea says, reading his thoughts. "We all have our time to cross over. Some like Jersey here, have been waiting for a long time. Those cases tend to go a bit quicker. Now, focus! We must start all over again. Block out the rest of this place and just focus on the little girl crying for her momma."

CHAPTER 19:
LET'S BE FAIR

Earth – 4 Days After the Explosion

From the back of the church, Brian watches anxiously as the Mass finally ends. Father Moran purifies the chalice almost like he's in slow motion. Brian can't believe how long this is taking. The fair starts in less than an hour and they still have to drive there. He has researched these fairs online. They are first come-first serve. There will be 20 or so psychics in a room, each giving readings every 15 minutes. He noticed Shelly Southport got top billing, so he knows she'll be on everyone's list. The more time goes by, the more worried he becomes that he won't get the chance to meet Shelly Southport. He also wants to see her speak and hear what she has to say about her new book, which he has seen advertised online.

For the last twenty minutes of the liturgy, Brian has let his mind wander to his idea of what the psychic fair will be like. He imagines that the Sheraton Starlight Room will look like a sultan's palace. Shelly will have to be a hybrid of *I Dream of Jeannie*'s Barbara Eden and *The Munsters*' Yvonne De Carlo, whom he'd seen in his dad's nostalgic DVD collection and in reruns on cable.

When he snaps back to the present, he sees the congregation grinning as Father Moran jokes with them.

"We have a wonderful congregation here, we work together, we support each other, and I hope I'm still your priest when I'm an old fart."

Brian snickers in his seat. Kimberly will be satisfied.

The congregation begins to file out, shaking hands and paying respects to the priest as they exit. Father Patrick motions him to the back of line. Upon his turn, Father Patrick asks, "How are you feeling?"

"OK, I guess." Brian responds, shrugging his shoulders. Father Moran then tells him to follow him down the stairs so he can change quickly and they can escape out the back before an impending wedding takes over the premises.

The priest has gone to change, but just as Brian is about to sit down on a hallway bench Father Patrick flies by, automatically inserting his white collar in his polo shirt. He excitedly says, "Come on, why are you still sitting there? I thought maybe we could go to Denny's and have a chat—or is there something else you had in mind?"

Brian answers, "So glad you asked, Father. I kinda had an idea."

The priest smiles back at him mischievously. Together they walk to the priest's car. Brian sadly notes as he gets in the back seat that this old Chevy probably won't go very fast. As they buckle their seat belts, Father Moran, true to his no nonsense form asks, "OK, Brian, if it's not food then what's your idea?"

"Well… during Mass you said that our loved ones who have passed are watching over us in Heaven." Brian begins to kick the front passenger seat a mile a minute.

Father Moran immediately identifies the kicking as the same distracting noise he'd heard throughout the entire service.

"Yes, I meant that specifically for you to hear. I'm glad it wasn't lost."

"Well, do you REALLY believe that? Do you think we can communicate with them?" Kick, kick, kick.

"People do it every day, kid." Father Patrick wonders how long Brian's going to keep up the kicking.

Pleased at this reply, Brian comes clean about his motives. "Good. Because I'd like you to take me to the Sheraton Hotel where there's a psychic fair. They advertised that all are welcome. Last night over pizza you said that my father would always love me. Well, I think I'd like to hear that from my Dad." Kick, kick, kick.

"Did you talk to your mother about this before I picked you up?"

"Yeah, and she's fine with it, if you're fine with it."

Father Patrick can't believe Christina wouldn't have called to clear this with him. It's not exactly where he wants to be seen. But for some reason, he doesn't he reject the idea either. He feels this could be a good excuse to face his own curiosity about psychics. After all, taking a parishioner might deflect pressure from this priest, who's already caused a lot of tension within the diocese when he did not publicly condemn same sex marriage in one of his sermons. Actually more than one of his sermons... Some already considered him a "problem priest"— just what the Church didn't need these days.

He sees the determination in Brian's face. He knows that he's not about to let this kid go unaccompanied. He'll text Christina and let her know what's going on.

Brian can see the priest processing the opportunity. He furthers his argument, "My dad always says that it's really important to find the facts. So this is a fact finding mission."

"I'm not sure if it's a good idea for me to been seen at a place that the church would not be sanctioning, but as your spiritual director we can consider this a mission. Then we'll talk about the experience over lunch. Where is this fair?"

Brian answers, "OK." He pulls a crumpled paper from his pocket, "Sheraton Hotel, Starlight Ballroom. Starts at 11 a.m. so um... can we go now?"

Father Moran firmly says, "Not until you stop kicking that seat!"

He takes a breath then continues, "I will help you explore whatever this is that you're interested in that you think is going to maybe connect you with your father, under one condition— that you explore a deeper connection with 'the Father.'"

"You mean like the big guy?" Brian thinks this over for a

moment. "Well, I already started by going to Church today, so I guess we have a deal."

Father Patrick Moran and Brian approach the hotel where the Psychic Fair is being held. They get out of the car, and Brian starts to sprint toward the end of the long line. Father Patrick pauses. Brian looks back wondering why the priest isn't moving faster.

"Hurry up, Father, we're late!"

Patrick pauses. "Brian, I don't want you to get your hopes up. But what we can do is take a moment and put a positive outcome in our minds."

Brian cocks his head skeptically, "We're praying, aren't we, Father?"

"You betcha."

"We're not gonna Tebow are we?"

The priest laughs, "No. You don't have to get on your knee to pray. And by the way, the proper term is 'genuflecting'–not Tebowing."

"Yes, yes! Let's do this." They pause a moment with their eyes closed.

Brian and the priest are finally almost through the line, just now stepping indoors. Brian is wearing his version of "Sunday best"—loafers, khakis, and a white button up shirt, about two sizes too small. Ironically, Father Patrick has shed his black and white "clerics," or traditional church garb, and looks more like he's going to a ballgame—loud red shorts, louder blue polo shirt with his white-and-black collar sticking out, and a Chicago Cubs hat. They are, by far, the most eccentric people on line.

Patrick is surprised of the prominence of middle-aged women, who are conservatively dressed. He expected to see a more peculiar crowd. The group, who has gathered, spans generations and ethnicities. However, Father Moran notices that there are no other children; Brian is definitely the youngest. They stand out as if they are the only black and white cartoons in the color funny section of the newspaper. It's going to be hard to blend in.

It seems like everyone is staring at the priest's Roman collar. Father Patrick feels as if he's being spotted walking into a strip club, and he might as well be, as far as his bishop will be concerned.

Also noticing how the priest's outfit seems to stick out in this bunch Brian asks innocently, "Father, were you wearing this underneath your robes the whole time?"

Father Moran answers, "Just the sandals."

The other people standing in line, who can clearly see the white clerical collar, start to murmur. Father Patrick standing on line is already starting to notice the glances of recognition and can only imagine the phone calls going to the bishop.

Finally, the no nonsense woman sitting behind the table unemotionally says, "Next." Brian approaches ahead of Father Moran.

"We don't allow children. Sorry. NEXT!"

"Wait, wait, that's my Dad... Father?" Brian says sheepishly as he points towards Father Patrick, who has fallen behind, too caught up in what people around him are thinking.

Father Patrick rolls his eyes and thinks, *Great! The diocese will have a field day with this. First, I am at a psychic fair, and now I have a son.*

Father Moran looks at the woman.

"It's $20 for the two of us, right?" He says mildly.

She scans this odd couple trying to figure them out. But 20 bucks is 20 bucks so she nods her head. Father Patrick is not angry, but is impressed by the inner strength and focus Brian displays.

Brian sheepishly admits, "Sorry Dad, but I'm a little short."

Father Patrick whispers, "It's all right. Where do you think the collection basket money goes?"

The collector, who notices his collar, gasps.

"It's a joke."

Brian laughs nervously. Father Patrick tells Brian to put his money away and hands the woman a $20 bill.

In return they get a photocopied, black-and-white pamphlet with a schematic of where all the psychics are stationed and what their specialties are.

They walk in as the room is filling up quickly. Pamphlet-covered tables all along the edges of the room each have a psychic behind them. They can see that dialogue has already begun among a few of the psychics and the attendees. Brian looks around the room for his Barbara Eden/Yvonne De Carlo fantasy and sees there's nothing that comes close. His new "Dad" is the only one making a fashion statement.

Brian puts his nose in the map looking for the booth of the medium who he researched online, Shelly Southport. He locates her at the back of the room and says, "This way, Father, I mean, Dad."

Brian grabs him by the arm and leads him through the crowd.

Father Patrick, completely out of his element, digests every moment scanning the room for his parishioners. Not that he's making any judgments, but he doesn't want them to misunderstand his mission. In all honesty he feels like this journey is important for him as well, for his own spiritual enlightenment. Brian isn't the only one with questions.

Just then, his precognitive moment is validated and he taps Brian's shoulder to make him stop in front of a blond woman he's familiar with from the parish.

"Oh, hi, Father Moran. Wouldn't have expected to see you here. Looking to get your fortune told?"

Brian answers earnestly, "No, he's here trying to help me connect with my father. We're going to see Shelly Southport."

"Oh… Are you psychic? I know she likes working with young psychics."

Father Patrick takes over. He can't have her having any wrong ideas. "No. He's just on a mission." He whispers to her, "His father was just in that huge South Africa explosion."

She responds with a head nod. She's points the way to Shelley's booth and says, "Hope you find what you're looking for."

Brian momentarily tears up, but thanks her and continues on. Father Patrick quietly notices his eyes, but appreciates how quickly Brian regains his composure. This is no ordinary grieving 10-year-old.

"You know, Father, what I really hope is that I can't make a connection. That would give us the most hope that he's still alive."

Placing both hands on his shoulders, he makes eye contact with Brian.

"Whatever the outcome, this is God's plan. You might have to accept a psychic medium may not be able to connect and unfortunately, given the circumstances, his body may never turn up either. But there is one thing that can be validated —your father loves you either way and love is eternal."

"I know, Mom said we have to be realistic, but it's way too early to give up hope. That's why we're here. Father, you believe in miracles, right?"

They arrive at Shelly's booth, only to find her not there. A line has formed, longer than the others and a young guy is scheduling her appointments. They overhear that today's appointments are already booked. They are now getting on a list to be contacted at a later time for private readings. They also hear that the private readings start at $800.

Brian is visibly shaken. He freezes, his eyes well up. He's losing his dad all over again.

"Father, I *need* to talk with her."

"Brian, there's plenty of other psychics here. I'm sure one of them can help." Father Moran looks into Brian's eyes and sees all the pain he's been hiding.

"No! She's the only medium who passed Dad's researching criteria and testing. Not all psychics are mediums, to quote Wikipedia. I researched her all night and she was tested by a university. If anybody here is real she's it. She's the one that can help me. I just know it!"

The people ahead of them have moved out of the way and as her assistant has come forward Brian erupts with a desperate plea.

"Excuse me, sir. Um, I need to speak with her, please!"

"I'm sorry, but she's booked for the rest of the day." The assistant affirms. "She's only here today to do a book signing and lecture along with a few readings."

The 6' 4" college-aged assistant with a box of tissues (standard at all booths), sees Brian's distress and kneels down.

"Hey, look, Shelly's in Ballroom C. Come with me, I will walk you in as my guests. She's just about to start talking about her latest book, *Find What You're Looking For*." He points to the lecture schedule in the program.

Father Moran starts to get emotional at the young man's empathy, and doesn't just take a tissue, he humorously grabs the whole box.

The assistant talks as they walk, "Shelley's philosophy is, 'Whatever is supposed to happen will happen.' She will do a few readings during her lecture. If you are supposed to meet her and make a connection, you will."

Father Moran guides Brian with his hand on his back as they follow the assistant through the crowded ballroom.

When they are back at the welcome desk, the assistant points towards Ballroom C, which is directly in front of them. He nods to the priest and walks away.

They pause a moment outside the door. They hear laughter coming from the room that ends as quickly as it began. They both look at each other curiously. Then Father Patrick opens the door, and they walk in. Despite their efforts to sneak in, a squeaky door announces their entry.

Shelly Southport is pacing back and forth on the stage talking into a microphone. They are standing under a speaker so it sounds like she is talking right to them, "I have a father figure who crossed in a sudden tragic accident. And he wants to connect with his son."

"Oh. My. God..." the priest utters with a shortness of breath.

"Whoa, can it be my Dad?" Brian says looking up at Father Patrick for approval.

"Well, I don't know if it's your Dad..." Father Patrick replies. "But that's my high school girlfriend—Michelle."

CHAPTER 20: COLLADI-SCOPING WORLDS

Jack's World

Still standing in the hallway, Jack allows Anthea's energy to blend in with his again, and she is able to home in on the source of the little girl's cries with ease. All of a sudden Jack hears a car horn—Christina's car horn. Jack looks around to see where it could possibly be coming from. *Is there really road rage in Heaven?* Jack wonders.

As if to answer Jack's thought, Anthea echoes Christina's alarmed, "WHAT THE… HEEEEEEEY!" in Christina's own voice.

Anthea now knows the story of the little girl and its outcome. She pulls her hands off Jack's chest.

"Jack, the girl is connected to your family. Your wife, Christina has a concern for this child and you are feeling her through Christina's energy. You two are very connected. That's why no one else here is hearing her. The little niña is not here Jack, not yet."

"What do you mean 'not yet'?" Jack looks at her with a concerned gaze.

"Jack, there's a lot you have to learn about this place, yourself, your lessons, and how it's all connected. I can't just tell you the answers to all of your questions. It's up to you to discover who you are and why you are here." Anthea gazes through him, her eyes are huge.

She is the only energy that Jack has encountered in this place with whom he feels comfortable. Besides his Grandpa Joe, of course, and his uncanny attraction, sense of peace, and history with Annie.

Reading his mind, Anthea says out loud to him "Dr. Brooks, Jack. You mean Dr. Brooks." She finds his informality with Dr. Brooks somewhat curious.

Jack would be blushing if he could. Anthea really is connected to him and again lets him know it. She stops walking and turns back around to look at the entrance to Jack's room. She senses something off-putting. Her face shifts to a look of annoyance.

"What is it? What's happening? What are you seeing? That is not a look that I want to see on your face, Anthea. It's kind of alarming." Jack makes sure she makes eye contact with him.

"Jack, you understand energy, yes?"

"Um, yes. Scientific journalist! Author! Lecturer! Should I go on?"

"Please don't, but pay attention, Einstein," Giggling she's now back to her effervescent self, if only to put Jack at ease.

Anthea feels something coming in the same way that a dog is able to sense an epileptic seizure before his owner has one. She firmly asks Jack to stay put as she disappears. In a flash, she is gone.

Jack hears scurrying behind him. He looks and sees the white rabbit that Grandpa Joe had been holding in his dream on the plane. It runs quickly down the corridor and makes a left into one of the patient's rooms. Jack feels an irresistible urge to follow it. Just as he is about to, Anthea reappears.

"Jack, I want you to watch what's happening." She says.

Jack looks at her, but there is nothing happening except for "Ayudame" cries—and a white rabbit somehow willing him to follow. "See with your soul's eyes, Jack, not your earthly eyes. Your soul speaks to you all the time. You need to listen."

Before Jack can make a wise crack about how his soul speaks, or if it can speak a foreign language, Anthea responds. "Jack, remember we don't hear other accents or languages here. You will hear it in your last incarnation's language. It is all perception. You think that I am speaking American English right now. I am not. I never knew English. I am communicating with you soul to soul."

"Right… I seem to keep losing grasp on my soul-communication skills," he says in exasperation.

Anthea is all teacher, all the time. "I'm sorry, was that too much technical information? I tend to be a teacher, but my job is really facilitator for the director. The facilitator. Perhaps I should go by TF."

"Nah, you have such a beautiful name though. Why go by a title?" Jack asks.

"Nice one, Jack… nice. You are not only listening, you are answering with your soul as well. Very good." Anthea says, smiling.

"My soul is blushing. If that's possible."

"Happens all the time. Own it." She laughs.

Just then the rabbit rematerializes in Jack's gaze. He tries to apply Anthea's lesson and trust his gut to follow it. The rabbit begins to lure him down the hallway. Anthea understands why he follows like a moth to a flame, and she shadows him. She's not about to let Jack out of her sight right now.

The rabbit leads him simultaneously towards the child crying out for help, louder and louder. The rabbit hightails it into an empty hospital room. But when Jack crosses the threshold this room transforms.

The antiseptically clean room morphs into a dirty, dark, claustrophobic bedroom with one small broken window, which has bars on the outside. The smell is hideous. Scattered all over the floor are some Happy Meal toys, which Jack can confirm by the McGarbage evidence everywhere. In one corner, next to some of the half-eaten nuggets are animal droppings, which Jack silently hopes are from the white rabbit and not rats.

A tiny child-sized mattress lies on the floor with a dank blanket wrapped around a crying trembling little girl. Jack notices some crayon drawings taped to the wall, some resembling Dora the Explorer, other of families and yellow flowers.

On complete instinct Jack says, "Daisy?"

The young girl uncoils and looks over in his direction. She seems to stop whimpering for a moment, but Jack realizes she can't see him, only sense his warmth.

The empathetic pain he feels from the little girl is too much to handle. Jack turns to leave her tiny room, expecting to be back out in the hospital, but he's not. He's still in Daisy's nightmarish world. He walks down the hallway towards the living room-kitchen area. He can look out the barred window and see the same skyline visible from his own home. He realizes he is in an apartment on the outskirts of Chicago.

As Jack looks around the apartment, his parental feeling kicks in. *Who is looking after this child?* He turns the corner into the room and sees a peeling wallpapered wall of disheveled photos of Daisy and her grandmother from a happier time. Jack knows their stories immediately. Titi had been the only source of love in Daisy's life until she passed three months earlier.

Jack turns around and sees Daisy's semi-conscious mother sprawled out on a torn couch. He knows she is strung out on heroin. The mother looks like she hasn't eaten real food in weeks. Standing at the kitchen counter is the fat, muscled, white tattooed man Christina had honked at after summer camp.

Just then a scared Daisy cries, "Mama!" The low-life stops cutting up his heroin.

The boyfriend gets up to silence Daisy, and on the way kicks her mom, just to make sure she's still breathing. She is. Jack watches him walk towards Daisy's room and can feel the level of anger that is about to descend on her. He feels like he has to try something. He steps in front of this druggie hoping to take the beating instead of Daisy. In this world however, Jack is physically not there and the man walks right through his energy. The druggie charges into the room and slams the door behind him, rattling the rickety apartment. He feels like the character Sam in *Ghost* and doesn't like it one bit!

Jack hears Daisy cry, "Mama, help me! Titi! Ayudame!" He pops into the bedroom just in time to see this thug backhand Daisy, the sheer force launching her into the wall. She folds down the wall, like a limp doll.

Jack's rage triggers the same kind of 19th century movie-like flashback as before, except this time he's not touching Annie.

In a long waistcoat and top hat, a gentleman pours a powder from an apothecary jar labeled arsenic into a vat of stew cooking on a wood-burning stove. He mutters angrily to himself, "That should do it."

The two images bleed into each other. The man in the waistcoat vanishes, and the man with the heroin leaves the bedroom, satisfied Daisy will be quiet for the time being.

Jack panics when he sees a trace of blood on the wall.

"Jack screams. "No!"

Out of control, Jack screams, "I have to save my baby!"

The apartment suddenly transforms back into the Jack Richmond Memorial Hospital. Concerned, Anthea calls the team to sedate him. Dr. Brooks administers the syringe, which actually just contains a placebo, but just the suggestion of the drug causes Jack to sleep.

The doctors look at Anthea. Dr. Lesley White, who works on kindness, pipes up, "What the hell just happened?"

"It's his soul." Anthea says, vanishing. "I need to report to TD immediately." Although asleep, Jack's mind races backward and forward, encompassing the scenario he had just witnessed. He teeters for a moment between reality and unreality, not clearly grasping which is which or where he is, or even *who* he is. At least right now... His discomfort is palpable, yet somehow his unconscious mind is drawn toward an unknown destination. He realizes then that he is bleeding—that it feels like bleeding, though he knows that he can't be. Impossible. And yet— His very soul is bleeding away, as if through the skin of his physical being.

Then, with a jolt, as if shocked by electricity, Jack's consciousness collides with a deep awareness of *everything* in a blinding moment. It doesn't last very long before he sleeps again, and has a glimpse of peace.

CHAPTER 21: EXTRACURRICULAR ACTIVITIES

Earth – 4 Days After the Explosion

The ballroom is over-crowded and there are people standing against the walls. The 40 rows of folding chairs are filled with people seated except for a middle-aged man in the third row who begins to stand. A balding man is now standing halfway between Brian and Father Moran, and the stage where Shelly is giving the reading. He takes a microphone and claims the message is for him, "Yes, my dad passed in a tragic accident."

Brian panics that this man is stealing his message, but listens intently and is overwhelmed by how much he needs this process to be real.

Brian notices Shelly is also not the ethereal TV icon he had conjured up. In fact she looks more like Lucy's friend Ethel. And by the laughter they heard through the door, she might be just as funny. She appears to be looking directly at Brian and Father Patrick, and not the man she's currently reading.

Shelly tells the man, while continuing to stare at Brian and the priest, "He's fine. Don't dwell on how he passed. Remember all of the good times. That's what he wants."

Brian wonders if it's possible she's supposed to be talking to him. He looks up at the Father and sees he is emotionally rocked, standing there with his jaw dropped. Energetically the room might be filled with people, but Brian, Patrick and Shelly might as well the only ones present.

Shelly refocuses her attention to the man. "Was he a photographer or really into photography?"

The man answers, "No, but I have his photo with me that I purposely brought today. I don't normally carry it."

Shocked, Brian looks up at Father Patrick and begins to kicks off his right loafer. Father Patrick looks at him curiously but then sees a tiny photo booth shot in the heel.

Shelly continues, "OK. I don't really like to call that a validation because I know that there's probably many other people here who also brought photos, thinking that it would help them make a connections, but what's with the shoes?"

The man excited says, "He was a shoe salesman!"

Both Father Moran and Brian stare at each other.

"I'm also seeing a C or K name. And this person is on your same level, like a wife, sister, sister-in-law or cousin?"

The man questions, "Here or on the other side?"

"Still here, I think, a sister maybe?"

Brian is in a fog, but Father Patrick mouths to him: "Your sister!" If it's possible, Brian's jaw drops even farther than before.

The man shakes his head to indicate a definitive "no."

"Don't you shake your head. I hate that. This C or K name is connected to a Libra." Again the man cannot acknowledge this fact and for the moment neither can Brian or Father Patrick.

"Look I'm sure it's a Libra connection. I'm a Libra I don't miss that sign. I see the scale. This person has a birthday between September 23 and October 23."

Brian gulps, "That's my Dad! His birthday is October 5!" Father Moran can't believe this is happening.

The man in the third row man begins to cry, "That's my birthday—October 15."

Brian and the priest are baffled. They seem to wonder together, *Is this all coincidental?*

Through tears the man says, "I miss him so much. Is he OK?"

"I'm sure you do. This process is just beginning for you.

Mediumship isn't a cure for grief. I just want to give you pure facts that he's with us. I can't tell you what you want to hear, just because you want to hear it. You get that?"

The man laughs through his tears. "He always said to us, 'I can't tell you what you want to hear, because you want to hear it.'" The crowd gasps at this amazing validation.

Since Brian doesn't understand this message, his disappointment level is shown by him putting his foot back in his loafer and tapping it.

Shelly curtly says, "Thank you." The audience applauds with approval. She motions for the man to sit down and takes a sip of water. "Now I think that about wraps up the hour." Shelly redirects her attention to the middle of the crowd and once again it feels like she's talking directly to Brian and Father Moran. "Some of you may have felt that the messages here today were for you as well as the people who got the reading. There's no accident that you're here in this room now. This is your family's way of helping you communicate with them."

Brian and Patrick smile at one another.

"Thank you all for coming and it warms my heart that you're all interested in my new book. Keep your heart open and you'll see their signs and messages." The audience applauds and then begins to shuffle out.

"It's over?" Brian can't believe he missed another opportunity.

Father Patrick is still frozen in shock.

Many people, still wanting a moment with her, move toward her on the stage. Going against the tide, Shelly steps off the platform, right past this group and beelines it straight for Brian and Father Moran. Brian sees this and his heart begins to race. *Yes, this is the moment!*

Shelly isn't charging towards Brian, but to Patrick. She walks right up to him and puts her arms around his neck and kisses him square on the lips. Now Brian's jaw is the one that is dropped. "Patrick, this is unbelievable. It's so good to see you."

Father Moran is so stunned he can't speak. He looks

around at the people who have taken notice. *Great, add kissing women to the dioceses' check list.*

"Michelle, I had no idea you were psychic."

Noticing his collar, she replies, "I didn't know you became a priest." Winking at Father Patrick she adds, "I so wouldn't have predicted that!"

Uncomfortably Father Moran says, "Well, good to know you haven't mellowed."

Shelly laughs and then looks at Brian. "Who is this?"

Brian speaks up seizing the moment, "I'm Brian. I Googled you and am hoping you could help me find my father."

"His father was in the South Africa explosion the other day," Father Patrick adds.

Shelly closes her eyes, puts her hand on Brian's shoulder and says, "I am so sorry for what you are going through. I think it's fantastic that you're here looking for answers. But a medium can't cure your grief, I'm afraid. That's not what we do, as much as I want to. I might be to help you find some closure but it might take time, it's a process. Especially with such a recent—"

Brian jumps the gun. "How about Denny's for lunch, you get a break right?"

"I don't think that's the place either." She redirects her attention to Father Patrick. "I think that it's too soon after this tragedy for anyone to be reaching out to a medium, especially... How old is he?"

Brian, who's intently listening, quickly says, "Ten!"

Shelly continues, "Ten? How'd did you guys even get in? Listen, he has to take this all in. Call me, and we can set something up in a few weeks. Plus, we have so much to catch up on." She hands her business card to Father Moran. "Glad to see you still have a flare for fashion and great legs!"

Brian says, trying to claim her attention, "Hello! I'm ready now. I don't even know if he's dead! You have to tell me he's gone before I can grieve!" Brian is upset that he's losing his opportunity.

She looks at Patrick for support. "I don't really sense his

energy around you. So we can't do this now anyway."

"So, what does that mean?" Brian is annoyed.

Shelly takes a deep breath and answers, "It just means I'm not making a connection with him. It takes time, honey."

"Look," Father Patrick says to Brian. "This has already been an amazing coincidence."

"There's no such thing as coincidence, Father Patrick."

"Right. Brian, Shelly and I go way back and I promise you, we will go forward with Shelly as soon as we can.

Both Shelly and Patrick blurt out at the same time, "I promise."

"Fine." Brian says, disheartened at not making a connection today." But you both know there are no coincidences. There must be a higher power at work here, and we should follow this experiment to its conclusion. That's what my father would do. I know he's out there."

"Brian, I know you came on a personal quest," Shelly responds. "But, believe it or not, connecting with your dad will become even more important to you later in life."

"I'm more interested in right now," Brian replies, semi-ticked off, thinking she is trying to dismiss him.

Then it penetrates, maybe he does know what she means. He feels as if coming here has begun—or confirmed—that he is on the path to understanding to see beyond the veil that now stands between him and his father.

One day, Brian tells himself. *I promise.*

CHAPTER 22:
DRESSING DOWN

Jack's World

The Director sits at her oversized mahogany desk, absorbed in transferring her notes from her rounds to more clinical entries in an old IBM desktop computer. The office seems out of place with the rest of the sleek modern hospital décor. After being the director and witnessing centuries of progress, her decorating choices span various and disconnected motifs. Her leather arm chair looks like something that J.P. Morgan might have sat in, while her square lamp looks more like a sculpture out of the Museum of Modern Art. Without looking away from the screen, she says, "What do you think you are doing, Anthea?"

Anthea has appeared and is sitting across the desk from her boss.

"Think? I didn't think. I did exactly what I've been trained to do—protect you and our patients. I thought I was being tested once again. I sensed a dark energy emerging around Jack. I would have thought you would have too, but since you weren't doing anything about it, I felt I had to jump in. You could have stopped me! I know you know what I'm doing at all times! You've made that very clear, Madame TD."

The Director feels her mind racing. A dark presence can only mean one thing. Gregorios. Damn him.

"You overstepped me, and I don't like it. Now I have much more work to do correcting Jack's course. You may go for now." The Director hits her print button, not looking at Anthea.

TD is formulating a new plan, behind many walls, in her mind. The presence of Gregorios changes everything. Though she has known it all along, she has kept it as her secret and attempted to control her thoughts and to fake out the enemy and turn him from his purpose with her moves. Jack Richman's case is now her number one priority.

Anthea looks at The Director in confusion. Powerful as she is, Anthea knows that TD is constantly aware of a possible drain on her energy. That energy drain goes by the name Gregorios, and he is hungry—for the energy represented by souls.

"But, TD, you know as well as I do that Jack was going to follow that rabbit wherever it took him." Anthea says. "He's curious and trying to figure this place out scientifically. The fact that he is trusting his gut, rather overthinking, is a step forward. But we can't make his choices for him. He runs, I run after him."

"It's when you run after him that counts. The process has to unfold before you interfere. I sent you up there to *facilitate* his move to Level 5, not to bring him back to the earthly dimension. He wouldn't have even been in the hallway if you hadn't lead him there, by hand no less, Miss Facilitator." The Director assembles her printouts and shoves them into the "updates" folder. She knew Jack will never get to Level 5. Already she was seeing the end game but has to monitor her own thoughts so that they wouldn't be accessible to Gregorios.

Anthea thinks, *Wow, she really doesn't miss anything.* "It's Anthea, Madame TD. And the other doctors just left him there, scared, alone and unprotected."

"Exactly. When are you really going to trust our process? You think you're a team player, but clearly you're not. You don't have to be the star. You are here to assist me, Anthea. And by the way that name is no more beautiful than plenty of others."

TD hands Anthea the updates folder.

"Take these to Dr. Brooks' team, and ask Dr. Brooks to come see me."

Anthea grabs the folder and is gone. Outside TD's office Anthea wrestles with being dressed down. She's humbled once again, realizing she doesn't know everything TD does, but something still doesn't seem right.

Why would TD allow Jack to cross back to Earth at his level? Anthea remembered her family on Earth and how she loved them. It was difficult to see them come through her hospital, one by one for generations. She had to help them transition on into the light of God's Kingdom, while she was tethered to The Director for what might be an eternity.

Every time she would ask TD when she might be able to join up with her family's circle of spirits she was told, "You have not finished your work here." Anthea had heard that response for aeons, just like Dr. Annie Brooks had heard the same while searching for her own children for over 200 Earth years. Anthea knew that everyone's path was his or her own to follow, and she was dedicated to The Director and trusted her guidance. But she didn't have to like it.

The Director swivels a 180 degrees, away from her computer. She leans back and gazes towards the sky like ceiling, with a tear in her eye. She knows that Jack's soul is in jeopardy. If it comes down to protecting the secret she bears, or his soul, she knows which choice she will make... again.

If we are all capable of learning the lessons that are presented to us, why don't we? That is, why don't all of us just 'get the message'? That question has haunted her for too many earthly generations to count. If she could just crack the code, so to speak, perhaps she could solve the most difficult problem she faces. The fact and face of evil, of the dark energies, is undeniable and overwhelmingly powerful. It is present and potent here, in her facility!

The Director immediately shuts down the thoughts that could lead her to reveal what her soul's eyes see so clearly—more than she wants to, more than she can afford to at this time—to anyone, even to herself.

The printer comes to life again without The Director doing a thing. She watches it print out one sheet that says, "Thanks for being such a good teacher. – G."

TD looks around the room and sneers knowing that her job just got more complicated. Out loud, she confirms her fear, "Gregorios."

CHAPTER 23:
TOUCHED

Jack's World

Anthea, folders in hand, finds Dr. Annie Brooks and her team gathered around Jack's bed. He is waking up—or coming back to full consciousness.

"That was so strange." Jack mumbles as he reaches for water to quench a parched throat.

Anthea says, "Dr. Brooks, here are the Updates from TD."

Brooks takes them and looks them over, sharing them telepathically with her team.

"There was a girl and a drugged monster in a crack house? Wait, you were there." Jack points to Anthea.

"How is he supposed to go anywhere right now? Look at him." Dr. Gareth Roberts retorts.

"Go where? Can we save her?" Jack asks aloud—and loudly.

"No need. Follow us. Dr. White, help him." Dr. Brooks commands.

Dr. White kindly helps Jack out of bed. Unsure of the consequence of her touch, Jack pulls away. But she takes his arm anyway and says, "It's OK." Once again, Jack notices that no time traveling occurs as it has when Annie touches him.

Dr. Brooks looks at Anthea, "You're coming too, apparently." Anthea is confused, but trusts the instructions TD has just given to Dr. Brooks.

They all proceed to the room next to Jack's. The doctors

file in and surround the bed. Anthea stays back, standing next to Jack in the doorway, observing. A beautiful young Latin child is materializing in the bed. A bright, warming light pours in, growing brighter as the child appears in the bed. She is a new arrival. Jack realizes he's witnessing something miraculous. When he witnessed Angie cross over earlier, it had been through a window. But now he is inside the room, watching the process up close. He can only compare this feeling to the one he'd had being in the delivery room with all three of his children. He feels like he wants to weep at the magnificence of what is occurring, here at Jack Richman Memorial Hospital.

"Sorry, Jack. In this room, she is a member of the Daisy Estrada Memorial Hospital." Anticipating his next question, she continues, "And before you ask, the old woman sitting in the corner is her Titi. The same one from the pictures you saw earlier."

Jack realizes, *So it wasn't a dream, after all. Daisy's beloved Titi sits in the corner, gently stroking a white rabbit that sits calmly on her lap.*

Anthea smiles serenely as they watch the team of doctors energetically nurture this gentle soul who battled abuse throughout her short lifetime. Their hands seem to hover over the place where Daisy's torso materializes. Jack watches the way Dr. Annie is assisting, talking and working on Daisy's energy. Daisy starts to morph from this child into a beautiful, mature adult. It seems as if a time-lapse photographer is orchestrating the ease and grace of her crossing over. Daisy cannot see Jack standing there watching, learning and evolving through her experience. This bothers him a bit, makes him feel like a "peeping Jack." Anthea gives him a nod as if to say it's all right for them to be present.

"All part of the plan right?" Jack says, still feeling a bit uncomfortable. He continues to watch as the residents introduce themselves to her, just like they had done with him. He knows he needs to listen and watch to learn more about this place.

Knowing this child's history Dr. Chin begins by bolstering

Daisy's ego, "Daisy, you're safe here. You are now the strong, confident woman you were meant to be."

"Know this, Daisy, you can afford to be kind here. You won't be punished for it." Dr. White says, smiling gently at the girl.

Dr. Avanti offers, "The truth is, love is the answer." He steps to the side, so that Daisy can now see her Titi in the corner, though the rabbit is invisible to her. They smile sweetly at each other.

"That's why your most important relationships flourish here in Heaven." Dr. Robert finishes. As it turns out, he can be quite soft and compassionate when he wants to be.

The rabbit jumps off Titi and scurries right to Jack. A rejuvenated Titi stands as her granddaughter rushes into her arms. They embrace tightly, as everyone, including Jack, feels warmed by the power of the loving reunion.

"Titi! I was so scared. Every day," sobbed Daisy.

"I know *mi nieta*. I was there, watching over you. I'm sorry I couldn't do more."

"But you did. I felt you. It was the only thing that kept me going. *Gracias, gracias.*"

Titi can't explain the amount of comfort Daisy's words provide her. She had felt so helpless watching over her. But that Daisy could feel her? That meant the world to her. Now that Daisy was safe and out of harm's way, she would be able to move the next level.

The two remained hugging, crying and laughing, lost for this moment in their bubble of love and warmth.

Dr. Brooks gets back to business, quickly skimming through Daisy's chart, looking for something specific. Anthea knows this routine all too well. She knows what Dr. Brooks is searching for.

"She's looking for her kids?" Jack questions, as he reads Anthea's mind,

Anthea, always the teacher, comments, "Well aren't you a quick learner? Nicely done, Jack. But all in good time."

Jack scoffs, "Well, if I was a quicker learner I'd understand why everyone can see Titi and embrace her relationship with Daisy, while my Grandpa Joe is invisible to you. Why didn't anyone think I needed to be greeted like this by my grandfather or *anyone* for that matter? I don't understand that—or why this rabbit is around." Jack tries to move his foot to shoo it away, but it doesn't flinch.

Dr. Brooks makes eye contact with Jack and sees through him into his pain. Her thought exchange explains to Jack that each situation is unique. *A beaten little girl needed her grandmother's presence to ground her here. You have a totally different set of circumstances.*

Continuing to use his newfound telepathic abilities, So, the harder you had it on Earth, the better things are for you here? Is it because I had a great life that I'm having such a hard time here? Did I not suffer enough? That doesn't make sense. If this is truly heaven it should make everyone feel safe and welcome. This little girl should feel peace, but I should, too! And I haven't felt peaceful or safe since the moment I got here.

Annie lets the others take care of Daisy. This girl's case is tragic, but simple, nothing like Jack's. She walks over and touches him to convey her understanding. Annie knows on some common level that they are not allowed to have this moment of connection like others do, but it keeps happening, magnetically. Somehow, they are part of a unique sect of people in the afterlife who are different. People who have gone through life without ever finding what they are looking for.

Just as Annie touches Jack—it happens again.

A man is lovingly looking at Annie in her 19th century nightgown and desiring her essence and body. Jack can feel the man's powerful emotion and knows the man loves Annie, without question. The feeling is overwhelming and powerful. It's a timeless, intimate connection. The man leans in to kiss her passionately as she gazes at him submissively.

At this touch, Anthea's and the team's attention turn to Dr. Brooks and Jack, who are staring at each other. They are clearly having an intimate moment in the room, they've clearly forgotten their surroundings. The team of doctors can feel the intensity; the temperature of the room climbs by the moment. Dr. Avanti tugs at his tie to loosen it.

Anthea is trusting the process and not taking over the situation, despite her gut feeling. *This shouldn't be happening...* She and the other doctors are stunned and paralyzed. Then TD appears.

"What in God's grace is going on here? Anthea, why are you just standing there?" At this moment Jack and Annie separate, instantly knowing the doctors had felt their desire.

"Madame TD, you just scolded me for interfering with the process. You were the one who ordered Jack and me to be here now. I thought this was your plan."

"Your thinking is the problem. You must think what I would do in situations."

Daisy and Titi have been locked in their own embrace, energetically shielded in a cocoon of privacy, until this moment. Titi walks towards the doorway, picks up the rabbit and hands it to Jack. Her need for it has been fulfilled.

"Thank you for helping Daisy cross. You opened a portal, which enabled her to get here. I hope you also find what you're looking for." She puts her hand on his arm and it's the first time since Jack has been here that he feels true peace and comfort. He'd had a purpose and had truly helped someone.

The Director watches this exchange and telepathically tells Anthea, *That's what this moment was supposed to be about. And I'm not sure if I hadn't interceded that it would have ever happened.*

The room has cooled as quickly as it had heated up. Everyone is humbled by the glory of the moment between Titi and Jack. The higher purpose prevails. TD prevails.

Relieved, The Director sighs, "Jack, it's time for you to leave Daisy's hospital and move to your next level. Dr. Brooks, my office please. I hope the rest of you understand the lesson here."

Titi returns to Daisy and they continue to find solace in their energetic bubble.

Following TD, Brooks rattles off, "Dr. White, Dr. Chin and Dr. Avanti, please escort these two to their next level. We've already accomplished a lot here. Dr. Roberts, let's get Jack back on track. Please escort him to Level 2."

The three doctors, Titi and Daisy move out of the hospital room and down the hallway toward doors marked "Exit."

Jack proceeds with Dr. Roberts in the opposite direction but looks back, jealous of the others as they head toward the most beautiful myriad colors of light. It's as if they are walking into a rainbow...

Why can't I go to with them? Jack wonders.

Dr. Roberts answers telepathically, *Remember Jack. This process is highly individualized. Everyone's path is different.*

Jack is always the one to call for careful exploration and experimentation, but all he wants is to be done with process and move on to where Titi and Daisy are going.

Dr. Roberts answers, *You are moving on, Jack. I know it can be hard, but just trust.*

Intellectually, Jack is beginning to grasp the notion that Gareth Roberts and the others are teaching him. But he turns to look back once more at the awesome rainbow-like path the others have taken to—where? Somewhere real and beautiful. Somewhere that beckons Jack, too, with its awesome spiritual siren song and its promise of peace... Peace.

CHAPTER 24: FOOD FOR THOUGHT

Earth – 4 Days After the Explosion

"A parent's embrace is eternal, Brian." Father Patrick says as the two sit in a booth impatiently waiting for their lunches. Brian is connecting the dots on his placemat with a crayon, absorbing everything the priest says. It's his first real conversation about Heaven and the afterlife.

"So you're saying that my Dad is hugging me right now—I just can't see it?"

"Can't you feel your father hugging you? That's how I connect to God the Father."

"No, I can't." Brian thinks for a moment. "Do you think that's proof enough that he's still alive? Shelly said she couldn't feel him either."

Perplexed and not knowing how to answer Father Moran declares, "Where is our food? We've been waiting for over half an hour."

Brian simultaneously realizes that his dot drawing is of a clock and starts connecting the dots of the next puzzle. "Tick, tick, tick. Well this gives us more time to talk. There's no such thing as coincidence, remember?" He winks mischievously.

"True. But an overcrowded, understaffed restaurant might be stretching the point a little."

"How do you know? Maybe we're here right now for some larger purpose."

Stunned, he remembers the moment the other night

when he caught Angie and the sequence of events leading up to that. Maybe he is here right now to catch Brian?

Just then, a waitress walks by with a huge tray of food (not theirs, as it turns out) that's beginning to tip right toward the priest and Brian. Father Patrick puts his arm out and catches it just in time. The woman graciously thanks him, uses her other hand to steady the tray and carries on.

"See. I told you. You saved the day." Brian says with a smart-ass smile.

"No, I just saved the soup of the day." Father Patrick cracks himself up while Brian giggles heartily.

Redirecting the conversation Brian asks, "So maybe there are accidents, but definitely no coincidences, but there is a Heaven right Father? And you think my father's there?"

"I believe with all my heart that there is a Heaven. And it's an amazing, loving place. In the Bible, John 14:2, Jesus refers to Heaven as a mansion with many rooms, and that he is going there to prepare a place for John—who represents each of us. I don't know where your father is, just like you don't, at least not specifically, but I believe that he is in God's heavenly kingdom and preparing a place for when you will see him again. Up until that time, Brian, I'm here for you. Many people seek closure with death, I am hoping to help you find connection with it, your Dad and the Holy Father himself."

Brian sits up straight and without blinking looks at Father Moran and asks, "Is there a point system, Father?"

"A point system? In Heaven?" The priest tries to answer him on his level. "You mean like high scores in a video game?"

Without skipping a beat Brian delivers a joke. "Yeah, like the priest with the most followers gets a prize?"

They both laugh.

"Yeah, something like that. You know, I do have over 17,000 followers on my Twitter account. Not too bad, huh? I mean, I'm no Kim Kardashian or Lady Gaga, but it's impressive for a priest in a Chicago suburb don't you think?" Father Patrick is actually looking for a bit of validation from the tech-savvy preteen.

Brian nods with approval. "OK. Well, we're definitely going to follow up with Shelly, right? Like next week... or tomorrow?"

"Listen, first things first. I am going to have to talk with your mother about all this."

"Yeah, um, good luck with that."

"Don't worry, I got this. I will talk to your mother about it and we'll make plans."

Ever the 10-year old, Brian returns to connecting the dots on his placemat. Right away it's obvious to Brian that the next one is a telephone. He's really getting too old for these things; they're so easy to figure out... He pulls out his iPhone that he was previously only allowed to take when he went to camp or on a field trip and turns it on. The device starts pinging and buzzing, alerting Brian there are new emails and text messages, as well as voicemails.

Father Moran thinks to himself, *Good idea.* He starts to pull his phone from his pocket, but since the booth is so narrow he is forced to stand up to retrieve it. It's a very awkward scene, which garners attention from the other customers. Brian is embarrassed and shrinks into the booth trying to hide. He notes the phone is now off, must have happened in his pocket, or it died. He certainly did not turn it off on purpose, since he was always "on call" for his parish... As he turns it back on, it too started to make a ton of buzzes and beeps.

Father Patrick Moran sees he has 20 text messages and five voicemails. He quickly scans the text message inbox. All the messages are from Christina:

"When can I expect you back?"
"Would love to have you over for dinner."
"Where are you?"
"How come you haven't called me back?"
"I'm worried, this is not ok!"
"He's only 10 years old, I should know where he is!"

"It's your mom. She must not have gotten my earlier texts. She's really worried. We need to get you home immediately." Brian can only imagine how worried and angry his mother must be. The last text message makes it completely clear that she's really mad: *"Where the hell are you?"*

The priest hits his call button and the phone goes straight to voicemail. "It's her voicemail."

Brian grabs the phone from the priest. "Hi, Mom. I'm fine. I made Father take me to a meet a psychic, at a place called a psychic bazaar, or something like that. Well, I met this lady, her name is Shelley, actually her name is Michelle and used to date Father Moran. And anyway, we are at Denny's eating, and then he is going to bring me home. And… She said that maybe Daddy is not dead after all! Well, she didn't say *that,* what she said was she didn't see him around me. OK? Love you! We're coming home now."

Father Moran takes the phone back. "Christina I just got all your messages. So sorry and—" *Beep!* The message times out. He tries dialing their house, but he's forced to leave a message there as well. When he hangs up, he signals to their waitress.

She walks over to their table. "I'm sorry it's taking so long —"

The priest cuts her off as his adrenaline rises, "We need to go right now. Please wrap up our meal quickly and bring the check."

She nods, understanding without further words.

"What happened to patience, Father?"

The priest, more boisterous than ever replies, "There's a time and place for everything. Right now we need to get you home. I can only imagine the wide array of questions I will be dealing with not only from your mom in the next hour, but from the diocese if anyone reports they saw 'the pastor of the church with his *son* at a *psychic fair* being *kissed* by a famous TV psychic'." Father Patrick sighs deeply but realizes that this is all part of his mission to help his flock. That comes above all else.

"I'm sure she'll understand once you explain that I had

my phone off, and your shut off on itself after we went inside the fair."

"I hope so. But you have to understand, your mother is very sensitive right now. She too is dealing with her grief, and the thought of a lost child could send her over the top. As much as we're focusing on connecting to the afterlife, we must prioritize how we can help the ones we love here, now. That is within our control."

Brian says, "Got it, Father. I'll try my hardest to keep my mom and sisters in my mind. I'm sure Kimberly is going to be mad at me for not bringing her today."

"And I'm sure she won't let you forget it, either. Am I right?"

"Father, you have nooooo idea."

The two laugh together.

The frazzled waitress comes by and rips off a check, placing it on the table. "Your food will be waiting at the register. Sorry about the wait. Have a nice day."

The pair slides out of the booth hurriedly and head towards the exit. Patrick's pocket buzzes and beeps, buzzes and beeps.

CHAPTER 25: LEVEL 2

Jack's World

There is an awkward silence as Jack and Dr. Roberts walk down the hallway, which is especially odd in a place that is constantly filled with sounds, images and tastes attached to all his thoughts. To break the awkwardness, Jack asks aloud, "I am being transferred to another place within this hospital, aren't I? It's not where Daisy and Titi are going? I apparently did something to offend The Director and it clearly has to do with Dr. Annie Brooks, so now I am heading to Level 2? What can be accomplished on Level 2 that can't on 1?"

Dr. Gareth Roberts escorts him into an elevator and without touching a button it starts to move. "It's just the next step, standard protocol. It's not that different from Level 1, but here you and I are going to focus on assessing your relationships with others."

"Great. Am I the only person who seems to notice that there is no shortage of questions to be asked, but a clear drought of answers to be found? At a certain point, the student needs to be taught, Dr. Roberts. You can imply and experience, inference and transference also might apply, but people have to communicate. If one of my children was plagued with a lesson in school, and she was struggling with a subject, and her assigned teacher was not doing the job of educating her, I would go above their head and get another teacher, a tutor, something to assist them. I need help here, doctor." Jack is flabbergasted by the lack of information about his circumstance and the constant bombardment of new information that makes no sense.

Good, Jack. You are asking the right questions and thinking correctly, Roberts telepathically replies.

When the door opens it buzzes and beeps just like Father Patrick Moran's cell phone. Jack questions, as they step out, "Did you hear that? That was specifically a text message alert. Whose cell phone is that?"

Dr. Robert's doesn't hear the alert that Jack does. "I can assure you, Jack, that you are not hearing a cell phone from this realm. As you can see, hear and feel everything, there is no need for that type of communication device here. You understand that, right?"

"I do... but I know that I am not supposed to have the body that I had at 18 when I'm 35 either. But I know what I heard." Jack remains alert after hearing the text message sound. It reminds him of home.

The elevator stops, the doors open and a rush of wind and energy pour in. This rush of energy is accompanied by a pool of orange light that is too bright to see through, but becomes increasingly darker. When he focuses his vision, he turns to Dr. Roberts. "Level 2 sure does look a lot like my childhood home."

"Jack, it is your childhood home, your living room, eh? Circa 1982?" Dr. Roberts asks with confidence.

Jack walks off the elevator like the Pevensie children walking through the wardrobe in Narnia for the first time. Each step he takes off the elevator brings him closer to the vibration of his past. This is time travel at its sci-fi best—a three-dimensional experience that carries the sensory perception of being the director in your own modern-day reality show.

"Not *that* different? I can't believe it. Oh my God! Look! This is amazing!" Jack says with astonishment.

Dr. Roberts stands with Jack to monitor his energetic vitals as he is connecting with this plane in space and time. In the background, the high-pitch sound of a picture tube in the 19-inch Sylvania television is blasting an old episode of *Three's Company*: "Oh, Jack. Stop it."

"It's my mom." Jack looks at Roberts in disbelief. "It is my mom, but she is so young. She is younger than I am, or was, now."

Dr. Roberts turns toward the sound running down the hall.

It is Jack, the little boy version from that time. Jack runs in toward his mother wearing his Star Wars pajamas. "Mommy, I'm hungry."

"Back to bed, you," says his mom, Anna, barely looking away from the antics of Jack, Janet and the Ropers on the TV screen.

"But I just wanted to see Daddy when he comes home!"

"Well he's not gonna be home for a while. He's tied up at the lab. So back to bed."

"Will he be here in the morning?"

"That depends on what time you wake up," his mother says, indicating that if he were to get up early he could catch him.

Jack turns to Dr. Roberts, "I remember always asking for him, but he wasn't there. I promised myself I'd never be like that with my kids."

"You can't change your father's mistakes, but you can and you did make the correction in your own parenting," explains Dr. Roberts. "Additionally, your poor father missed all that quality time with Chrissy and Janet. Mind if we take another look?"

"Is this about your relationships or mine?" Jack interjects sarcastically.

"Yeah, yeah. Come on, time to move on," the doctor says begrudgingly.

"Can I just peak at my old backyard? I loved my tree house."

"Follow me." As Jack follows him, he turns for one last look at his childhood and to remember that image of his mother. The two walk through "little boy Jack's" living room past the family photos, the large one of Grandpa Joe and Jack always out on display near the back sliding doors in the dining room. When they walk out of the doors, they are standing on the top row of bleachers on a football field. Dr. Roberts and Jack are behind Jack's mom, and his dad, Dr. Jack Richman.

They are just in time to hear the announcement:

"Jack Richman, president of this year's graduating class and the recipient of our science award."

Anna says to her husband, "I wish your father had lived to see this."

"Don't worry, Grandpa Joe's right here next to me," Suzanne innocently says as she clings to her bunny.

Jack's mother just pats her on her head and smiles. Suzanne always talked about Grandpa Joe (whom she'd never met) as if he was her imaginary friend. Anna just thinks it comes from all of her son's stories about him to her.

Jack looks around to see if he can catch a glimpse of Grandpa Joe here on this journey through his life, but he doesn't see him or even feel him. *It's like Grandpa Joe is not allowed to connect with me when any of the doctors are near me, only when I am left alone.*

Dr. Roberts senses this thought in Jack and makes a note in Jack's chart. This is odd, indeed, but at least it explains some of his earlier questions and comments. Roberts and Jack witness the entire scene as "graduating Jack" is handed his award and diploma. He waves to his family up in the bleachers.

Every ounce of Jack's being sends love and a casual "Hi, guys" to his family. Seeing them all together makes him miss them so much.

Dr. Roberts explains, "You see, Jack, our soul relationships don't end. The energetic form of communication just changes. Just now on Earth, they felt you."

Dr. Richman's pager buzzes and beeps with the same sound that Jack heard in the elevator. Jack's mother shoots him a deathly look as he checks it.

"Dr. Roberts, there's that noise again. Did you hear it?"

"Your father's pager? Yeah, but that was the first time."

Confused, but wondering whether this is Daisy crying all over, Jack waits to see if it happens again. When it does, he'll try what Anthea taught him—to listen with his soul.

Jack cranes his neck around to check his old school grounds. With a blink, the setting changes and he sees the Southern Illinois University Saluki dog mascot running into his old college science building.

It is the first day of the second semester and Jack is watching "college Jack" struggle to find the building his class is being held in. Jack explains to Dr. Roberts what was actually happening in this moment of his life history. "I was mindlessly digging the toe of my Air Jordans into the turf and turning circles in the middle of the quad."

"Jack, I do have eyes. I don't need a narration," Roberts says as he sits next to Jack on a nearby bench taking it all in. "College Christina" approaches "college Jack."

Christina is thinking, "This poor guy..." So she walks right up to him and asks, "Freshman? You need help?"

"Is it that obvious?" Jack asks bashfully looking down at his feet.

Jack turns to Dr. Roberts, "This is starting to get creepy and a bit intrusive, even though it's my own life."

Dr. Roberts puts his index finger to his lips to quiet Jack, then points back to the scene at hand just in time for Jack to reply to Christina.

"No, not at all. I was just trying to stop you from getting dizzy and falling over."

Christina smiles at him as he looks up. Their eyes meet and suddenly it is like they are in a movie. The rest of the world gets blurry and the camera encircles them, creating their own little bubble apart from the rest of the world.

Before Jack can whisper excitedly to Roberts, the doctor says in monotone, "I know, this is your favorite moment of your entire life—even better than the birth of your children, because without this moment, there would be no children. Blah, blah, blah. I'm not the sentimental type. Wake me when you've figured out the lesson."

"Fine. But can we watch some more? I don't want this to end."

Although he is feeling somewhat schizophrenic, flipping from one world and one life moment to another—and back again—Jack cherishes each insight and snapshot that he is being given. It's as if he is watching the movie version of his life, but he is also the writer and director—as well as the star... He keeps watching and can't keep his eyes off Christina, the love of his life.

Christina, it turns out, is going to a class in the very same building Jack is looking for, so she escorts him in a classic role reversal. "So what brings you to the Agriculture Building?" Christina asks.

"Oh, some stupid science core class." Then Jack adds sarcastically, "On agriculture, I believe."

Christina wrinkles her nose cutely. "Ha ha! Well, my class is actually Bio 102, so you're joke isn't as funny as you think. I guess they didn't have room in the Biology building."

"She never did stop calling me out on my lame jokes." Jack laughs. "And the rest, as they say, is happily ever after. I'm a lucky guy, that is, until I was blown up."

"So you get it, Jack? Do you understand, you were lost and

then you were found?"

"Yes. She completes me. That I get. And do I complete her?"

"No, Jack. You are missing the very obvious point in our journey. You were lost and she helped to find you." Dr. Roberts is now spelling something out for Jack like a teacher giving answers for a high school standardized test and Jack is not getting the point.

"I was lost, in more ways than one," Jack said ruefully.

Dr. Roberts walks Jack past this scene towards the entrance of the building and they wind up in the back of a labor and delivery room, watching Christina's and her obstetrician Dr. Brimaldi. Now the "movie" of his and Christina's life was getting all too real.

"Dr. Roberts, I don't know if I can watch anymore, my heart hurts from feeling."

Jack turns away from the "Daddy-to-be Jack" coaching down below.

"OK. Breathe. Another contraction's coming right now. Just push, honey. Push. You can do this." Sure enough, baby Brian's head crowns, and Christina screams. "Breathe! Push!" Jack urges.

Starting to get angry and emotional about connecting with all these earthly emotions, Jack erupts. "What's the lesson here?"

"You tell me, Jack. I never did get to be a father myself, so you're gonna have to explain this one." Dr. Roberts genuinely hopes to continue his lessons through Jack's experience.

"Well… at this time, I didn't realize how my life would change forever. I was no longer just someone's child, I became someone's father. This someone was going to depend on *me*. It was the scariest moment of my life to know that I was responsible for another. Would I make the same mistakes my dad made? Would I be able to love a child? Would I be too selfish and not want my life to change because of it?"

These are real emotions pouring from Jack and he is actually starting to feel like he is crying, yet there are no tears. Upon further analysis, the tears were his memories, and ultimately they were good memories—of intense love, unconditional love.

"Jack, you've taken that role of father very seriously. It's evident in your all children. And it's validated by the way they think of you. It seems to me that you have been successful... yes? Evolved, would you say, from your past?" Dr. Roberts makes some notes on his clipboard.

"So A+ on relationships?"

A distracted Dr. Roberts explains as he's ogles the nurses in the delivery room, "Sure, if that's how you want to look at it. But remember there's always more to learn."

"Dr. Roberts, I cannot help but notice that you have a pretty intense appreciation of the female anatomy. I thought matters of the flesh are not important and it is all about the soul and energy in this realm? Am I mistaken?" Jack asks.

The doctor's countenance shifts for a split second, and Jack sees him as if for the first time. In that moment, Jack knows that Gareth has spent countless lifetimes where his sexual side on the earthly plane delivered his future and manifested his life. He has made multiple mistakes over centuries, and an earthly penis has ruled them all.

"Jack, let's just say that we are all working on evolution. Some souls just take a lot longer than you might care to." Dr. Roberts got back into his soul zone and Jack has a new appreciation for him. Gareth had revealed himself to Jack, and he feels like Gareth Roberts is no longer a stranger, but a friend on a similar journey.

The delivery room begins to bleed away to the Jack Richman Memorial Hospital's hallway and the elevator door closes behind them. It has felt like a lifetime reviewing these moments, when in fact it has been no more than the few seconds it takes for an elevator door to open and close.

Just then a feeling of worry overcomes Jack. He hears the

buzzes and beeps of a cell phone again. "Dr. Roberts, the cell phone noise is happening again. Help me find out where it's coming from. Something's pulling me. I feel inside me that something is wrong with Brian. I know it."

"You have to have faith, Jack. Stay positive. It's gonna be OK." Dr. Roberts puts his hand on Jack's shoulder.

"I don't want to have faith. I want to help my son. You just watched my son be born into my life. You just saw that I struggled with the concept of being a parent and being a good one. It is an issue for me, a life lesson, and now you want me to say a prayer and have faith? I need to help my son. *Help me, Gareth—please!*" Jack pleads to his new friend, not to the Dr. Roberts who escorted him to Level 2.

"Jack, you are not ready for this, yet you are like calling the shots at the same time, which is weird. Listen to me. We can get in a lot of trouble. There are rules here for learning and you have a knack for wanting to break them. You already have stuff happening around you that I have not seen in all my crossovers here in the hospital… and dare I say it intrigues me." Roberts now had an idea of why TD was so mad at Anthea before. "So, *concentrate* on what you are hearing—the audio frequencies."

Jack closes his eyes, and as he does, the sounds get louder and louder. The frequency morphs from a quick alert of a cell phone to a longer, familiar sound—a sound that he has heard before and often—a doorbell, his doorbell. He thinks, *I am going home.*

CHAPTER 26: FAYE DROPS IN

Jack's World

Ding, dong!

Ding, dong!

Dr. Roberts has already zeroed in on the source of the doorbell. He panics; Jack should not be allowed to re-enter the earthly realm.

"Something isn't right. I need to check in with TD. Stay here, take it all in." And just like that, Gareth Roberts disappears.

Worried, Jack looks around and realizes he's in his family's present-day suburban home. Instantly, he forgets about Dr. Roberts' concern and gets excited that he's going to be able to see his family.

Ding, dong!

Jack eagerly anticipates who will be standing at the door. *Grandpa Joe? Christina? Matilda?*

Instead, as he opens the front door—which he had installed himself with Brian as his little helper—he sees a stranger. Standing with a look of confusion and despondency is a woman who feels familiar only because she is a beautiful version of Mrs. Doubtfire (the loving woman the actor Robin Williams brought to life). Jack is correlating the similarities in stories because, as a father in the movie, Williams couldn't bear to be away from his own kids, either.

Jack is wondering, *When did Christina hire someone to help out?* He dismisses this notion as quickly has he thought it.

Visual similarities aside, Jack's soul knows that this situation is no comedy. His parental paranoia over Brian, returns, full force.

Unknown to Jack, this woman has just crossed over herself, and it seems as if she has lost her way and found herself in Jack's afterlife experience.

"Hello," Jack says.

"Hello? Who the hell are you, and where am I?" She says, looking at him suspiciously.

"Well, you're in my house, where I lived up until about four days ago."

"Mrs. Doubtfire" processes this then barks with a Brooklyn twang, "Do you have any coffee, kid?"

Jack stands aside as she pushes her way in his house.

"Come in? Uh, coffee? Ma'am, my name is Jack Richman." Jack realizes so far the only people that can talk to him are all crossed over, so he begins to try to tell this woman where she is. Why this duty is falling on him, he has no idea.

"Ma'am I think I have some unfortunate news for you." He says hesitantly.

"Really? Ya think?" the woman says sarcastically. "One minute I'm making coffee in my kitchen, and the next minute I'm fully dressed in my coat, purse in hand. And I can assure you that I would not be wearing this outfit today in 90-degree Miami humidity." She pauses, then repeats, "Do you have any coffee?"

"Mrs.? Um?"

"Call me Faye, Faye Bingham."

Jack looks around, hoping he is going to see Christina or Brian come around the corner any minute. Nothing. It is his house just as he left it, but nobody is there.

"Jack, you say? Where are we?" Faye asks.

"Yeah... about that, well... I think we are in my house." Jack puts out his hand to greet her with a handshake. At their touch they both feel a jolt and watch the events leading up to the last scene of her life. *Finally, this has happened with someone other than Annie, he thinks.* Jack is fully aware of the special connection and does not take it lightly.

Years ago, Faye had a premonition that she would be living out her life alone, but she didn't want to be in her big old house by herself. Thankfully, she and Harry were well off enough that she didn't have to depend on anyone for anything now that he was gone. After her premonition, she had gotten Harry to sell everything and buy the condo in Miami where she has spent the last 15 years living. Since she is alone, every day her daughter, Deb, calls her in the morning, afternoon and evening, like clockwork.

"Mom, you really need to sleep in the bed, not some old chair. It is going to take a toll on your back," Deb says with tender annoyance.

"Yeah, I know. Thanks for calling, honey. Have a great day at work." Faye hangs up the phone.

Truth be told, Faye is fearful of the bedroom. She hasn't been able to sleep in her bed, which her dear Harry had passed in. Finding him there, dead, scarred her for the rest of her life.

Faye stretches her legs, rises out of her chair, and begins to feel a bit dizzy. She thinks, Nothing that a black cup of coffee can't fix. *As she walks past her bookshelf, she remembers that she wanted to download a few new books to her Kindle.*

Every book on the shelf, and DVD for that matter, is a gritty crime drama. Faye laughs to herself, You know, Harry, I need at least two dead bodies in the first three pages or I'm not happy. *She shakes her head. She hadn't been challenged by a good mystery in a few years. She's glad she has long since retired from the tedium of the book editing world so she can read what she wants to, not what she has to.* These days everybody writes such predictable nonsense, *she thinks.*

The dizziness hits Faye again, but this time it's accompanied by a wave of heat and nausea. "Deb..." is the last thing she says as she collapses in the kitchen of her duplex on Collins Avenue.

Faye cuts to the chase, "Am I dead?"

"I think so," Jack responds. He's so confused. This isn't the way he transitioned. Daisy and Angie came through the hospital like he had. *Why am I the welcome wagon for someone I don't know? Just when I thought I had* something *figured out…*

"Son, you don't greet someone newly departed and say you think so. Did your wife's OB GYN come in and say, 'I think you're pregnant?' Or did he come in and say, 'You're eight weeks pregnant' based on the sonogram?"

"How did you know I had a wife or a child?" Jack is curious as to how this woman had any information about him at all. *Maybe she works for his hospital in another capacity and this is all just an exercise or test?*

"Nothing gets past me. I don't miss a thing. Investigative mind." She taps her head for emphasis. "I edited crime novels for 30 years. It's how I think. As I walked into your home, I just looked around. It is clear that you are married, and have at least two kids—one boy and definitely one girl. There is candied flavored lip-gloss on the table. Adult women don't wear candied flavored lip-gloss. Young girls who want to act like adult women wear flavored lip-gloss. It is how the wives allow the young girls to wear starter makeup and prepare the daddies, like you, to deal with it. From the looks of the high chair in the kitchen, you have a young one, too."

Jack is quite impressed by her evidently well-developed investigative mind.

"What are you, a doctor of some sort?" Faye asks.

"No, why do you say that?"

"You just feel like a doctor to me. That's all."

"Well, actually, I am a science writer, a journalist."

"Figures. I die and I *still* have to work with writers in the afterlife."

Jack finds her annoyance funny. "Faye, I can see you're a straight shooter. So let me blunt. I am not really sure why we are here together in my living room. I came back here with the intention of finding my son. I'm very worried about him. All I know is, I died in an explosion in South Africa and then woke up in a hospital that had my name on it. I was working with some of the doctors on transitioning from Level 1 to Level 2. Personally, I think I was being moved because The Director of the hospital didn't want me to learn something about one of the other doctors, Dr. Brooks, but they said moving me was 'just part of the process.'"

Before Jack can continue his attempt to explain what is going on, Faye interrupts him. "Do you hear that?"

"Hear what?" Jack is not hearing anything. Now he knows how the doctors had felt when he was hearing Daisy and the cell phone. He feels sorry for Faye that she has to experience this too.

"It's my Harry. He is calling me." Faye moves from the entryway to the living room, to the kitchen. She is looking around trying to find where the voice of her deceased husband is coming from. She is pulled to the answering machine. As she nears it, it turns on:

"Christina, it's Father Moran. I left a message on your cell too. Brian is still with me. My phone was acting up and apparently you didn't get the texts I sent you. We're fine. We ran an errand after Mass, which led to lunch. I will have him home shortly... lots to discuss." Beep!

Faye turns to Jack and sees his jaw drop. This confirms that his worry was a manifestation of Christina's anxiety over Brian's whereabouts, just like he'd heard Daisy's cries because Christina was concerned for her, too.

The echoes of Harry stop, and Faye finds herself right in the middle of the thing she had been craving most: a mystery. "Who is Father Moran? And why is he having lunch with your son without your wife knowing?"

"I have no idea. I didn't know him. Christina's very worried. I can feel her."

Faye takes off her wire-rimmed glasses and puts one stem in her mouth. "Don't worry. I'll figure it out!"

"Thanks. And while you're at it I'll try to figure out how

you got here and where you're supposed to go next." Jack is thinking two things, *Maybe she's here to help—and why hasn't Gareth returned?*

CHAPTER 27: BACK TO THE NEST

Earth – 4 Days After the Explosion

Christina has been waiting for over two hours for word on her son's whereabouts. She had expected him home around 11 o'clock, shortly after Mass was over. She knows that Brian is safe with Father Moran, but when neither of them responded to texts and calls she begins to get worried. It's been less than a week since she had the love her life ripped from her existence, leaving her to be both mother and father to her children. Her worry and stress is intense. She cannot handle this today.

As she steps out of the bathroom, she feels as if she is free falling and is about to hit the ground.

"I hope you really give it to him when he gets back!" Kimberly says to Christina. She is annoyed that Brian is getting any extra attention.

"Kimmy, I know Brian is all right, it's OK. I am glad he is with Father Patrick." She tries to assure her daughter while assuring herself.

"Well... I don't like him." She rolls her eyes and sits down on the couch brushing one of her dolls' hair. "He isn't like the priests that spoke at our school. They were nice and healing. He is way too—"

"Real?" Christina interrupts her. "He's a person, Kimberly, who has a job. You weren't very nice to him. He's only trying to help us heal as a family and hold onto our faith, something that we need. Something that your dad and I didn't really concentrate so much on with you kids."

Two Hours Later

The car pulls up and Christina walks towards the door, but Kimberly gets there first.

"Do you think it is all right to make us worry about where you were?" Kimberly says, her eyes flashing with sassy attitude.

Father Patrick Moran hurries through the Richman home's front door. Brian struggles to keep up. He is excited to report back about his day. With enthusiasm he hugs his sister briefly and disarms her sassiness. Then he hugs his mom in the entryway. Christina clings to him tightly for a long time.

Father Patrick apologizes to Christina for not being more forthcoming with Brian's intentions. She quietly nods an acknowledgment of both it being OK and to say thank you.

Brian, sensing a new emotion within his mother, struggles to get away. "Mom! I'm fine. Sorry about the little technology hiccup. Father Patrick sent you messages, you just must not have gotten them."

"Well how about you fill me in on your plans *ahead* of time from now on, so that we don't have these issues again!" Christina says firmly directly to Brian. She knows poor Father Moran was just a pawn in his scheme.

"You had Mommy so worried!" Kimberly yells from behind Christina.

The priest looks at this mini-adult with her arms crossed, acting angrier than Christina herself. Brian sure hadn't been exaggerating. Father Moran looks at her and says, "Kimberly, you look pretty in your yellow sundress."

She rolls her eyes, turns and begins to go upstairs. Two steps later she comes back, obnoxiously grabs her doll off the couch in the living room and then heads up to her room. Matilda is sitting in her bouncy swing watching the Wiggles sing "HOT POTATO, HOT POTATO" on the big screen TV in the living room.

"I'm sorry, Mom. I just didn't know how'd you'd react."

Christina looks immediately to Father Patrick for clarity.

"I'm sorry, too, Christina. I should have made sure we had an actual conversation about it before we went."

"Well, let's sit down and discuss where you guys actually went and why I wasn't given the courtesy of a phone call or asked for my permission." She has to address her discomfort, but she really is intrigued to see the light in Brian.

As they walk down the hallway to where Matlida is watching TV, Father Patrick catches the evil eye of Kimberly from the top of the stairs, who has come out of her room and sits listening from afar. Father Moran looks down at his feet, trying not to laugh and thinks, *Man, she's good. I do not want to be around for her teen years.*

As they pass the kitchen Brian sees and smells the tasty food cooking and starts, "Uh, Mom, we kinda already—" Father Moran gives him a nudge as if to say, go along with it. So Brian adds, "I mean, it smells so good!" Father Moran casually places their takeout in the kitchen counter and continues towards the living room.

Christina laughs, "Well, you know I either organize or cook when I'm nervous and I'd already finished going through your dad's files so here we are, a late lunch or early Sunday dinner. I hope you like spaghetti and meatballs, Father."

"It really does smell delicious," Father Moran says.

After they sit down on the couch, Christina is all ears. Kimberly "sneaks" down to the bottom of the stairs and eavesdrops from the end of the hallway the whole time.

Brian knows that he has to explain himself very carefully here. He wants to inspire and explain to his mother how this came about while not sounding crazy. He looks towards Father Patrick for moral support and then at his mom, all the while playing with the bottom of his sleeve.

"Well, I wanted to know if it is *possible* to talk to Daddy. I googled 'talking to the dead' and the fair came up in the local search." As he is talking, there are a few moments where his voice loses its authoritative tone, and cracks with emotion, revealing he is just a boy missing his dad and grasping at straws. "I was very skeptical myself, just as Daddy always taught me to be, Mom. I really researched this, I applied all of Daddy's criteria for researching articles, and I wanted to go there and check it out, make sure it was you know, real, and credible before I told you about it."

Christina listens in disbelief that a man of the cloth would take a ten-year-old to a psychic fair to explore something as real or ridiculous as this. Truth be told, she is a bit jealous that she didn't think about this first, or even go with them.

Brian puts his hand on top of Christina's, remembering Father Patrick's words that he needed to remember to prioritize the ones he loves who are here now. He winks at Father Patrick.

"Uh-huh." Christina feels like she's got a little scam artist holding her hand. "And what about you, Father, how did you feel about all this? Surely the diocese wouldn't have wanted you to attend such a mockery of faith?"

Father Moran laughed aloud at the irony. "Yeah, well I'm sure I'm going to have to explain a few things. You see, there were a few of my parishioners at the fair, and, well, Brian might have alluded that he was my son because they wouldn't allow children into the fair without parental permission. I am sure there is a message on the rectory mainline requesting a call to explain my attendance. That's the thing about social media, within moments, you can be on the Vatican watch list."

"There's a Vatican watch list?" Christina is shocked, not realizing he is joking. Concerned she scolds, "Brian Richman, how could you be so inconsiderate? Do you have the slightest idea of the problems you may have caused for him? I'm so sorry, Father."

Father Moran smiles and waves his hand in the air, "It's not a problem really. That's the least of it."

"There's more?" Christina is now fearful of what they are going to tell her next, but she prepares for whatever shocking revelation is coming.

Brian, in fact, had no idea that any of this could be a problem for the priest. Not only is he just 10, but also this whole church and God thing is very new to him. "Father? I thought it was OK. You totally could have said no. I'm sorry." It is in that moment that Brian realizes how special this priest really is. He is sacrificing his own reputation to help a boy he barely knows. Brian knows that he is the real deal and really cares about his parishioners' spiritual well-being.

"It's fine." Father Patrick says to Brian. Then he redirects to Christina, "It's fine really. I wouldn't have taken him if I didn't think I could explain it and it was worth it."

"So. Is anyone going to ask what actually happened at this psychic thingy? Like, what did this psychic say?" Kimberly questions skeptically from down the hall.

Father Patrick begins methodically. "Brian sprung this idea on me right after Mass. It was a spur of the moment decision and it turned out to be quite enlightening even for me. The way it is set up is there are two banquet rooms. You pay admission to get in, and-"

"Father, I am so sorry. This cost you money as well? Whatever it cost comes out of Brian's allowance." Christina gives Brian a stern look.

Father Moran nods to empower her maternal rule, as he already feels he has been disrespectful to her parenting by not including her earlier. Father Patrick continues, "On one side of the fair there are psychics sitting at tables and they do readings every fifteen minutes. On the other side of the fair, in the other banquet room, there are lectures going on. The one person he wanted to see was busy and let's just say that your son can be quite persuasive."

Excitedly Brian jumps in, "First, we went to see a psychic *medium*. That's one who can talk to dead people. All her appointments for the day were booked up, but her assistant got us into the lecture she was doing. She was doing a reading that sounded like it was Daddy coming through and talking to us. That was the whole reason I went there, to hear from Daddy."

Christina immediately looks at the priest for validation, and he nods that, yes, what Brian is saying is an accurate depiction. She begins to smile, but he shakes his head as if to say that it was not Jack coming through.

Brian notices the exchange and continues with the reason he is excited. "Mommy, the best part is that this woman knows Father Patrick. She walked right up to him and planted a big wet kiss on his lips. You used to date her—right Father?"

Now fifty shades of red, Father Moran is blushing in an uncontrollable manner. He sheepishly shrugs that this is true to Christina, and she tries not to smirk but can't help herself. "Guilty," is all he can eke out.

Brian resumes, "Like I was saying, it turns out she used to date Father Patrick here and she was *real* happy to see him." He laughs out loud.

"Ewwwww!" Kimberly says as she approaches the couch. Father Moran just looks at her not really wanting to reenact last night's dinner.

Christina eyes the priest and adjusts her ideas of him. He now seems more real to her; someone who experienced the real human emotions of a relationship and lost it, or chose to end it to dedicate his life to God.

"Mom, I think we need to go see her privately for an appointment."

Christina sits in disbelief and as she's overcome with nausea. She doesn't know if it is the pregnancy, the concept of talking to the dead or the idea that this woman could be trying to scam them for an expensive private session.

"But most of all, she said she couldn't sense anything around me. And then Father Patrick asked me if I could sense his love around me or whatever and I couldn't either!"

Christina understands immediately, knowing how her son always wants to see the good in situations.

"Brian, we are all grieving and missing Daddy. We will be doing this for the rest of our lives. So I understand where you're coming from. But, I am not thrilled that *one*, you didn't discuss this with me, and *two*, you dragged Father Moran into this. I don't want you getting some type of false hope that you will be able to talk to your dad like it's a Hollywood movie. Brian, your dad was a scientific thinker, he didn't even really believe in an afterlife. He used to make fun of the people you went to go see today. He even wrote a piece on exposing them as frauds and how they use tricks to get people to reveal things. Now take your sisters and wash up for dinner, I have to have a word with Father Moran."

Brian's energy level drops. "I know. But, there *is* something here, Mom. And something is better than nothing. It's something." He begins to walk away and stops. Defeated, he looks at his mom then turns his attention towards Father Patrick. "Thank you, for caring about me enough to help me try and find my dad."

He quickly turns so nobody can see the pain and tears welling up in his eyes. He takes Kimberly and Matilda down the hallway toward the bathroom.

Father Patrick takes over. "Christina, I know this is hard. And I do want to apologize again, but he really made a breakthrough today honoring his feelings and—"

"Honoring his feelings? You call giving a 10-year-old false hope 'honoring his feelings'? You are lucky I don't call the diocese or the pope myself." Christina is overwhelmed, shaking inside and out.

Father Moran stands up and with an unapologetic tone looks at Christina. "We watched this psychic medium give an amazing reading. I've never seen anything like it myself. Since she's a good friend, I know we can trust her. If she says she can talk to the dead, I know she at least believes she does. She's not the scam artist type. I promised Brian I'd reach out to her to set up a real one-on-one reading to see if she can get anything, with your approval of course."

Christina looks at him as if he did not hear a word she said. As he awaits her answer, Kimberly yells from the hall again, "I'm in!"

"Me too!" chimes in Matilda, without even knowing what she is in for.

Feeling defeated, overwhelmed, and now overruled, all Christina says is, "I will think about it."

Just then the phone rings. "Let the machine get it, I'll show you out, Father." This man isn't invited to dinner anymore. She eyes her eavesdroppers at the bottom of the stairs. Christina needed to be alone with her kids.

After four rings the machine picks up:

"Hey, guys! It's Nana Grace & PopPop," starts Christina's mother.

"And Grandma!" chimes in Jack's mother.

"And Grandpa," Dr. Richman says sternly.

"Eh, this is PopPop Frank here. Honey, we've got the Richmans in tow, and we're planning on spending the night in Lexington, Kentucky at the Comfort Inn. We'll get up early in the morning and see you around 2 p.m. for the Tenth Annual Richman Labor Day Barbecue!"

Before Pop Pop can hang up, Anna, Jack's mother, yells, "Can't wait to see everyone—and kids be ready, we've got presents!"

Beep!

Brian, Kimberly and Father Moran all turn towards Christina curiously, while a sudden look of guilt sweeps over her.

Brian slowly comments, "Mom, they sound awfully cheery... I didn't know we were still doing the barbecue."

"Well, yes, of course. It's tradition. Your father wouldn't have it any other way. Right, Father Patrick?" She looks toward the priest for support.

"Absolutely. But, Christina, I agree with Brian. I'm assuming you haven't told them about Jack, have you? They have the right to know."

"I know. I know. I'm terrible. But I just didn't know how to tell them. I haven't been up to it. And I thought maybe it would be better to tell them in person…"

"Presents!" Matilda shouts.

Father Moran looks at her, then at Brian, Kimberly, Matilda and Christina. "What time should I be here tomorrow?"

This is exactly what Christina wants to hear. "Oh Father, you've already spent so much time with us. I'd hate to impose further." She is no longer angry with him, she needs him too much for tomorrow. Forgiveness is one of the cornerstones of religion after all.

"Not a problem. I know I'll be needed. You have to tell your in-laws their son is gone."

"Father, correction, *possibly* gone," speaks up Kimberly.

"Either way, this is gonna be hard on them. It's not the natural order. 2 p.m. OK?"

"Yes. Thank you."

Father Moran hands Shelly's card to Christina and walks out the door. He hopes he made a difference today and is helping this family to find their balance. He thinks to himself, *Through all the tragedy they've been given this life branch of hope. And without hope, how do you survive? I hope Shelly can come through.*

As soon as the door closes and Father Moran leaves the house, Kimberly punches Brian's arm. "I can't believe you did that to Mom, to me and Matty. You could have just told us!" She runs upstairs.

"Kimberly! You apologize right now! You are not the parent here. I will deal with him," Christina yells out.

From the top of the landing Kimberly yells, "Then act like it!" She runs into her room and slams the door.

Matilda "runs" up the stairs, *which she struggles with*, as she's still not quite big enough to manage them yet. She idolizes her big sister and brother and hates to see either of them upset.

Christina looks down at Brian sitting on the bottom step, in both physical and emotional pain from his sister hitting him. He doesn't want to meet her eye. He knows she was only playing nice because the priest was here.

Calmly she says, "You, mister, I will deal with tomorrow.

Now go upstairs and apologize to your sister. You have no idea what this afternoon was like for us. I can't even think straight. I did not need this today."

Yelling he could handle, seeing the emptiness and sadness in his mother he could not. "OK. I'm really sorry, Mommy. I just miss Daddy so much." He proceeds slowly upstairs.

Matilda is standing outside the door trying to turn the locked knob that she barely reaches. "Go away, Brian!" Kimberly yells from inside.

Brian whispers to Matilda, "Tell her it's you. She'll never open the door for me."

"Kimmy, it's my room too. You have to let me in." Matilda whines and then winks at Brian. She's going to be just like Kimberly.

Kimberly sighs, gets off her bed and comes to unlock the door to let her in. Just as she does, Brian steps in. Kimberly shoots him a look of disgust, turns her back and crawls onto her bed. Brian waits for Matty to come in and then closes the door.

Christina stands at the bottom of the stairs, hoping a fight doesn't break out, but hoping that they can work it out. *It's funny. This whole thing might make them closer than ever.*

Brian looks at Kimberly, whose face is red, puffy and streaming with tears. "Why wouldn't you think I'd wanna talk to Daddy too?"

The tears are so much worse than anger. But he sympathizes completely. As he sits down on the bed next to her he explains, "I had hoped, but I just didn't really believe it was possible, honestly. I didn't want to tell you guys and get your hopes up, only to have them dashed, like mine were when she couldn't connect with him."

"You talked to Daddy? When's he coming home?" Matty asks innocently while breaking Brian's heart.

"No, Matty, I didn't. I don't know when he's coming back."

"Oh. I miss him. I can't find Moosey anywhere and he always helps me find him." She sticks her tongue out at Kimmy.

Kimmy rolls her eyes, "Ugh, yes apparently Moosey has

disappeared, and I've stolen him."

Brian, trying to be the big brother he knows he has to be now, "I'll help you look for him tomorrow, OK?"

"But you don't know all his secret hiding spots. Only Daddy does."

"Well, we'll just have to look *everywhere* then, won't we?"

Matty smiles and nods, pleased that someone is finally going to help her. "Kimmy once we find Moosey, you can borrow him to cheer you up. He's very good at that."

She smiles, feeling a thousand years older than her four-year-old sister and sad that she may never even remember their daddy. "Brian, what if this lady does make a connection with Daddy? What if he never comes back?"

"I don't know." He looks at Matty picking up on Kimmy's exact thoughts. "Then we're just going to have to act on our best behavior, help Mom out. And talk about Daddy a lot! So that we never forget him." He feigns a smile and pauses. "But I'm not ready to think about that yet. I can't imagine, won't imagine, not having Daddy in some way."

Matty climbs up onto the bed and squeezes herself in between her big brother and sister. "Never give up hope. That's what Moosey always says."

The three sit there, hugging, Brian and Kimberly knowing that life has changed forever and Matilda sensing the same thing, but not understanding why.

The three Richman children quickly look to the left as they think they catch a glimpse of a white rabbit scurrying across the floor... Brian and Kimberly look at each other in disbelief and Matilda yells, "Bunny!"

CHAPTER 28:
VENTILATION

Jack's World

Anthea hurries down the hallway of the hospital. She is heading toward The Director's office to make a quick confession. In her head she is going over what she saw, and she now realizes *she is* the one responsible for the crack in the foundation of Jack Richman. *I will tell her directly.* She then thinks that TD might already know, as she knows everything. She changes her plan. *No, I will wait to see what happens.*

Something had shifted in Jack when she allowed him to connect with the hospital energy. It was as if Anthea had forgotten the power that she was wielding. She had been trying to help jump start Jack and his afterlife journey, but now it was getting more complicated.

All she had wanted to do was to demonstrate for him the possibilities of this world. She wanted to help him to move on in his process, to meet up with his family and friends who are waiting for him, like his grandfather. She has been keeping her eye on him, watching things unfold, hoping to anticipate and prevent anything from diverting Jack from his path. But things have gone awry, for sure.

Since their little hand-on-her-heart chakra moment, Jack had dragged another person into his life review and caused energy to bleed between multiple realms.

Dr. Annie Brooks has been summoned to The Director's office once again, for her latest infraction of energy merging with Jack Richman. The Director doesn't even know where to start. In reality, Dr. Brooks isn't doing anything she wouldn't normally do with a patient. It's fine to touch patients, it's fine to reassure them but The Director knows Annie's *intentions* are against the rules.

In a world of energy, intention is of supreme importance. The Director sighs, sensing more things awry with Jack Richman. Realizing she needs Jack's whole team, The Director bellows an energetic command for all doctors and staff who are working on Jack Richman's progress to report to her office immediately.

Within nanoseconds Anthea is standing in front of The Director as she is dressing down Dr. Annie Brooks, Dr. Gareth Roberts, Dr. Lesley White, Dr. Umberto Avanti and Dr. Susan Chin, both telepathically and out loud.

"I need you all to listen to me, very carefully. Jack Richman is obviously a special case. I felt it when he came in, and I cautioned you all then. But instead of heeding my words, and handling him with care, the team of you has proceeded to allow him to entangle two more souls into his own realm. Can you not see that his own soul is in danger? He's bleeding out into everyone else's life, and what he needs to do now is make a clear choice, to choose his own path. I need you to keep him focused on his own life!"

The doctors on Jack's case insist that they have not told him anything about Faye or her life review. Dr. Roberts defends his every move with Jack on Level 2. They maintain that *they* have tried to keep him on track, but then all look towards Annie.

"What?" She is peeved by the implication that she is in some way holding him back. "Why am I the one that is getting the glaring looks?"

The Director looks at Annie and raises her eyebrow. Her energy is fierce. Anthea just watches. She is afraid to move or even think because she doesn't want the attention to turn to her since it was *actually* her fault.

"Madame Director, it'd be absurd to think that I am retarding a patient's progress. You know how important my work is to me. Why would I do anything to stop me from finding my children!" Annie blurts out in frustration.

Sometimes, Annie Brooks is nearly paralyzed by her obsession. It can sweep over her like a tidal wave of emotion. Just like any mother, her children are the focus and purpose of her life—have been since she bore them. Now, on the other side, in a world no less complex and demanding than on the earthly plane, her singular purpose—to find the children who had been murdered and torn from her heart—is no less urgent.

That is the source of her catastrophic frustration, the cause of her eternal restlessness... which will never end until she has found them. One look at her now tells the story of a woman possessed of a purpose that no one and nothing can answer. The only solution for Annie is to find the answer to the dark mystery of her past life.

The doctors look at each other and start to quiet their own energy, feeling relief that they were no longer in trouble. Annie has always been tightlipped about why she searches and searches the floors of the hospital.

Dr. Chin walks over and put her arms around her colleague. "Why didn't you tell us?"

"Tell you what? That I failed my own children and couldn't save them? That I allowed their monster of a father to poison, not one, but all of them?" Annie spoke from the depths of her soul.

Normally the least sensitive of the bunch, Dr. Roberts kneels down on the other side of his mentor, attempting to console the very woman whom he has been anchored to for what felt like eons.

"Look, Doc, we all want to be able to move on, but we need to work together. You unlock your doors, we unlock ours. We all move on and see our families. If you never tell us what we are looking for, how can we assist you in doing your job?" Dr. Roberts asks.

Annie has her head buried in her hands and is doing the heavenly equivalent of purging emotion. They can all feel it very palpably; even more than they could on Earth, for their beings are connected in more powerful and meaningful ways here. This spiritual plane allows for increased communication and understanding well beyond the physical senses, fully utilizing energies that have been reawakened.

The physicians look from one to the other, sympathizing with Annie Brooks but unsure what they can do to relieve her anguish in this moment. Knowing that this would now be handled among the team The Director sighs and suggests, "Dr. Brooks, why don't you take your staff and make rounds. I have some business to address with Anthea."

Dr. Brooks and her team vanish and all of The Director's attention is focused on Anthea.

"Young lady, what do you think you are doing? You are dabbling in areas that you are not equipped to control. You showed Jack how to connect with other people's energies and now he has, for all intents and purposes. *And*, it's with some *Murder She Wrote* editor who is going to stick her nose into all our business and possibly mess everything up."

The Director puts both her hands on the desk and yells, "Clean this mess up immediately! Get him back in his bed! And back on track! This is exactly what the Board and Council of Elders have been warning me against."

She sighs, feeling the impending pressure from the Council that will surely be applied. "Please, please, please, don't make my afterlife any harder than it already is."

All Anthea can eke out is, "Yes, Madame Director. I am sorry."

"That I know. I could feel your fear from down the hall,

my dear girl. What I cannot feel is Jack Richman, and that means that Gregorios is hard at work. You and I are the only ones that can get that situation under control and re-banish him. Ugh, how did he find his way in?" Gregorios is the embodiment of evil on this plane. Pure trickster energy, bent on a dark purpose. But TD knows that he wouldn't dare show up here at the hospital.

"You think it's Gregorios? I am sorry—I hadn't realized that Jack's soul was hanging in the balance to the extent that Gregorios would try to..."

"I know it's him. I've had lifetimes of fighting him for souls. And I don't want to lose this one, Anthea!" TD said fiercely. "He wants another soul to add to his army."

"But Jack's not evil!" Anthea protested.

"No, he's not. Jack Richman has had a full, positive life and he's always tried to make good choices. But we're all an amalgam of our past lives. And in the past there have been... weaknesses, the kind Gregorios preys upon."

"It's got to have something to do with Dr. Brooks, Madame. That's exactly the kind of energy that Gregorios feeds off of."

TD shook her head wearily, revealing a side of herself that harkened back to her weaker, human days. "She's an excellent doctor. She does good work. But if she can't let go of the past she'll never be able to move on. I've spent an eternity trying to get her to realize that on her own."

They both look at each other as they sense what is coming next—Dr. Brooks is going to reveal her whole story to her staff.

In the eternal scheme, perhaps Annie Brooks' tragedy is not the worst ever experienced in the human, physical realm— not in the afterlife, either. But for this group of active energies, in this moment of time, there is nothing more important—and it will either bond them in common purpose forever, or it will tear them apart and scatter their souls like motes of dust in the solar system if the dark energies represented by Gregorios prevail in this struggle.

Even TD senses that the battle lines have been drawn and forces of energy are aligning to force a confrontation.

CHAPTER 29: FAYE SHE WROTE

Jack's World

Jack stands next to his new murder-mystery afterlife friend, Faye, in his "home." Both are lost in thought—Jack over the worry he is feeling from Christina and Faye trying to gather the facts so she can verify that she's dead and praying that she is so can see her husband.

Faye wonders whether or not her daughter, Deb, has tried to call her and realized something is wrong. Since her daughter lives so far away, it'd probably be at least a day before anyone found her. She didn't like the idea of being left alone there. But living far away was her choice. She had no one to blame but herself. Her mother would have thought it unthinkable, to be left alone like that.

She shrugs, figuring a few of the Jewish traditions clearly weren't going to be met. She doesn't like the notion that her family would have to feel badly about that. *Maybe that was why the pearly gates were absent and instead she just got Jack's front door? Pff, all that stuff about angels and gates is crap anyway, right?* She wonders who from her family will show up to sit Shivah with Deb, there aren't many left. She prays Deb doesn't have to do it alone.

Jack and Faye are both so wrapped up in their own worlds that they do not notice Dr. Gareth Roberts reappear behind them.

Fresh from being yelled at by TD, Gareth has returned to

Jack, determined to be the one to get him back on track. He refuses to be in the same kind of trouble Dr. Brooks and Anthea are in. Gareth has zeroed in on Jack's energy at his house and is surprised to find him with another recently crossed over soul.

No wonder TD was mad. How did Jack manage that? This has to stop, now, he says to himself. But, his curiosity at how Jack is able to pull Faye (or anyone) into an afterlife realm after such a short time causes him to second-guess himself. He's never seen this blatant cross-contamination of souls before. *Surely there must be a reason the higher powers are letting it happen in the first place?* He is beyond confused, but knows he's got to set things back to normal.

Gareth clears his throat to announce his presence. Jack turns around and looks relieved to see him.

Finally, someone who can explain!

Faye stands, head cocked to one side, trying to figure out where this guy came from and why he's dressed like a doctor. But then again, who is she to judge? She's dressed like it's 20 degrees inside the house.

Instantly, Gareth knows Faye's story, but still can't understand how she got here.

"Dr. Roberts, finally. What's going on? Where'd you go? Who is this woman? I mean... sorry, this is Faye—but why was she at my door?"

"Jack, please. One at a time. First off, it's a pleasure to meet you, Faye. Welcome to your, well, um, actually let's call it *the* afterlife. I'm Dr. Roberts, and I'm one member of a team of doctors who are going to help you assess your recent life and get you moving on to your next. I know you're a bit confused, and I assure you this isn't normally how we do things—but we'll get you back on course in a moment."

Jack thinks, *Not likely.*

Thankful that Faye hasn't learned to communicate telepathically yet, Gareth responds to Jack's thoughts: *Enough. When are you going to understand that no one has* all *the answers? Everything always leads to more questions.*

"Pleasure to meet you, Doc. You guys definitely have some explaining to do. I want to talk to your supervisor immediately. I have a ton of questions that need to be addressed. Jackie-boy over here is kinda like a deer in headlights, you know? I only worked in New Age publishing for about a minute —and all that mumbo jumbo about seeing lights and a tunnel— not for me."

Jack laughs. "Well, I never cared for it much, either. Now I wish I'd paid more attention to things like that. Then maybe I'd have a clue as to what's going on around here."

"Nah, I'm a mystery gal. I always need a dead body or two in the first three pages of all the books. I even testified as a witness in a few murder cases. Did you know that, Jackie-boy?" The very first, faint inkling of potential telepathic means of communication springs into her head, unbidden. Faye feels as much as hears Jack's response.

"Oh?" Jack asks curiously.

Dr. Roberts interrupts, "Ah, of course. Totally understand why you're annoyed. Let's get you both back to the hospital."

"Hospital?" Faye questions.

"Yes, we find the hospital setting and its infrastructure allows our patients or souls to understand the process of your Life Review. I'll explain more once we're back there. Please take my hands, both of you."

Faye looks at him like this is not her first rodeo, and she is not taking anyone's hand. She is *not* that kind of gal. Dr. Roberts realizing this, grabs her hand and holds firmly. A surge of energy passes between them, startling the newcomer.

Jack gets back to the task at hand. "Wait. Christina is very worried about my family, my son and some man I don't know is leaving messages on our machine. Tell me how to help her."

Gareth feels Jack's determination and knows he'll never get anywhere if he doesn't help him. He drops Faye's hand, but looks directly into her eyes her to tell her she's not out of the woods yet.

"Jack, take my hand and concentrate on Christina." Gareth says.

They zero in on her and feel... relief.

"It's gone?" Jack asks.

Faye watches the two men and tries to readjust her thinking to sci-fi mystery. Clearly *anything* is possible. *Well this just got a lot harder*, she thinks.

"Yes, Jack. Everything is fine. It's all worked itself out. Now come on, you know better than I that being a parent means you're always worried about your kids, although some times are worse than others. The best you can do for Christina when you feel these things is concentrate on your love for her. She'll feel it, and it will comfort her to know you're with her. Now come on. Faye, your hand please. We've *got* to get back."

Faye takes his hand, and as quickly as she does, they become surrounded by the hospital walls. Faye notes that the stitching on Dr. Roberts' lab coat says Jack Richman Memorial Hospital. Reading her thoughts, Jack notes this as well and finds it curious since he had seen it change before when he was with Daisy.

Faye asks, "Dr. Roberts, I was hearing my husband's voice while in Jack's 'house.' Can you help me find him like you helped Jack here?"

"In due time."

Faye looks at Jack, and he gives her the yep-get-used-to-hearing-that look.

"Sir, can I explain to you who you are dealing with? My name is Faye Bingham. I have edited and published over 200 titles in the genre of true crime as well as mystery, crime thriller, and the occasional erotic crime title. And sixteen of those books have won Edgar Awards." Faye sounds a bit Mae West-y on that last part. "So, I didn't get to where I am because I just sat back and waited for someone to give me information. I went out and found it. Did the research. Connected the dots. Dotted the i's and crossed all the t's. So, Sonny, stop dickin' me around and answer my questions."

Not missing a beat—and not wanting these two to continue to interact—Dr. Roberts take charge. "Jack, this is your room." He nods to the door directly behind them. "Please stay here." His tone is begging. Jack complies... for the time being. "Faye, if you'll follow me, we'll get you properly admitted on Level 1, and we'll explain everything to you." They head down the hall and get in the elevator that Jack and he had taken earlier.

Dr. Roberts and Faye walk into the empty room. "Faye, this is your room. Please stay here for a moment and I will go get the rest of the team." He leaves, and moments later Dr. Chin walks in.

"Welcome Faye. I'm Dr. Susan Chin. Nice to meet you. Sit down on the bed for me, so I can test your soul's vitals.

Dr. Chin is silent while she scans Faye. To Faye, Dr. Chin's arm moments around her body look ridiculous, and she can't understand why this woman has nothing to say. "You think I am going to sit here in this bed and just wait for you or someone else to tell me what's going on here?" Faye offers sarcastically.

"As soon as Dr. Brooks arrives, she'll answer all of your questions, and you will understand what is going on." Dr. Chin smiles back nervously. She knows immediately that Faye is not going to allow things to unfold naturally.

"Why is it that this whole facility is named for the guy that is so gaga over the British chick? What's her name again?" Faye begins her process of interrogation.

"You noticed the hospital is named for Jack... interesting." Dr. Chin is now in almost a panic, which alerts Dr. Avanti as he strides into the room. She must report back to Dr. Brooks immediately that she is part of Jack's hospital and that must be because Jack Richman had brought her in.

Plus, they need to figure out what Jack has told her. *She already knows about Dr. Brooks? Maybe Gareth mentioned her briefly? Dr. Chin is confused by what's happening here.*

"Hi, Faye. Allow me to introduce myself. I am one of the doctors here and I..."

"Wow! You *are* Dr. Good-looking. Seriously? I cannot take you seriously at all. Get me someone who looks like Marcus Welby or someone I feel can give me information not ideas."

Faye's tactics seem to work, as Dr. Avanti turns red and heads out to find Dr. Brooks. Dr. Chin is left alone with this viper on a mission.

"So. Do you think in Chinese here, and then it comes out in English for me to understand?" Faye asks.

"What?" Dr. Chin is very surprised she's picking up on this. But she supposes anything is possible... since she's connected to Jack. "Um, actually, yes. We speak in our last lifetime's incarnation and being that I was from southern China I think in Cantonese—not Chinese."

"Oh, I am so sorry. How prejudiced of me! You would think I would ask you if you were a bad driver in your last life, as well." She laughs out loud and continues, "You know, stereotypes are bad on Earth, are they here as well?"

"There is no judgment here, just truth. Truth is revealed when the patient is ready to accept it." Dr. Chin writes on Faye's chart.

"You know, sweetheart, I was quite the accomplished writer and editor down there—or over there, or wherever the hell *there* actually is. Think you can you shut a drape or something? That damn light shining in could wake the dead if everyone here wasn't already dead."

"Well, I can do nothing about that light; just be happy you are actually seeing it. If you had come in through other channels, well, you might not see any light at all." Dr. Chin giggles to herself.

"Young lady, that was rude. Are you telling me that you don't think that Jews go to heaven?" Faye scolds her.

Dr. Chin is mortified and caught off guard. "That's not what I meant, at all! I meant that if you would have come through your own path, and not through Jack's you might be seeing something different. And, well, you are kind of tied into his story now... and not, not, um... "

Dr. Chin is no match for Faye. She succeeded in making Dr. Chin nervous and downright uncomfortable at a job she has been doing for more than 60 Earth years.

"What in bloody hell do you think you are doing, my dear?" Dr. Brooks chastises from the doorway, sounding just like TD.

"Well hello, Dr. Brooks. Let me introduce myself." Faye gets up and extends her hand. "I am Faye Bingham, and apparently I am now dead. I am trapped or stuck in some limbo-land in a hospital named after a schmuck who is walking around here infatuated with you, all the while wondering about his wife and kids who live in my old neck of the woods. And you are exactly who here, my dear?" Faye waits for an answer, which does not come in the way she expects.

"Faye, you have been brought here by mistake. You were supposed to be admitted quickly and then swiftly moved to Level 9, where you would have been processed and met your beloved husband and sister. Now, they are still waiting for you. So, don't be alarmed. I just need you to acknowledge a few things about your last lifetime, and I will have you on your merry way." Dr. Brooks is frank and direct. Not at all the maternal energy her colleagues are used to.

"Well, thanks for finally answering my questions, but no," Faye says.

By this time, all of Dr. Brooks' residents have arrived in the room and begun their work. They're taken aback by Faye's blunt refusal to follow instructions. Every person who comes through "the door" is herded like a sheep through his or her life review and then they're off to their next evolution. Since Jack arrived on this side, everything has been completely off. The question, of course, is *why?*

"Pardon me?" Dr. Brooks replies, questioning Faye's negative statement.

"*No.* I know that I have rights because I have beliefs. As a result of my beliefs and my own control over my fate, I feel in the core of my whatever I am now—being, soul, spirit—that I am entitled to be empowered here, not dictated to." Faye sits up and addresses her feet. "I used to have bunions the size of Ellis Island. No, seriously, I had to cut holes in all my shoes to accommodate the monsters. So happy to see they are gone here. And I feel like I am about 40 years old again. Now, I can tell from looking at the rest of me, I still look about 75, and I'm OK with that on the outside, as I liked myself the best at this age. You can say I came into my own when my Harry died. Forced to... but I made quite the life for myself professionally. You have to channel all that sexual energy somewhere..."

Faye acutely looks at all of the doctors, who stand there in shock at her lecture. She has their attention, that's certain. They are so used to being listened to, but they now they have just been taught how to pay attention.

Dr. Gareth Roberts quickly succumbs to the thoughts and sexual images Faye is conveying and cracks first.

"Yes, I still remember those moments fondly, even being here as long as I have." He looks towards the floor with a raised eyebrow and crosses his leg over the other and folds his arms against his chest.

Dr. Avanti nudges him back to reality. Avanti observes with compassion and listens keenly, wanting things to work out for the best. An inkling of his childhood braces him and almost takes his breath away. Why is he having this sensation here and now? *I feel like I'm being told something or led toward an answer. But I don't know the question!* Avanti kept his thoughts to himself, as he always did.

"But, I must say, the exchange of energy here, Faye, is far superior to the physical exchange on Earth. I'm sure Harry will be more than happy to explain it when you reunite." Roberts smiles, full of himself.

Faye, for a very brief moment, is speechless. She watches the other doctors in the room react to Dr. Roberts' moment of reckless honesty. She is able to assess each and every one of them. And in this place, see, hear, and feel their energies in a way that sparks her desire to know more and dig deeper. All of her investigative and editorial skills come into play in ways she had not anticipated in the least. As frustrated as she is, she's having rather a good time with these... er, people.

After gathering her own thoughts, Faye presses further, unknowingly picking up on everyone else's thoughts.

"Dr. Brooks, what is this that they are all buzzing around with here about you losing your children? Tell me, mother-to-mother, how did that happen? I can help. I know this. Tell me the characters and the plot."

"She will do nothing of the sort, madame!" TD shouts standing in the doorway.

TD can hear Gregorios laughing in the background, taunting her that he is winning at her own game. He wants to bring her down. And every time she acknowledges him, the light from the outside shining in seems to have a cloud pass in front of it for just a moment. When it comes back, it's just one shade dimmer, still as bright as ever, but noticeable nonetheless.

She struggles to control her thoughts, not wanting to leak anything that could give Gregorios and the dark energies he represents any further advantage or insight into her mind. Unspoken—even un-thought—is the idea that the avatar of dark energies is closer to her now that he has ever been. And that is a most dangerous threat to her and all who are in her charge.

Faye, in her inimitable way, is undaunted.

"You must be the big cheese. Allow me to introduce myself, I am Ms. Faye—"

"Bingham. You resided at 46201 Port Paravel Avenue in Aventura, Florida. You left the physical world on September 4, 2011. Passed from a sudden and massive heart attack leaving behind your daughter Debbie and a long list of people you pissed off."

Faye Bingham started visibly. *Now here's a woman after my own heart! Direct and to the point.* "I love a woman who does her research. You know, if more of my editors and writers did that, I would not have been nearly as successful." Faye sits back and admires her perfectly shaped feet and purple nail polish.

"Faye, you will not interfere here." The Director said icily. "You will not insert yourself in areas where you are not welcome nor belong, and you will not interfere with progress of other patients. Do I make myself clear?" A pin could drop in this room waiting for Faye's agreement. Instead she puts both her hands out in front of her, admiring her manicured fingers that were smooth and not riddled any more with arthritis.

"Exactly who is Gregorios, and why does he want so badly to take you down?" Faye asks.

TD's eyes narrow as she glares back at Faye. "You're a new arrival to this world. You have family waiting for you on Level 9. I wouldn't want you to miss your chance to reunite with them. Dr. Brooks, conclude your business with Ms. Bingham and move her on her way."

Faye smiles as TD turns and walks away, fuming. Dr. Brooks and her team look at each other, then back at Faye.

"Now, where were we? Oh that's right, Annie here is going to tell us a story. The floor is all yours, my dear. All good stories have conflict. It's the plot twists and turns that we need to focus on. Tell Faye what transpired."

With that, she take's Annie's hand in both of hers.

CHAPTER 30: ALWAYS HERE

Jack's World

Back in his room, Jack sits down on his bed and attempts to wrap his mind around what is happening. He tries to think about his family and send them his love as Gareth suggested. *But how will I know they feel me?*

"Concentrate, Jack. And you will see them." Out of nowhere Grandpa Joe's voice reaches him. Jack feels comforted and greatly relieved by his presence. *Finally,* he thinks. It seems like a week since he's heard from him, besides seeing the white rabbit, which he thinks has something to do with him, but isn't sure.

As much as he has received answers to so many of his critical questions, there are depths to the mystery of this new form of existence that of which he has yet to even guess at... That's why he needs Grandpa Joe so much.

Jack attempts to concentrate on his family, but he has too many questions for Grandpa Joe. "Why can't anyone else see or hear you? What's going on? I need you to be here and part of this." He just wants to feel the comfort Daisy had felt when she saw her Titi.

"I'm always here," Grandpa Joe whispers.

"Grandpa, I just don't know what to do. I helped Daisy, somehow, but how do I help Faye? How do I help myself?"

"Go to her, Jack."

Now Jack knows for certain that he should listen to

Gareth Roberts. He seems trustworthy. He has helped him. But Grandpa Joe... there's no one else he trusted more in his life because of the night he had saved him from the bullies on Halloween.

He thinks real hard about Faye and tries to remember how she felt to him. And just like that he's standing by her bedside moments after the doctors have finished her intake and left.

"OK. First things first. You need to show me how you all pop in and out of places." Faye starts to laugh. The discoveries and mysteries before her are getting her so excited. Dr. Brooks and her team have just left. And she doesn't know what it is about Jack, but she knows he's the guy to help Annie. In fact, she's never felt so sure about things before. And she knows she can help him with her, now that she knows Annie's story. She always trusted her gut, it's the top characteristic of any good detective after all, but this is different. She's so sure of herself.

The Director reclines in her oversized armchair, thinking over the current issues that are crowding her consciousness and inhibiting her progress. Never, in all her time as TD, has she had so much go awry at once.

First, there is Jack and Annie—that is semi-anticipated, but the order of events is not. Next, there is Annie's fixation on finding her children—while the timing is bad, it is about time her team knows what's going on. Then there's Faye Bingham, flagrantly defying the process. No one refuses to move on to Level 9! And most disconcerting of all: Gregorios—who knows where he is and what information he is privy to. Jack Richman's soul is the connection among all of these issues. But TD is most troubled by the suspicion that Gregorios *might* know everything she knows. Terrible. The thought that she might have to lose Jack's soul as collateral damage disturbs her, but she is prepared to make the hard decisions, as any leader must be.

TD knows it is only a matter of time before the Council of Elders intervenes. And one does not want that. She types up a memo on her retro IBM computer.

Dear Most Honored Council of Elders,

I want to assure you that, although things here may seem to be off track, I have everything under control. Your patience in these matters is greatly appreciated, as always.

Sincerely,
The Director of Earthly Transitions

As she finishes typing a pop-up box appears which reads, "SENT."

The Director sighs, hoping this will stall them a bit and give her time to think of the appropriate course of action against Gregorios.

The printer comes noisily to life and begins to print. The Council's reply is expected:

Sure you do...
-     G

TD's eyes widen with fury as she hears Gregorios cackling in the background... The laughter of her nemesis penetrates to the core of her soul. The Director gains a glimpse into the utter void he controls.

CHAPTER 31: ETERNITIES

Earth – 5 Days After the Explosion

Christina lies in bed staring at the ceiling. She is lucky if she has slept three hours last night. It's 7:30 a.m. She figures she might as well get up, but just can't do it. Between Jack, his family, her family, and the baby—saying she had a lot on her mind would be putting it mildly. This is too much to deal with all at once. One thing alone could spiral a person out of control... Nevertheless she remembers her grandmother always telling her the universe never gives you more than you can handle. *Glad the universe thinks I can handle this, because I sure don't.*

She hears the doorknob begin to turn, to her surprise it's Matilda, all dressed for the day, followed closely by Brian and Kimberly, also already dressed. *Is it much later than I think it is?*

"Mommy, Moosey is missing. We're at Def Com 4, and we're about to turn this place upside down!" Matilda says very seriously, as if the world really is in such a state. Christina supposes that for them, it is.

Brian adds, "Mom, I told her we'd look everywhere. But have no fear, we've already had some Pop Tarts, and we're gonna get started looking now. Come on, guys." He turns and leads his sisters out of the room.

Christina sits stunned but manages to get out, "Hey, guys, just don't make a mess, please. There's a lot to do get ready for this afternoon."

Kimberly answers without a trace of attitude: "We know,

Mom. That's why we're gonna do our thing and do our best to stay out of your way. We'll put everything back. Promise."

It's moments like these that really make a parent proud. Christina's only worry is that they all seemed like they've aged about 20 years in the past few days.

At 2 p.m. on the dot, the doorbell rings and the kids race to the door to welcome their grandparents. However, it's Father Patrick Moran, right on time–just as he promised. "Hey, guys."

Brian says in his most responsible-sounding voice, "Hey, Father, come on in. Mom's in the kitchen." He shouts, "Mom! It's Father Moran!"

Father Patrick walks down the hallway into the kitchen and says hello to Christina. One look at this mom lets him know how overwhelmed she is. The kids return to the living room where they are meticulously picking everything up and putting it back in the search for Moosey. Father Moran looks curiously over at them and then back to Christina who has caught his gaze. She explains, "They're looking for Matilda's toy. It's gone missing."

"Ahh," replies Father Moran.

"So," Christina starts as she wipes her hand on her apron. She's in the midst of making potato and macaroni salads. "What's the game plan, Father? Like how do I do this? Right off the bat, later at dinner? What do I say?"

"Anything I can do to help?" He says, as he takes a moment to think about her question.

Christina hands him the potato salad. "Here mix this."

Father Patrick begins to mix. "Well my guess is they are going to wonder where Jack is, right off the bat, so you'll probably have to tell them immediately."

"Right. So I'm probably making all of this food in vain. No one will want to eat." She stops stirring the macaroni salad and sits down.

"Well, I'd love some to take home, at least. Now, were you both raised Catholic?"

"Ah, no. Jack's mom is quite resolute in her faith, but his father never allowed Jack to go to church. Believes in medicine more than miracles. And I went to Sunday school for a bit as a kid, but then I just stopped. Haven't been to church since I was about eight or so, except for weddings, funerals or christenings, of course."

"OK." The clergyman realizes this is gonna be a tough room. "I think you've just gotta tell them the facts. Why Jack was in South Africa and what you know. But be realistic. Tell them he's not confirmed dead, but neither are hundreds of unidentified bodies. And that you have your cousin in the FBI—Bobby is his name, right?"

Christina nods.

"That he's looking into things and you're still waiting to hear."

"Yeah, easier said than done."

From the living room Brian yells, "Don't forget about the psychic medium who we're gonna talk to, Mom!"

Christina rolls her eyes.

"And don't forget Moosey is missing," Matilda chimes in.

Christina puts her head on the table, burying her face in her arms. *How am I going to do this?*

Unsure what he should do, Father Patrick pats her on the shoulders. "It will work out, Christina. Have faith."

"Father, I don't even know what that is."

While Father Moran looks at her and sorts out how to explain the concept of faith, the doorbell rings again and the kids stop what they're doing and run to the door again. Christina and the priest follow slowly behind.

The kids bombard them. The kisses and hugs are plentiful. When Grandpa Frank, Christina's father, manages to get in the entryway of the house he drops the bags he had in his hand and gives his daughter a hug.

"Chrissy, dear, where can I put all these presents?"

At the mere mention of the word, the kids grab the bags and take them into the living room. Everyone follows behind grumbling, tired from their trip. Christina's mother, Grace, is always quick to criticize.

"Chrissy, I really don't understand why you don't just get some drapes for the windows? The rooms would look so much more inviting."

Annoyed and tired, Jack's father, Dr. Richman barks, "Every time we come over you say the same thing, Grace. And every time we tell you it's because Jack has claustrophobia. He needs to see outside."

"Yes, but she could still do some valances or something, don't you think, Anna?"

Not one to disagree with her husband and start fights over little details, Anna, Jack's mother, sees the distress in Christina's eyes and quickly changes the subject.

"My, my, look how big you've all gotten!" She exclaims, looking at the children.

"Not looking too bad there, Squirt. I'm gonna have to give you a new nickname soon," Frank says to Brian. His wife shoots him a look for not backing him up. But he just waves her down the hallway.

Having been the only one to notice the additional guest, Anna introduces herself to the priest. "Why, hello. I'm Anna, Jack's mom and you are Father—?"

"Moran. Pleased to meet you." He appraises her pleasant, yet tired demeanor and makes a mental note to remember her this way, as he knows it's only minutes before the grief takes over.

"Oh sorry, everyone. This is Father Patrick Moran. He's a priest at our local Catholic church. I thought it might be good for us all to start going. Father these are my parents, Frank and Grace. And Jack's parents, Dr. Jack Richman and Anna."

A round of hi's and nice-to-meet-ya's ensues. Anna is the first to speak to this revelation, "Christina, I'm so pleased to hear that. How do you kids like it so far?" Anna has faithfully gone to church every Sunday since childhood. It's how she was brought up and how she fought to raise Jack. But being a man of science, Dr. Richman had forbidden it. She is delighted to see that Jack and his family are finally embracing religion's possibilities.

Kimberly snottily answers, "I wouldn't know. Brian's the only one that got to go so far."

Christina shoots her the "behave" look and she quietly begins to open the present that her Nana has just handed her.

Dr. Richman has taken his seat in Jack's recliner and is beginning to look quite comfortable. "So where's Jack? Out back getting the grill started? Tell him to get in here to watch his kids open up their gifts."

The kids all freeze in their excitement. Father Patrick catches Christina's eye. This is noticed by both of her parents, who give each other a concerned glance. Something is up, and they know it.

Christina's father looks up at her and the priest standing awkwardly in the room with fake smiles plastered on their faces. Direct and to the point he asks, "Hun, what's up? Something's wrong. You've got a priest here for Christ's sake. Uh, excuse me, Father." He looks out the back window. "Where is Jack? He's not outside."

Matilda unwraps one of her gifts. It's a new stuffed white rabbit, and all it does is remind her that Moosey is missing. "Daddy is gone... just like Moosey," she says sadly.

Brian and Kimberly get up. Kimberly says, "Come on, Matty, we'll keep looking. Let's try upstairs we've pretty much looked everywhere in here." Brian looks at his mom and she nods a "thank you" to both of them

All eyes are on Christina. She wants to sit down but all the spots have been taken. Frank and Grace sit on the couch, Dr. Richman in his son's recliner, and Anna on the love seat. Father Moran takes a seat on the opposite side of her so he can keep eye contact with Christina.

The four grandparents sit uncomfortably in their seats, waiting for what seems like eternity.

Jack's World

As Jack sits with Faye in her room, he once again feels Christina's angst. He concentrates real hard on her, closing his eyes and envisioning his family sitting in their living room as they watch *Shrek*, again. He thinks about nothing but his love for her and his kids.

Earth

Christina finds the silence is choking her. She can't speak. She closes her eyes and feels a burst of energy. She clenches her fists and somehow manages the strength to begin.

"Well, Jack was never going to be here today. He went off to that Alzheimer's conference in... Johannesburg, South Africa." She opens her eyes, waiting to see if the mention of this city causes any reaction.

Her mother gasps. Frank looks at his wife curiously. Anna looks over at her husband who seems just as clueless as Frank. Grace asks, "When did he arrive?"

"The day of the explosion."

Dr. Richman leans forward as Anna sits paralyzed. "Explosion? Christina, what's going on?"

"There was a gas explosion... right by his hotel. Hundreds are dead. It was huge." Christina stutters out.

Her mother grabs her husband's hand. "I saw it on the news. I take it—" She looks at the priest, his real purpose having been made clear. "I take it you haven't heard from Jack?"

Christina crosses her arms in an attempt to keep herself contained. "No. We haven't heard anything. He could be one of the people who is wounded. My cousin Bobby is looking into the situation for us."

"Oh good." Grace says quietly, knowing how capable her nephew is.

Father Patrick looks at Anna sitting next to him. She's gone pale. He scoots over next to her and put his arms around her. She collapses into him. "How could you not tell us right away? He's our son!"

Dr. Richman stands up, "But you told the kids, didn't you?"

"Yes."

"Jesus!" gasps Anna.

"He's their father, they have a right to know what's going on. I'm sorry."

"Well I'm *his* father!" Dr. Richman, who is unaccustomed to allowing himself to feel emotions, explodes, "How could you not call us and tell us what's going on. He's my son!"

Father Moran sees this as his opportunity to jump in. Christina's eyes are welling up with tears—fast.

"Sir, I think she just thought it was the kind of thing one did in person. And she knew you'd be coming in just a few days. We'd hoped to hear one way or the other by now."

Frank and Grace sit holding each other, their hearts breaking for their son-in-law, for the kids, for Christina, but mostly for Jack and Anna. Everyone remains quiet; the only sounds that can be heard are sobs and heavy breathing.

Through tears and knowing the answer she still asks, "So you haven't heard? Well, he's—" Her voice cracks.

"He's my son, Christina. *My* son!" Frank quickly stands up to go support Dr. Richman who is beginning to sweat. He grabs his left arm and begins to fall forward just as Frank reaches him.

Anna screams, "Jack!"

Father Moran whips out his cell phone and dials 9-1-1.

CHAPTER 32:
ANNIE'S STORY

Jack's World

Faye sits in her bed laughing at the strange events of the past hour. She died, ended up in a stranger's house, was teleported to a hospital named after said stranger, was told she was here to review her past life, and then touched her doctor and saw her past life instead. It is certainly a lot for her to take in. She's barely had a moment to process Annie's story when Jack had popped in.

"No, seriously, Jackie boy. How does everyone pop in and out of places like we're in *Star Trek* or something?"

Jack laughs. She is reacting just as he had not too long ago, albeit she's just doing it with more attitude. He likes her. He feels oddly comforted by her.

"Simple, just think about the energy of the person you want to see or the energy of the place." Jack walks in and goes to sit on her bed. "Mind?"

"No not at all. Pop a squat. Now what do you mean energy?"

"I'm not sure to be perfectly honest. I may have a scientific mind, but I never had to capacity for quantum physics. Um, as you're here longer you'll realize people feel one way to you. So you think about that then you're there. I'm still getting used to it. This trip to your room was my first solo try."

"Well good for you." Faye couldn't think of what to ask next. She has a million things going through her head. Most about why he seemed so preoccupied with thoughts of Annie. *Wait, he's not actually saying anything to her*, she notes.

"Yeah, we're capable of reading minds here too. Pretty neat huh?" Jack says having felt her thought.

Holy crap. This is getting to be too sci-fi for me.

You're telling me! I'm a journalist who works in medicine and science. If there's not an experiment with proven results, I don't believe it. And yet, here we are.

Faye pauses, taking in her newfound ability. She is getting a little frustrated. She always told her writers that they needed to establish for the reader the world in which the story takes place and its parameters right off the bat. Now if it's Earth present time, than that's not hard to do, but a whole other universe? That would require introductory chapters, plural. All she got was a paragraph synopsis, 'We're in heaven, assessing your last incarnation, yadda, yadda, yadda.'

And now she keeps getting little "parameters" thrown at her with every turn she takes. This is not how this is supposed to work. Oops, need to speed up the story so allow the characters to pop in and out of rooms. You can't just change things to make it's convenient for the author. This is not some Greek tragedy with a *deux ex machina*.

Faye decides to just get back on track to figuring out yet another weird sci-fi moment she experienced.

"Jack, this may sound like a crazy question, but has Dr. Brooks ever touched you and shared her past life with you?"

"Is that what that is?" Jack exclaims. "I mean we have touched a couple of times and I've seen these little vignettes or moving pictures, but there's no story or a sense of a lifetime in them. It happened to you too?"

In fact, this is not what happened. Annie had purposefully and completely shared her life with Faye, who had seen it all unfold, beginning to bitter end.

"I suppose... but not exactly like that. You do know she's looking for the souls of her children in the people who come through this hospital?" Faye says.

"NO! I mean I'd picked up on a thought or two from the other doctors that she was looking for her kids, but I didn't know exactly what it meant. How do *you* know that?"

"I read minds. That's how. OK, so I didn't realize that's what I was doing, but that's all the doctors were 'saying,' so I asked, and then she held my hand and I saw her whole life."

Jack sits stunned. He doesn't know what to think. For one, he's actually a little jealous. He could tell that he and Annie had a special connection, but perhaps it isn't that special at all if Faye has it too. Secondly, this woman has been here for half a second and she's already figuring things far faster than he did.

Answering his thoughts, Faye supplies, "Investigative mind, Jack. Not everyone has it."

"Well I thought I did have one."

"Yeah, but you work differently than me. I operate under the assumption that anything is possible. People are crazy and irrational. You, however, just said yourself that if there's not data you won't believe it. Everything in life isn't so black and white." Now all Faye has to do is continue to remind herself that "anything is possible" in this world so she stops wasting her energy on being frustrated. That's the parameter.

"Yeah, I guess I'm starting to understand that... So, please tell me what Annie, er, Dr. Brooks showed you."

"Jack, it was very personal, and very painful. I'm not sure it's my place to share."

Frustrated, Jack says fine and begins to zero in on Annie's energy. Just like that he disappears. Faye is annoyed, but figures he must have been thinking about Annie, so she tries to teleport herself.

"Ah, I see you've figured it out," Jack whispers as Faye pops in right next to him. He's standing outside an office where Dr. Brooks is sitting with her residents. They all have their backs to him and Faye, and although they can't hear the doctors in the traditional sense, they feel their every thought.

"Come on, Jack, we shouldn't be here. I'll tell you what I know. I'm sorry I held out on you." For Annie's sake she's going to give Jack the abridged version. The two pop back to her room.

Annie's Office

Dr. Roberts is the first to break the silence in the room. Dr. Brooks isn't saying anything; enough is enough already, "Well. Out with it. We may have an eternity but please don't make it feel like it."

"I, I just don't know where to begin."

Dr. White attempts to help her along. "You said your kids were poisoned, right? What were their names? How many did you have?"

Slowly, Annie begins. "Five. Their names were William, Elizabeth, Henry, Frank and John. William made it. After I died I was able to see him, thank God he'd been helping a friend that day. I know he's lived a decent life. But the other four..."

Faye's Room

Faye begins, "She had five kids and four of them were poisoned, including Annie. Though they all died right around the same time, they were just far enough apart that they were separated in the hospital. Annie never saw them again. She was hoping to meet them there again and apologize for what she let happen to them. The guilt has taken over her afterlife. So she searches the files of all new Level 1's hoping she'll recognize their souls in a different incarnation."

Annie's Office

"All I've ever wanted is to apologize for failing to protect them, to meet them and hear about their lives. As I'm sure all of you want to see your families again. Just one moment, and I know I'll find peace."

"Dr. Brooks—" Dr. White says calmly. She and the other doctors have heard thousands of life stories. White knows she's easily affected by the tragic stories, and she always works hard to maintain her professional distance. This is something that she feels must have come from her childhood experience,

205

though memories of that time are faded and quite dim for her now. The events of the last few days, however, seem to be moving quickly toward some conclusion or revelation that disturb and excite her. *What is it? Why am I feeling this way, almost like the child I once was. The child I no longer know...*

"Please, call me Annie. If we're going to do this let's at least forget the pretexts."

"All right. Annie, we all want to see our loved ones, and your story is tragic, but we all know there are many tragic stories here. Why do you think you can't move on?" Dr. Roberto Avanti speaks up, "Annie, we need to know the whole story. What's the moment where you feel it all went downhill?"

Annie thinks about this for barely a moment. She's had eons after all to rehash her life. She takes a deep breath and resumes. "Easy. The day I met Dr. William Palmer, my future husband. Now keep in mind I was the illegitimate child of a highly decorated army lieutenant colonel and his housekeeper, my mother.

Faye's Room

"She was quite the scandal in 1827 England. So life was never easy. Her mother had received a small inheritance when her father died, and it was to be given to her husband as her dowry. You know, back then people didn't marry for love, but over time it developed."

Annie's Office

"Despite my husband's vices, I did love him. William purchased a quaint two-story house. From the front there were two windows on the first floor and three on the second floor. It had a gate and a little front yard. It was in town and close to everything. I was so happy. Finally, I was getting a fresh start. And I was going to have a loving family. However, it was just after our marriage at St. Augustine's, that my husband discovered his inheritance wasn't what it was supposed to be. He drank. So had my mother."

Faye's Room

Jack knows something about parents who drink... never, ever did his father do this when he was still practicing medicine, but as he got older and worked less, he compensated with the bottle. Perhaps this is one of the reasons Jack connected with Annie so much.

Faye continues, "She was used to it, but he gambled also, and was at the pub every night. She was married at 20, and by 27 she had had five kids whom she loved immensely. But it wasn't long before they began to struggle."

Annie's Office

"I took them to church and tried to raise them the best I could, but I had very little nurturing myself as a child. Maybe if I had, I would have noticed..."

Annie pauses. That was the easy part. "History knows my husband as the Rugeley Poisoner. He was eventually hanged after our deaths, thank God—but not for our deaths. For another. He must have put his poison in our dinners before leaving the house. He always came home later and never ate with us. We all got very sick, except William, who had missed dinner that night to help out a friend."

Faye's Room

"They thought the whole family had cholera, like so many others, but it wasn't. Annie knew it wasn't. William would have gotten sick too, and it wouldn't have happened quite so fast."

Annie's Office

"One by one they all died in my arms within a two-day period." Annie is now visibly crying on the inside and out. She takes a long deep breath and continues. "I barely remember… I was so sick. I don't even know if they heard me tell them how much I loved them."

The other doctors all look at each other. Collectively they wrap her in their energetic embrace.

Together they sit, taking in the moment. The doctors collectively make Annie's mission theirs. They won't—can't—let her down.

Faye's Room

Faye finishes and looks at Jack. He is visibly stunned.

"The man I saw when I touched her—that must have been him, right?"

"I suppose, but I don't know what you saw, Jack. This woman's in a world of pain. Now do you understand? Be easy on her. Just do as she tells you."

He nods.

"Jack, why are you here? Why am I here? We need to get to the bottom of this to move on, right?"

"I don't know if I want to move on, to be honest with you. I don't feel done. I want to be with my family. Do you feel the same way? Maybe that energy is how we're connected?"

"Careful there, you're beginning to sound like them. *Energy!*" Faye laughs. "And no, I don't. I desperately want to see my husband. My daughter is grown and takes care of herself. I've been old and lonely a long time. Best thing that ever could happen, I drop dead with the snap of a finger, instead of being a burden on my family with some long drawn-out illness. So… I guess that's not it."

"Well, at least we've eliminated a possibility."

"Just as important sometimes. Of course, there seem to be an infinite number of possibilities around here, so I'm not so sure how far we've gotten."

"We both passed quickly? I was in an explosion. My body will probably be found in like 100 places."

"Eww, Jack. T-M-I. Anyway, let's step back. You open the door to your house and there I am. Who were you expecting to see?"

"My family."

"Well, I've never met you in my life before or heard of you. Next!"

"You know, I was wishing for someone who could help me figure all this out, and I am very thankful that I have you to talk things through with. Someone with a logical mindset."

"Maybe that's why I'm here. Just because you needed me." She smiles at him. "Now why are we waiting around here. What's the next step in this 'review'?"

"Gareth and I discussed my relationships. Next, I believe Dr. Chin is supposed to help me assess my ego. So I guess I'm waiting on her."

"Guess that means I'm waiting on Gareth? When they are finished with Annie, they'll be around to collect us. You'd better get back to your room."

"You're probably right." He hesitates. "Thanks for letting me know Annie's story. Let's meet up soon, if we can.

"I'm just a thought away, apparently," Faye adds sarcastically as Jack pops out of her room.

Annie's Office

"I never got to say goodbye to my daughter," Lesley says. "I tried to hang on until I saw her, but I just didn't have anything left. I understand your pain."

"Thank you, Annie, for opening up to us." Gareth has been with her the longest and through all the patients. But it isn't until this moment that he understands love. Of course he'd had a grasp or inkling before, but during this embrace, as he feels what Annie is feeling and the empathy from his fellow doctors, something clicks for him.

The newest doctor, Roberto, feels quite similarly. But he experiences something quite different... He feels the love of a mother as a son would feel it. Very distinctly, as he has never quite felt it before. Roberto remembers his past lives. His first incarnation had been short; he'd died as a toddler... his name had been John...

He looks around to see if anyone else has had a similar realization, they hadn't. And they hadn't sensed his thoughts either. He sees the white rabbit hop out of the room.

CHAPTER 33: LET THE LEARNING BEGIN

Earth – 7 Days After the Explosion

The Richman house is in chaos. After learning about Jack, Christina's parents refuse to leave her. Their baby girl needs their help, whether it is taking the kids to the park or cooking. They know Anna can't be left alone, either. The poor woman has lost her son and now her husband lies in an ICU after a massive heart attack. The doctors still aren't sure if he is going to make it.

From the upstairs hallway: "Mom! I don't understand why we have to go to school today. We should be at the hospital with Grandpa." Brian whines as though he's a real ten-year-old and not the mature child he's been the past week. Kimberly chimes in with her agreement.

"Brian, we lost your dad and now it looks like we're about to lose your grandfather in the same week. You already missed the real first day. And I don't want to add you guys falling behind in school to the list of things to worry about, OK?"

Nana Grace, always one to rescue and remedy a situation adds in, "I know it's gonna be hard. Just try not to think about what's going on here and focus on what you're supposed to be learning. That's what your daddy would want you to do." She looks at Christina and raises her eyebrows with hope and a hint of exasperation.

Matilda is all smiles. Finally, she gets to go to school like her big brother and big sister—well pre-school, that is.

"Bri, I am going to have the best first day of school in the history of the world. And you are going to be jealous!" Matilda says.

"Yes. So jealous. You are going to be eating cookies and brushing a doll's hair all day while reciting the alphabet, big deal." Brian is jamming his folders and a pen case that he pilfered from his dad's desk into his book bag.

"And it's not really school yet, Matilda. That will be next year, when you're in my school," Kimberly chimes in.

Matilda takes offense at both of her siblings. She grabs her bunny off the couch, which her Grandpa Jack had just given her, makes a face that lets the world know she is done with them for now, turns around and goes to stand by the door signaling she is ready to leave.

"Matilda, I think it's a great idea that you take Bunny with you. He will remember all the things that happen today that you forget, sweetie pie." Her Nana Grace, kisses her on the forehead and has a flashback to when Christina was that young.

Brian rolls his eyes, "Seriously, your first day of school and you want to take a toy with you? Really? You'll get distracted and lose Bunny just like you lost Moosey. And Daddy isn't here to find him or fix everything like he used to."

Brian is not embracing this new beginning in a positive way.

Matilda walks from the doorway, nods in agreement and carefully puts him on the couch in the family room. "Now, stay there and don't go hopping around. You don't want to end up lost. You don't know your way around yet."

From the bottom of the stairs, Grace and Frank do their best to keep this as a cheery as possible.

Frank yells up to Brian and Kimberly, "Come on, kids, we need to take your picture!"

"Pop Pop, can you make sure you get my good side? This is my very first, first-day-of-school picture," Matilda demands.

Less innocently, Kimberly adds, "Yeah, me too."

Brian and Pop Pop exchange a smile as the three line up on

the stairs, oldest at the top, youngest on the bottom. Christina stands between her parents. Her mom's arm wraps around her waist.

Anna enters, trying her best to put a smile on her face. "Oh, you kids are getting so big. Smile big!"

"Say, 'Grandparents are the best.'"

"Grandparents are the best!" *CLICK.*

Christina can't believe Jack has missed this, just the first of many such occasions.

Sensing Christina's thoughts, Anna whispers, "It's all going to work out... you will see."

Jack's World

Jack sits in his room thinking about the kids. Suddenly, The Director walks in, with her swirl of energy and directness.

"You miss your kids, Jack, I can tell. Do you know where that comes from?"

"It comes from being a parent, holding them, loving them, taking care of them and protecting them. It is a privilege to be a parent," Jack answers off the cuff.

"Follow me, please."

"Where we going?"

"I want to show you how you how you will eventually be able to connect with your family on Earth. Consider it a movie trailer or a sneak peak."

The Director motions for Jack to follow her out of his room. In a flash Jack is standing next to her.

"What do I need to do? Click my heels three times? Concentrate really hard? Visualize my family and be there?" He squints really hard, half thinking that maybe that is how to do it.

"No, Jack." So he opens his eyes. "You made a connection once before in that world, did you not?" TD inquires.

"Um... kind of," Jack ekes out.

"Kind of? Oh, Jack, if I am going to give you this opportunity, I need you to be a bit more forthcoming in the trust department. So?" She commands him to respond truthfully, dangling the carrot of connection in front of him.

"Fine, yes I did! I've been trying to get you guys to explain it to me since it happened, but I figured out since everyone ignored me it wasn't supposed to have happened. My Grandpa Joe keeps appearing to me, but not like you guys. He's here, nearby and whispers to me, but hasn't materialized since my connection to Annie and the team has gotten stronger. It seems the longer I am here, the less he can break through to me. I feel like I am losing family on both sides," Jack answers from his soul as honestly as he can.   "I knew the answer already, Jack. I just needed you to be the one to verbalize and acknowledge it." She smiles at him playfully. "Your grandfather showed you a funeral Mass, correct?"

It's apparent that she has the answers to the questions already, but Jack still needs to go through the motions of answering them.

"Yes. It wasn't a scene that I was able to process too well. We were floating above everyone, and there was a bright light. Plus, to see my family in such a deep state of mourning and loss... it was painful for me when I first got here to see that. I'm better now. Actually, I feel like I was processing my death relatively well until I saw that. Can our family on Earth's grief affect me, er *us*, when we crossover to this side... you know, like hold us back?"

"Oh, Jack! You human newbie spirits are so funny. Thinking that your short time on Earth can define who you ultimately are as a soul." She takes a moment to laugh. "The truth is that you were, are, and will be an amalgamation of multiple lifetimes and families... not one defining you more so than the other. Here, think of it like this: A car is the sum of all its parts, but a tire can exist without needing the car to attach to. Grief is part of the Earth world, not the spirit world. When you are done learning what you need to learn in this place, you will be connected to your family in many ways, throughout their lives until they come through the doors of their own memorial hos-

214

pital."

The Director ushers him behind a desk at the nurses' station. It is empty whenever something impressive is going to happen, and bustling when there are newcomers coming through the portal.

"Madame Director, before we go any further, I just want to say thank you. I don't know what is about to happen, or what you are going to show me, but I just want to tell you that I appreciate you doing this. I know it's beneath your level of expertise." Jack fights the urge to hug her. "I need answers so badly."

"Not at all. Everyone here has his own set of circumstances and as such, we have various courses of action. But don't you dare hug me," she says.

TD turns on a computer that looks a lot like his iMac at home, but instead of the Apple logo, there is a halo.

"That's funny. It looks like the wave of technology ten years from now," Jack says.

"It is. Notice the sleek edges and the paper thin display. Our tech guides have been working very closely with some important thinkers of your world to match what we need them to be able to discover, develop and create to keep your earthly, human process of evolution going."

Jack is blown away. "Wow! Like Steve Jobs?"

"I am sorry, Mr. Richman, I cannot disclose such things. I will say this: Where do you think Apple got their ideas from? Divine inspiration is a very real thing, my boy. Now, place your palm on the screen."

Jack places his palm on the screen and a bunch of rectangles, squares and oval images of his earthly life came alive in front of him—from the birth of his grandparents and far into the futures of this great-great grandchildren.

"Wait a second. I don't think I want to see all of this." He pulls his hand off, and the screen pauses.

"I understand. It's overwhelming the first few times. You could get lost for eons doing this. The novelty wears off when you recognize the need for learning. The photos are just the shells or blueprints of what could be. Free will changes people's destinies every day."

"Right. So, not everything is fated?"

"Nope. Unfortunately, people like to surrender their decision making to God, or a higher power, instead of working with it to create and manifest their life. Sometimes, I watch what people are doing, and I want to stretch my hand down and whack them on their asses for being so stupid with their frivolous decisions."

"You seem quite vested in what goes on there. I would think people's mistakes would be so yesterday for you." Jack is trying to make her laugh.

"Listen, I have to deal and manage the souls of millions of people through their unique hospitals. I have to help them understand that their own choices determined their life outcome. It's the number one lesson my patients have to learn —taking the responsibility for their actions and not blaming other people in their lives for their issues."

"Your job is not an easy one, is it?" Jack is serious.

One photo on the paused screen jumps out at him. It is Matilda's first day of school. "The kids are going to school already? Madame Director, I really have no sense of time here. Can I see this day? How much have I already missed?"

"Jack, right now I am only going to show you your children. I can't show you anything else that you might have seen on your own. If that stipulation is all right by you, we can proceed."

"So, nobody else in my family? Just the kids?" Jack repeats.

TD nods. Just then, Annie Brooks appears in front of Jack, behind the computer and counter.

"What are you doing? Does she have you working here already? Is that why you are still hanging around here, old chap?" Her British accent sounds like music to Jack.

"Actually, I am about ready to take a sneak peek of my children and their first day of school. Come around, and I'll show you."

TD watches like a hawk and revels in her delight at the exchange. She loves it when things actually go according to plan.

"Annie, why don't you take it from here? He is only allowed to see his children. Can you help him with that?"

This is a soft spot for Annie, and she knows TD has orchestrated this whole thing on purpose. She cocks her head to one side and smiles at her. "Absolutely, Madame Director." Her energy also shares a thought with Jack. *If I cannot connect with the souls of my children, then I will have to appreciate the learning process through watching another.*

Jack feels a stab of pain for her. If he'd lost *his* children...

He presses "play" on the photo stream. His perspective changes, and he is there, watching his kids pile into the van with their book bags and lunch bags, just invisible. He is able to see the entire scene, but focuses on just the kids.

Jack points. "That is Brian. He is so me. He looks a lot like my wife's side of the family, but he really is me in energy and personality. And this is Matilda."

Annie laughs, "Oh she is just the darling of the family isn't she?"

"And that is Kimberly. And she's, well, she is kind of—"

"Prickly?" Annie suggests.

"Ha! Yes, you can say that. She's already won awards for being a debater at her age. You give her a perspective, and she'll argue it. We're thinking she's a future lawyer, maybe even a politician!" Jack laughs.

It is so good to see them. He can feel their love and warmth and hear Matty's little laugh. He supposes he could find peace here in the afterlife if he can learn to reach out to his family like this more often.

Annie and Jack only spent a few moments of Earth time experiencing the depth of family and children. But neither knows the healing that is truly taking place.

Earth

Christina returns to the hospital to visit Jack's father, crappy coffee in hand for herself and her mother-in-law Anna. She spots Father Patrick Moran at the nurses' station.

"Hi, Father."

"Hi, Christina. How's Jack's dad doing? Dr. Richman?"

"He's hanging in there. Making life a living hell for the nurses and doctors. Doctors never make good patients."

Father Patrick laughs. "I'll come and check on you guys later after I see a few other families around here."

Christina nods and moves on. She enters the room, and Anna rises to take a coffee from her hand. Her father-in-law is awake and looking a little better.

"Christina, we've just been talking," Anna says. "Do you think you could give Bobby a call and get an update? Anything's better than nothing."

"Yeah. I wanted to do that today anyway. I'm very surprised he hasn't called. Let me go to the end of the hall where there's better service."

She watches Anna return to the chair next to his bed and hold her husband's hand.

Ringing, ringing...

"Hello?"

"Hey, Bobby, it's Chrissy."

"Hey. Been meaning to call you."

"Any news?"

"Not exactly. It's mayhem over there. There's only a handful of confirmed, identified people." He pauses. "Eh, how do I put this? The government and organization is not the best in this crisis and they are presuming all at ground zero dead. It's that bad. He didn't make it. Chrissy, I knew this when you called me, but I didn't want to sound like there was no hope. I asked a friend to go to the hospitals and look for him. Gave him a picture. He just called me... he checked the hospitals, clinics, and Sangomas... Jack's gone."

"No, no, no! There has to be something," Christina says in disbelief.

"Chrissy, don't get your hopes up."

She begins to cry and allows herself one minute exactly. Then takes a deep breath, wipes her eyes and heads back to the room.

As she walks in, Dr. Richman and Anna perk up. Christina shakes her head and begins to tell them how much of a mess things are there.

"His friend is taking Jack's picture around to the hospitals and looking for him. But he says there's no trace of Jack. He's just gone." She begins to choke up.

Dr. Richman tightens his grip on Anna's hand. She looks at him and sees the tear trickling down his face. He is frozen and the machine flat lines.

Doctors rush in, pushing Anna and Christina out of the way. They stand next to the doorway watching the doctors work furiously.

"Code 999 to ICU! Code 999 to ICU! Charge to 100. Stand back."

BEEP, BEEEEEEP.

"Charge to 300. Stand back."

BEEP, BEEEEEEP.

"Jack!" Anna screams to her husband of over forty-seven years. "Don't you leave me! I need you! Don't you leave me! FIGHT!"

A nurse pushes her aside and she falls into Christina, who can barely stand herself. Together, they stand in the doorway. Christina feels like she is living her grief outside herself. How is it possible that her kids are losing their father and grandfather in the same week? She and Anna are ushered out into the hall and slink down to the floor against the wall.

Father Moran watches them from the end of the hallway,

then runs toward them.

CHAPTER 34: EGO

Jack's World

Jack and Annie continue to watch Jack's family through the screen at the nurses' station. An immense amount of healing is taking place that neither can really comprehend. Annie knows that while she may not be able to find peace, she can help others. However, she knows this will never completely make her OK.

After all her time in this hospital, she'll never understand why this screen only works for patients. The Council of Elders had long ago programmed it to only allow what they think is helpful for the greater purpose of each soul. Annie had only been given access to this once when she first entered Level 2 of the hospital. It is how she learned William would be taken care of. After the deaths in the family, he didn't last long living with only his father. Dr. Palmer's drinking had increased and finally when he was imprisoned and hung, her son found refuge with his friend's family and worked on their farm. All this she had seen and the comfort it brought her—knowing that he was safe —is what has kept her going.

This is what is happening for Jack. He only sees his kids laughing in the van on the way to school and entering the building. He only sees Christina take Matilda into pre-school. These are happy moments that will allow him to know that their life can go on and they can be happy. Yes, he feels Christina's worry, but he also knows that's part of life. People worry, people do go through difficult times, and he knows he will be able to send his love and help them get through those moments.

The screen turns off and Jack looks up at Annie. His look

conveys his new understanding of how this world can interact with Earth.

"I think you are ready for your next level," Dr. Brooks says softly. "Dr. Chin here will take you."

Dr. Chin has appeared down the hallway and walks towards them. As she approaches, she assesses Jack and Dr. Brooks emotional states.

"Well, it's nice to see things back on track. Jack, please follow me."

Before Jack obeys, he turns back to look at Annie who smiles and then disappears.

Dr. Chin and Jack enter the elevator. Dr. Chin loves when it's her turn to be one on one with patients. She gets to use her vast knowledge of Earth's pop culture and have people actually understand her jokes. The other doctors, White and Avanti, who have lately begun to seem more mature and focused, usually just stare and make comments about how weird she is—but with a sense of understanding and compassion.

"OK, Jack, we're headed to Level 3 where we assess your ego."

"Right. I'm not too worried. I'm no Donald Trump."

Dr. Chin laughs, happy that she understands his reference to *The Apprentice*.

"Maybe not, but you're a top scientific journalist, trust me you've had your moments. Like just now."

Jack drops his head, knowing full well he's allowed his ego to get to the better of him.

The elevator doors open, and suddenly he's back at the Alzheimer's Association International Conference. However, he's not in South Africa—instead it's last year's conference in Rome, Italy. At the front of the room Dr. Begley stands at a podium explaining her theories. Jack shakes his head. This was definitely not his best moment. Dr. Chin observes his reaction and makes a notation on his chart.

Jack sits in the middle of the hotel ballroom. His hand is raised waiting to be called on. When he first entered this lecture he was very excited. However, after listening to her theorize and hypothesize for an hour his excitement is all gone.

Dr. Begley points to Jack, and he stands to challenge her research.

"Doctor, can you please discuss the process of your experiments? How were the test subjects chosen?"

"Ah, Dr. Chin. There's no reason to continue further. I fully admit the way I handled this situation was bad. I acted like I knew better than her about conducting experiments but the truth is I'm not a scientist. Let's fast forward to just a few weeks ago when I politely asked her to have private discussion about her work. I believe, had I not been blown up in that explosion, I would have redeemed myself."

"Jack, although we can improve and make adjustments on our behavior we can't take moments back. You embarrassed this woman at her lecture. No matter what you did from then on, you can never erase that for her. Do you understand?"

"Yes," he says, uncomfortably. "You're right."

Dr. Chin smiles, and the scene before them changes.

Jack looks at himself as a teenager, barely younger than he appears now in the hospital. He stands just a few houses down from his childhood house.

"Wow, this street looks like it was the set for *Leave It to Beaver*," says Dr. Chin.

The cookie cutter development is indeed quite the picturesque development from the Leave It to Beaver *era. The leaves on the few young trees are beginning to change colors. Track star Jack is taking a leisurely jog and approaches a group of three boys picking on his neighbor, Tim. Every time the kid goes to stand up, the other older kids push him back onto his front lawn. Jack slows.*

Inside, Jack will always be the little scared kid from the haunted house, but he vowed a long time ago not to participate in that kind of ridicule of others. Inspired by his Grandpa Joe, he was not going to let his neighbor get picked on. Not today anyway. He is bigger, tougher and older than this group of 12-year-olds. This is a fight he knows he can win.

"What's going on, Tim?"

"Oh nothing." The other boys glare at Jack.

Jack glares right back. "You guys are finished here, right? I'm sure cool important guys like you have something better to do than stand around on a lawn, right?"

One of the kids replies in disgust. "Yeah." They turn to leave but not before giving Tim a deathly "this isn't over" stare.

Tim looks up at Jack. "Thanks. They'll just be back tomorrow, though."

"So don't be here. Find something else to do. Maybe you'd like to join me after school for a run? We'll train you so you can get away quicker at least?" Jack says with a teasing smile.

"OK! Yeah I'd like that. See you tomorrow!" Tim runs inside the house shouting out for his mother to tell her his plans.

"I'm confused. Shouldn't this be in my kindness evaluation? You guys did say that was one part right?"

"It could absolutely be included there. You were very kind to this young boy. But what were you thinking here, Jack?"

"I was thinking, I'm bigger and older. And I can win this fight."

"Exactly. You inflated your ego in order to be able to help this kid out and used it positively to help someone. You see, it's about intention. Even the nicest gesture, if done solely to benefit yourself isn't really worth much. Like rich people who just donate to good causes because it's a tax write off or because it betters their public image. In this case, your slightly egotistical moment really made a difference. And you inspired Tim to do the same for another kid when he was older."

"Really?"

"Yup. Let's go this way." The two turn the corner of the street, and as they do they are back at his house down in the basement office. He and Brian are sitting side by side. Brian is about five years old. He's looking up at his daddy with awe and admiration. Jack remembers this moment well. He was showing Brian how he did his research for his articles.

"So Google is the first stop. Got it."

"Right. But then you have to look carefully at each website. And see who wrote it and what their qualifications are. Anyone can write anything on the internet. Just because it's there, doesn't mean it's credible. Got it?"

"Yep."

There's a long pause while Jack clicks on a link and reads its contents.

With a big smile on his face Brian asks, "Daddy, you must be really smart. I think if you can look at all the websites, write the articles and take care of all of us, you must be like the best dad in the world. Right?"

Jack laughs. "Well I don't know about that, but I think I do OK. Thanks for your vote."

"Anytime, Dadd-i-o."

From the top of the stairs, Christina calls down: "Brian, come wash up for dinner!"

He runs out of the room and upstairs. Jack can hear the pitter patter of his feet overhead. Jack sits back and relishes the moment—even knowing it's only a matter of time before he has to punish Brian for some infraction or other, and he's suddenly the "worst dad in the world."

"I think I'll cast my vote too, Jack." Dr. Chin says making another note in Jack's chart.

"Thanks. But I lucked out, he's really the best kid. Well-behaved most of the time, a good big brother. And he's so smart. I'm mean clearly if he recognizes how awesome I am…"

"Watch that ego, Jack," Dr. Chin says playfully. "Now the lesson here is?"

"That I didn't let that comment go to my head? That I reminded myself how fickle kids are and knew he could turn around and say the opposite the next day?"

"Exactly. Some parents really do let these things go to their head. And next thing you know they are bad parents. Or they spend too much time worry they can't live up to that expectation."

"Right. Checks and balances."

"That's why it's important who we surround ourselves with in our lifetimes. We all need that person who is going to give it to you straight and give you a reality check when you need it."

"Ha, ha. Sounds like Faye."

Dr. Chin smiles. "Yes, she is quite straightforward isn't she…? But who do you think that was for you on Earth?"

"Oh that's easy—Christina. She never misses a moment to tell me I'm being a butthead."

"A butthead? Isn't that physically impossible?"

"It's a figure of speech, little bit nicer than using a curse word. As in the person isn't using their brain?" Jack shakes his head realizing this is probably a pointless conversation. "It's not pointless, Jack. I really aim to learn all of the current Earth lingo and culture. I think it helps, during the transition process. Thank you. Now let's get you back to your room. I think we're done here."

The hospital hallway materializes before their eyes and Jack, and Dr. Chin stand in front of his door.

"Wait here for Dr. White." Dr. Chin disappears.

Jack enters his room and wonders how long Dr. White will be. He's relieved that this process is finally moving forward.

Just then he hears Grandpa Joe's whisper, "They need you, Jack."

"Grandpa, just show yourself." Jack says.

"I'm not allowed."

"Then play by the rules and stop causing me worry. I just saw my kids go to school. They look OK. Of course they need me, but they'll be all right, I think."

Jack concentrates on Anthea. She's the only one who has tried to help with Grandpa Joe.

CHAPTER 35: THE LIFE OF JACK RICHMAN

Earth – 9 Days After the Explosion

Christina stands next to Anna in the front foyer of St. Hyacinth's Church. They shake hands and exchange hugs with those entering. It's oddly fortuitous that Dr. Richman had passed while up from Florida for Labor Day. This has made the logistics of having the funeral so much simpler. Anna and Jack had moved down to Florida after Jack had retired from his surgical position at the nearby hospital. Christina is grateful she'd been in touch with Father Moran prior to his death. This too, helped make things easier.

Brian and Kimberly stand behind Anna and Christina, attempting to keep Matilda entertained.

Father Moran approaches and let's Anna know it's time for the ceremony to begin.

Christina turns to her children, "Guys, follow us. We're in the first row where Nana and PopPop are sitting."

Father Moran remains at the back of the church, waiting to direct any latecomers. Another priest from the church is presiding over the ceremony. Father Patrick had thought that he would be best served consoling the Richmans, if need be.

Father Michael Walters steps to the podium. There is no casket. Dr. Richman had made it clear to Anna he wanted his organs donated and cremated. He had never understood the huge cost burden of a casket anyway and he wouldn't do that to his beloved Anna.

Jack's World

Jack sits in his bed concentrating on Anthea. He knows she will help him sort out things with his Grandpa Joe. He's also beginning to sense an intense worry and sadness from his family again. Now more than ever, he needs Anthea. He expects to be teleported to Anthea, but instead Anthea pops into his room.

"Yes, Jack? Sensed you needed me?"

Confused, but pleased Jack says, "Uh, yes. Two things really."

"Jack, didn't Dr. Roberts show you how to concentrate on your family when you're sensing their need for you?"

"Yes. But this feels different to me. It's much more intense. I'm also hearing my Grandpa Joe again, and last time I felt my family this intensely, on his suggestion, I went on a pretty wild ride."

This is news to her. "What do you mean wild ride?"

"I don't really know. I was flying or floating and saw scenes of my life flashing before my eyes."

"OK. Hmm. That is odd. But from the moment you arrived your case hasn't been exactly typical."

"Ha! I've sensed that."

"Well, let me see if I can help when you concentrate. Hold my hands."

Earth

Father Mike begins: "We are gathered here to celebrate the life of Jack Richman, father, husband and devoted grandfather, and to say our goodbyes. It is a testament to a man's life when so many people show up to honor his life. I join the family in saying thank you for paying your respects. I hear many of you wouldn't be here today if it wasn't for him. Although, he was an accomplished surgeon please take note that we're not referring to him as Dr. Richman. He didn't want that to be his legacy. His legacy is each and every one of you."

Father Mike motions for all to rise. Christina carries Matilda in her arms. Matilda puts her head on her Mommy's shoulder. Brian, Kimberly, and Christina all share the same look of emptiness. This funeral is a lot to handle. Christina wishes she could figure out what happened to Jack so they can also have a memorial for him and say goodbye. It's part of the process and one many people need to be able to move on (or so say her books.)

Everyone's thoughts are of love for Dr. Richman and his family. They think about the loss this family is suffering and how much they must be hurting. Some too, wonder where Dr. Richman's children are. Christina has kept Jack's whereabouts private, she didn't need to deal with people's worry and concern over that too. Anna however was determined to have the ceremony soon so she can get back to Florida with Christina's parents and be in her home where all her photos and memories aree.

As the priest talks of Jack being returned to the Earth... ashes to ashes... Matilda's head pops up off her mom's shoulder and questions, "Daddy?"

Christina turns around to look, sees nothing and kisses Matilda on the forehead.

An electric light on the side of the church explodes.

Matilda eyes are still scanning the church. She knows she heard her Dad's voice. She feels him. She squeaks out, "I love you, Daddy." Tears gently flow down Christina's cheek.

Kimberly, Brian, and Christina, as well as the rest of the people, know something weird just happened. But only two people in that church know for sure that Jack is acknowledging his presence—Matilda and the medium sitting in the back of the room next to Father Moran, Shelly Southport.

Shelly nudges Father Patrick trying to get him to look in the direction of the light explosion. She has seen Jack and another hard-to-distinguish entity. They float up towards the ceiling. Shelly can't believe what she is seeing. Never has she witnessed such a sight. And then as if by magic, she sees Jack again materialize to her left, this time not as clear and with a different entity, a female one.

Jack's World

Jack takes Anthea's hands, closes his eyes and concentrates on Christina and his kids. Walls begin to form around rows full of people, and he realizes he's back at his mother's old church.

He recognizes the scene as his funeral. He'd been here before. He communicates this to Anthea. *This is one of the places Grandpa Joe took me before. It's my funeral.*

Anthea who is standing with Jack in his vision looks around. She notices a woman to her right staring at her. She finds that highly interesting and curious but continues to search for clues in this scene. Then she spots it. At the front is a picture of an old man. *Jack, who is that man in the picture?*

Jack has just noticed this himself. It's my father – Jack Richman, Dr. Jack Richman. *I didn't see that before... My father's dead? Anthea, I need to see him.*

Anthea takes in the scene and looks at her charge. *I'm sorry, Jack. Let's go back the hospital and see what we can find out.*

One more second, please. Jack moves upfront to get a glimpse of his family. He closes his eyes and gives them all energetic hugs. Brian and Kimberly give each other a curious look, smile, and then return their attention to the priest.

Anthea has moved forward with him and says, "Now, Jack." And with that she pulls her hands from his and they are back in his hospital room.

Jack takes a moment to process the scene. "So—wait—when did that happen? Can we time travel? My kids look about the same age."

Anthea explains, "Jack, time is irrelevant here. So, when we connect to energies on other dimensions sometimes it's hard to pinpoint the specific dates."

"I need to see him. He must be here, right?"

"Everyone is at some point. I'll need to speak with TD about this and find out what's going on." Anthea smiles and telepathically tells him to sit tight.

Jack is left alone in his hospital, not knowing where to begin. He begins to cry. He has reached a point and just has to release. He cries for his father, for his family, because he's scared, because he's confused, and about Grandpa Joe.

"Why, Grandpa? Why didn't you show me the whole church?"

Jack isn't expecting an answer, he doesn't smell or feel Grandpa Joe close by. But he hears his whisper, "You just needed to see your family, and that's the moment we connected to. You only saw what you wanted to see."

Jack thinks about that moment when he'd first arrived at the hospital and he'd gone on his journey with Grandpa Joe. He was right. He'd floated to the top of the church and had seen the whole picture, but he jumped to conclusions and hadn't looked around. But that was because he was being told to go towards the light... Just when he thought he could accept being here, he is forced to question every moment since his arrival. What has he seen? More importantly, what *hasn't* he seen?

TD's Office

"Madame Director," Anthea announces firmly, as she pops into TD's office to report her encounter with Jack.

The Director scowls, "Interfering again?"

"Yes, I know, I know. You can scold me later, did you happen to make note of what Jack told me about his grandfather and his father?"

"Of course I noticed, it is to be expected. I suppose I can't yell at you. At least this time you came back to me instead of trying to figure it out yourself."

"I learn."

"Better late than never, I suppose... Tell Jack this was very recent, and after they both complete their intake, they will be reunited, along with his grandfather."

"OK…"

"What? Not good enough for you?"

"Well good enough for Jack, but I am hoping you can shed a little more light on the situation for me so I know how to handle things appropriately."

"That is all you need to know. You're dismissed."

Jack's Room

Anthea reports Jack and her heart breaks for this man, lying on his bed crying. She explains TD's instructions.

"I suppose I should have expected that answer. Thanks… Sensing he needs to be alone she leaves him.

Jack gathers himself together and thinks of Faye. He needs her help.

The Council of Elders

Anthea paces nervously outside of the chamber of the Council of Elders. She is risking everything by coming here, but she had never experienced anything like this before. Jack needs to move on. Why isn't TD helping him? Anthea does not want to betray her, but in good conscience, she knows she needs to help this man.

She enters the soaring chamber, bowing before the twelve enlightened beings who sit in a semi-circle behind a curving table, dressed in iridescent robes. The space is vast and she feels so small.

"Respectfully, I beg your wisdom," she says, her eyes downcast.

"You may speak."

"I'm concerned about the soul of a patient, Jack Richman."

"Yes, child?"

"He's not progressing forward. In fact, he keeps bleeding into his old world."

"And The Director is handling this how?"

"That's the thing, she's not. She's not handling him."

Twenty-four eyes stare at her coldly.

"That is what you see." The being at the center of the table says to her. "We see all. It was courageous of you to come here, but unnecessary. The Director has our trust and approval. You may leave us now, and place your trust in her hands."

When she was gone, the Elders conferred among themselves. They would speak to TD to be certain she knew the options that lay ahead for her on her path. It was time for change, time for growth. One day, if all went according to the Council's intent, she would take her place as a leader and guide others on their paths. An entire new world of experience and service awaited her... but it would have to be her choice, her will to accept what was best for her and everyone she would touch in the future.

CHAPTER 36:
MATILDA'S VISION

Earth – 9 Days After the Explosion

"Come on, Matty, in here." As fast as she can, which isn't very fast, Matilda hurries into Brian's room after Kimberly. Brian shuts the door.

"What did you see at the funeral? You said, 'I love you, Daddy.'" Brian questions Matilda with an intensity that scares her a bit.

"I saw Daddy. Bri, why didn't he come home with us?"

Kimberly and Brian stare at each other and then back at Matilda. Kimberly slowly asks, "You're sure?"

"Yeah. Duh, I know what Daddy looks like. And he was there with an old guy too."

"You mean Grandpa?" Kimberly asks, looking at Matty in disbelief.

"No, silly. He's dead. Mommy said so."

"So who was it, Matty?" Brian says slightly impatiently.

"I dunno. If I knew I'd tell you. Jeesh!" She rolls her eyes. Kimberly does not like a dose of her own medicine.

Brian starts to talk to Kimberly, "OK. So she saw him. When I was researching the psychics they said kids are very open to seeing stuff. But why couldn't we see him, we're kids."

"I dunno. We should call that lady. She was there, she sees dead people right, maybe she saw?"

"Yeah...Ugh, Mom hid the card so I didn't try anything."

"Can you blame her, Mr. I Can Do Whatever I Want?" Kimberly snottily replies.

"HELLO? Stop talking like I'm not right here!" Matilda yells. "Where's Daddy? Why will no one tell me?"

"Mom told us, remember? He's in South Africa and there was an explosion and we haven't heard from him, so we don't know if he's dead or alive." Brian explains matter-of-factly.

"But I saw him TODAY! I'm asking Mommy." Matilda starts towards the door to go find her mom among the house full of people.

"Matty, don't. She's not going to be able to give you the answer. We believe you. I felt Daddy, you did too—didn't you Brian?"

"I think so…" Brian is not so quick to admit this. Father Moran told him if his father was passed he'd feel him. And naturally he doesn't want his father to be dead.

"Matty, we can't explain. Some things aren't explainable. But let's just keep this our little secret, like the other day when we thought we saw that bunny run across the room?"

"OK. But if Mommy asks me about it, I'm gonna tell her the truth."

CHAPTER 37: REVELATIONS

Jack's World

Jack teleports himself to Faye's room. Despite her some-times abrasive manner, Faye's maternal instinct is strong. She takes one look at Jack's face and puts her arms around him, giving him a comforting hug.

"What happened, Champ?"

"It's my dad. He's passed over. But I can't see him," Jack says, brokenly. "Faye, why am I stuck here? You pass over, and they offer to take you right up to Level 9 to reunite with your husband. I've been here for days."

"Yeah, well—they keep saying your case isn't normal. " She nudges him gently. "What do you think that means?"

"I don't know. Maybe I didn't do enough good back on Earth. Maybe I didn't suffer enough...but my time was cut short. I still have so much left to do..."

"I don't know, Jack, I'm sure they see worse souls than you come through here every day, and they don't hang around."

"I saw my dad's funeral today. I saw it when I first got here, but back then, I thought it was my own. Today I realized that my father passed. But why wasn't I there to greet him? He's here somewhere and he needs me. If I'm dead, I should be able to see him." A new realization was dawning within Jack. But he also understood that more levels of learning lay ahead for him. His very human impatience rose to the surface again.

"Whoa!" says Faye. "Did you hear what you just said?"

"Yes!" Jack says in frustration. "If I'm dead, why can't I see him?"

Faye keeps looking at him. He is a special case. Especially here.

"Oh my God." Jack says, tears streaming down his face. "Is it possible? Can I still be alive?"

With that The Director materialized into the room. "Yes, Jack. But of course, it's a little more complicated than that. I'm sorry this has been so confusing for you, but basically, your life —and your soul—hangs in the balance here. You're in a coma. I wish I could say I knew how things will end for you, but I can't. And until then, I'll continue to fight to keep your soul safe."

"My soul safe?" Jack said. *Why would his soul be in jeopardy? Safe from whom?*

"His name is Gregorios," TD says, reading his thoughts. "He's chaos incarnate, on this level. And my whole life—each of my lives, actually, I've fought him, always hoping that he will make the right choice, and in each lifetime, he never does. You're linked to him Jack, through your many lifetimes as well."

"But I don't know him...I've never seen him!" Jack protests.

"You do, Jack. He's always been there. He lived one of his most recent incarnations as your Grandpa Joe."

Jack shakes his head in denial. Grandpa Joe is his hero. He was always there for him, always kind. The Director isn't to be trusted. This place isn't to be trusted—it is a nightmarish hospital and what he needs to do is to wake up and get out and return home to his family.

"No!" he yells.

"Jack..." TD says soothingly. "I think you know that we're a sum of all of our lifetimes, and while Jack Richman was a good man, you have a past deeper than that. A past that makes you vulnerable to Gregorios."

He looks at TD, not believing her, not trusting her—and then he bolts from the room.

TD looks at Faye, shaking her head. "You're here for a reason, Faye. You're the missing piece. I need you to get through to him, that he has to face the truth."

"But what's the truth?" Faye asks.

The Director knows this is the proverbial moment for Faye, who has been an energetic receptor of new information at every opportunity here. She has consistently ascended to new levels of awareness. Now, almost with tenderness, TD touches Faye to impart the necessary knowledge to her... after which she will never be the same.

CHAPTER 38: HOPE

Earth

Shelly Southport sits in her office with the Richman family. She has taken them on pro bono, as a favor to Father Pat. The pain in this family cuts right through her. Not knowing is always hard, and for Jack Richman to have simply disappeared in that South African explosion, with no remains found, no news in days—Shelly knows it must be simply brutal to live through. She looks at Christina, a beautiful woman, but clearly fragile with grief. And the kids! So young, and they still have hope.

Shelly is torn between wishing she could give them some closure, and hoping that perhaps she can give them some hope.

"Sometimes, the connections are very strong," she begins. She looks at Brian. "Your grandfather is coming through, loud and strong. He's crossed over, he was met by his parents."

She looks at Christina. "He wants you to know, that he needed you to give him that news about Jack. It didn't kill him, it released him. Do you understand?"

Christina takes a deep breath. "I do. I've agonized over that. I should never have gone in there and just told him there was no hope."

"It wasn't what killed him, Christina. He's taking on the responsibility. What killed him was high cholesterol and, he's showing me, he never learned how to manage his stress."

Christina has to smile at that. Jack, Sr.'s temper had been the stuff of legendary stories around their home.

"I know you want... I know you all want to connect with Jack Junior. But I have to tell you. I'm not getting him. Doesn't mean he's not there, I'm just not feeling him."

"So he's alive!" Kimberly says eagerly.

Shelly looks at her, saw the little girls eyes shining with hope, and felt an optimism flare within her. "I can't say that for sure, hon, but I don't think you should give up hope yet. OK? Keep fighting."

Christina sighed. "I appreciate your meeting with us. I really do. But I think I know what we need to do now."

Brian looked at her hopefully.

"We need to go to South Africa, together, as a family. I can't stay here and wait for news anymore. I think we need to be there. We need to find him. We need to find him together."

Kimberly moved closer to her mother, wrapping her arms around her waist. Matilda ran over to join them. Brian came last, big enough now to wrap his arms around all of them.

CHAPTER 39: HOMEWARD

Jack's World

Jack runs down the hospital hallway, trying literally to run back home. He careened past gurneys and doctors, past the nurses' desk. He can see the light coming through the emergency room doors—when Faye materializes in front of him.

"Jack!" she commands. "Stop.... Wait... Listen to me!"

"No, Faye. I can't believe what's happening here. I don't know who to listen to. I have to get home."

"Jackie, Jackie, Jackie... Every story has to have an ending. But not before the story gets resolved—and your story is not resolved yet my boy. You know there's more going on here," Faye pleads.

"You are not running from Gregorios, or your grandfather. Jack, you are running from the truth and the reality of what you just experienced back there. From facing why you are here, why I am still here as well." Faye places both her hands on his chest, gently.

Jack looks in her eyes, and he knows that Faye is going to force him to see the truth.

In that moment, everything goes dark all around them and he can still hear Faye's voice.

"Just allow it, Jack. Find her...." she says.

Jack focuses on the face of his wife, Christina. She's his love, and his life, and he holds on to the image. Her face is large and illuminated, smiling at him. She's beautiful to him.

"No, Jack, don't fool yourself. Go deeper." Faye's voice echoed in his consciousness.

Christina's face morphs into Annie's. Beautiful and radiant. She is smiling a coquettish smile and dressing for dinner. The same scene he had seen before. Dressed in her nightgown, and allowing her hair to flow down, she brushes it while flirtatiously looking at him in the mirror. A dance of energy and love is about take place as he caresses her shoulders and allows one hand to go down the small of her back, and the other tilts her chin back to kiss...

He shudders in fear. As he caresses her, as he leans in to kiss her. The realization of exactly who and what he had been in one his lifetimes dawns with a sickening clarity.

"I can't!" he says, closing his eyes in fear. "I love Christina. Christina's my wife."

"This is what Grandpa Joe does not want you to see," Faye says. "This is the real reason why you were brought here. Annie needs you to open up to the truth. This truth will set free all of their souls. It's why we were all brought together. Don't you get it? They need us!" Faye is gentle, almost maternal as she guides him on his path to understanding.

"How do *you* understand this so clearly? I have been here longer than you. Exploring and pushing for answers—and then you barge in here and just solve everything? Is that it?" Jack pushes away from her in anger.

"Listen here, right now, Jack Richman!" Faye says. "There comes a time in every soul's existence when it has to take responsibility for its actions over the many lifetimes.... That's why she picked me to do this."

"She picked you? What are you talking about? Who picked you? Annie?" Jack is out of control, confused.

"The Director. She needed someone to be brought here to help. You are the key, Jack. But you were so closed off to the possibilities that she needed me to help you start to realize them."

"I am the key?" he says incredulously. "I am a science writer from Chicago... I didn't even believe in an afterlife, yet now you are telling me that I am a key to unlock some universal mystery?"

"Not just one mystery, Jack, multiple ones." Faye looks to her left and slightly behind her. There is a pool of sparkling light forming there.

The Director follows Jack, materializing like a Hollywood special effect – she is glistening and revealing the true power she actually yields in this dimension. For the first time he looks at her with respect, awe and a feeling of blissful submission. Gone is her severe black suit. Now she is clad in swirling silver and white, looking like a fierce angel.

"In life, people are all connected in ways that they will never see, Jack Richman. We all have an invisible system of energetic synapses that fire, triggering lessons and development. People attract friends and family, situations to teach them the lessons they are required to learn. Many times it is the synchronistic encounters of these trigger points that you all call coincidences that push us forward."

The Director takes a step towards Jack, reaching her hand out to touch him.

"Stop! Don't come near me! Don't touch me!" Jack feels trapped. "I don't like this. I want my grandfather, not you! He is not what you call him, he is not someone that would choose to do evil... he's a good person."

The Director doesn't back down, and now standing behind her is Anthea, glowing and powerful in her own light. She smiles at Jack, and he remembers a moment in time when he did trust her, when she helped him.

"Jack, we are all here to help each other. You *can* trust us," Anthea telepathically imparts to him.

"No... no... no... no... I cannot feel this... I cannot feel this." Jack is shaking his head back and forth.

"Denial is a powerful weapon, Jack. You don't have to listen to them. Stand with me," Gregorios whispers in his ear.

He jumps at the harshness of his grandfather's whisper.

"Jack, he is here for your soul only! He is not looking to

evolve himself or anyone else here," The Director says urgently. "Jack, I'll tell you my secret. I love him. He is me. We have been together for eons—and will continue to be."

"What do you mean?"

"I mean sometimes we're tied to the energy of another being. I see Gregorios for what he is. And I know it's my duty to thwart him, as many times as I can. Sometimes it's a game we play, but here, Jack, the stakes are very real. This time, your soul is at stake. Gregorios has evaded me lifetime after lifetime, trying to plan his approach to gain more power and control here in this world... and I have always been the yin to his yang, protecting him, helping him. In his previous incarnation, before he was your Grandpa Joe, he knew what was happening here, in my world, and he went searching for a way to manipulate it. That, Jack, is what negativity does. It tries to feed and control, so it can feed its own purpose."

Additional pools of light start to form, containing Dr. Annie Brooks, Dr. Susan Chin... Dr. White, Dr. Roberto Avanti... and Dr. Gareth Roberts.

Jack looks over at them, but they are all shadowed. He can see them, but not as vividly as Faye, Anthea and the Director. Instead of shimmering pools of light, their pools are darker, murkier.

"Why can't I see them? Why are they shadowed?" he inquired.

Dr. Gareth Roberts stands next to Anthea. The contrast between her glowing vibrancy and Gareth's dull aura physically hurts Jack.

"I don't understand what is happening. I feel like you are ganging up on me. Taking me to an intervention in some way, like I did something wrong." Jack is pleading, like a child who knows he is going to get a shot at the doctor's office and doesn't want it to happen.

"Are you READY, Jack?" The Director asks with authority. "Are you ready to release the souls that are tethered to you, to allow all of us to be free of this level and dimension and move on to the next?"

"Yes…" Jack says.

Behind him is a long dark hallway with flickering light. It looks like a scene from a 1950's hospital or asylum. A magnetic pool begins to emerge in the dark. He resists it. The Director, Annie and all the doctors, as well as Anthea, all stayed in the light. He is told to stay in the light. He instinctively knows the Dark is bad.

Once again, Jack feels like he iss alone in Hell House on Halloween, but instead of being eleven years old, he is an adult.

"I am afraid of what happens next."

"You are safe, Jack. I am here." Dr. Annie Brooks whispers from the darkness. With that, scenes from her life start rushing into his consciousness. He knows all there is to know about her. Not fragments or pieces, but whole stories are being downloaded… vivid thoughts, images and feelings. Feelings of passion and jealousy. Feelings of control and family… flooding the movie in his mind….

"It's OK, Annie. Allow yourself to let go." Jack closes his eyes. As he does, the light around Annie illuminates and tears start to fall down her cheeks. For the first time in centuries, she is allowing herself to release and feel. He is taking on her pain, he is taking on her images, emotions and her last lifetime…

Jack allows the dance to begin. He watches what is to become the torture of her afterlife. The poisoning of her children. He feels the excruciating pain of a parent, one who loves his children more than life itself, and questions how one parent could take the life of his own child, the life of their mother… He allows these feelings to wash over him… The whole time feeling like he is some sort of soul filter and he is the conduit that is to help Dr. Annie Brooks be released from her search.

Once and for all—he will do this for her. He has to admit in this moment how he feels about Annie. If this is all true, they had been in love in another lifetime. He knows he loved her in a way that he can't possibly understand.

The details keep flooding him. Scenes of happier days and passion, births and hopes mix in with the growing darkness that will eventually destroy their life together. The evil doubts and anger and beginnings of a twisted reality that will lead to madness and murder. The final piece of the puzzle falls into place. Jack Richman finally understands his role. He is Annie's husband, known to the world as the Rugeley Poisoner. He gasps out loud, feeling that the impossible is actually possible.

How could I be such a heinous creature? How could I do that to my family? I love my family? He thinks in total anguish.

The Director looks at Anthea signaling her. Anthea is in her own way conducting this dance of energy as much as the Director. She looks at Gareth Roberts and nods. He walks over and stands by Annie, holding her hand. Annie looks at him, weeping uncontrollably.

"It is OK, Annie. Let all that pain go," Dr. Roberts responds.

Jack feels something inside him open wider. He can feel himself being pulled down into the darkness. He feels Grandpa Joe beckoning him. Jack knows he has to fight it. He opens more....

The love that washes over him is overwhelming and abundant. He amplifies a healing that can only be equated to finding the cure to AIDS or cancer in the Earth world. He breathes this force of unconditional love in, and when he did he opens his eyes to the truth.

There standing before him is Annie Brooks, a woman searching for her children, a mother who feels she let her children down and failed them, and who has been a battered soul, self-persecuted and needing to be released. In the light with her are her residents... All of whom look different. They are supportive and understanding, they love her.

Jack knows her truth now. He feels it in his entire being. He breathes it. He lives it with her.

"Annie, it's OK now. You are safe. You're all safe." Jack moves toward the light of her revelation.

Annie looks at him, shakily. She is relieved to release these emotions and feelings, even if she doesn't fully understand what has happened.

The Director and Anthea look at each other, knowing something is about to happen.

"Jack... I don't know what to say, I feel like I am supposed to be helping you—and instead, you became my greatest teacher. I feel unburdened and free. I will continue my search with an open soul and heart." Annie wipes her tears away.

"But, you don't need to search anymore, Annie." Faye responds.

Annie looks at her, and then quickly to the Director, who nods. The visceral shake that began at the core of Annie's being starts like a tornado. She looks at Jack, and in his shattered eyes she sees the truth.

Annie turns to her left and sees her residents standing before her. They have worked with her for ages, assisting others to cross over; she has helped each adjust from their previous lifetime. They had been assigned to her as residents to help others. But in that moment they all know and recognize the truth. She has found her children, one by one...she has been working with them. They just need Jack to help bring them together.

Annie wraps her arms around each them, one by one.

"I am so sorry. I am so sorry," She says over and over again. They hug her back. Jack is witnessing what he can only call a miracle. He feels humbled and grateful that he has been able to spare Annie any more pain. He shifts uncomfortably, feeling the magnetized pull of the energy that is materializing down the hall. It is becoming harder for him to resist.

He looks at The Director. She feels the pull as well, but is not acknowledging it.

"Wait... there's one missing... My fifth child. He survived. I know this. Will I get a chance to meet up with his soul as well?"

Annie wipes her tears away and looks toward The Director.

"You already have, Annie," Faye says, presenting herself simply. "If I knew things were going to go down like this I would have brought a Mother's Day card or something... maybe a challah bread from my last life, or a matzo ball soup!" She walks over and allows Annie to embrace her.

Jack is awed that his energy is so connected to all of this. He doesn't understand fully, but now he accepts, at least, that there are things he will never understand.

"What about Faye's husband? Will she get to see him now?" Jack asks, unselfishly.

"Yes, she will actually. We are all going to be moving on, myself included," The Director says reluctantly. "There are always consequences to energetic choices. Mine is to make sure that Gregorios becomes accountable for what's been done. He has a lot to atone for."

Anthea looks down. She has spent so long working for TD that she is not sure what would happen to her next. She does not know—yet—that The Director has made an ultimate, selfless decision to enter a lower realm where she can help Gregorios become a better being and turn from the impulse to create havoc and chaos. If she can, TD will save Gregorios, just as she has saved Jack. If the Council of Elders will allow her to make such a choice...

Jack's world has shifted. He looks around, and he is standing back in the hallway, right outside the room where his journey began in after the explosion. As the white light pours in, Jack realizes what it is about the light in this place that has intrigued him since his arrival: It is all coming *in*, and he cannot see outside. It is almost as if the light is an opaque liquid always flowing in but not allowing any vision to penetrate it.

To his left are his friends—no, family now. Faye, Annie, Chin, Roberts, Avanti and White. To his right is The Director and Anthea. Most of his questions are finally answered.

"Except for one," Anthea says with a giggle.

"Yes. What about me?" Jack asks. "I get that somehow I

had to act as some sort of conduit for Annie to reunite with her children. I know I made mistakes in past lives. But what about *me*. Do I get to leave here, too? Am I going to evolve out of here like the others? Or is this my purpose now? Am I that guy? The one that will be the problem solver in some way for people who come through here? I want to know that I will be able to see my family again, as well. One day they, too, will pass through this dimension. I want to be able to be there for Christina, Brian, Kimberly, and Matilda."

As Jack utters their names, he gets a stronger pull to hallway behind him. The energy is becoming darker and stronger. He can't believe what he is seeing. A man is walking toward him, calling his name...

"JACK! Is that you?"

"What the hell?" Jack mutters. Too much is happening, too fast. *What is happening?* How can Faye have discovered so much so quickly? Her powers of detection must be greater than he realizes. Or, perhaps her brain functions at a higher rate of speed here in this hospital realm.

"This story has to have an ending, Jackie. They all do." Faye implies he is still resolving something.

"Jack, look at me." Annie grabs his face. "Look into my eyes..."

He does. The energy between them is amazing, he can't deny what he is feeling toward her anymore, whether he wants to hide it or not, they have a connection.

"I forgive you, Jack. I forgive you!" she says simply.

He shakes his head helplessly, only hoping that she knows he has evolved, that he is no longer that mad, angry man who had destroyed them all. He sends love to each of them, the same love he feels for Christina, Brian, Kimberly and Matilda. William, Elizabeth, Henry, Frank and John: They are all his children, and his love for them, and his regret, is crushing.

There were no words that come into Jack's mind, nor from his mouth. Only: *My children. My. Children. Children. My life. My children...*

One by one, Annie and Jack's children from that lifetime come and give him a hug of understanding and forgiveness. Although it happens quickly, in Earth time, it seems to move with liquid slowness. Each child, now a mature being, each of whom had helped Jack in the hospital, each of whom had shared their love with him, approach him and look into his eyes. Little had he known… How could he have known?

They wish him well in his next evolution and free him of his soul's karma. Their generosity of spirit nearly crushes Jack in an embrace of love. The spirit squeezes his soul.

Annie walks toward the exit of the hospital with her residents, the children she has searched for forever. She walks into the light of the outside world.

"Jack, pretty amazing shit we just experienced her? Eh?" Faye hugs him and whispers, "I think you by far made up for it in your last life with your children, please release this now."

She kisses him on the cheek and runs out the same exit into the light…

"Well, that leaves three of us" Anthea says.

"No, we're all leaving," The Director responds. "All of our choices have brought us here, to a crossroads. Anthea, I am leaving this dimension. I must work with the Council to deal with Gregorios. We have new paths to walk. You are taking over here as The Director. I know you can do it." She gives Anthea a small, proud smile.

"But, TD! I can't imagine this place without you. I'll miss you. And I'll make you proud, I promise!" Anthea says, glowing with excitement about her promotion.

"And I will miss you." The Director hugs her ward. "I have one parting piece of advice. Get someone as amazing as you to assist you."

Jack wishes he could push a pause button right now. So much is happening that he can barely absorb it. First, the revelation about his children, then, The Director's decision to turn over the management of the hospital to her No. 2. His spirit is trying to absorb it all in a very short time.

Anthea smiled in appreciation and says, "How will I know who that person is?"

"I think you already do," Jack says.

Anthea looked towards Jack and smiles. "You're perfect."

The Director, sighs. Anthea is very talented, but she has not yet reached the state of all-knowningness. She interjected, "No! Not him... her!" She reaches out, laying her hand on Anthea's shoulder, and Anthea feels herself suffused with the ability to see and know all that was happening in her new domain.

They turn, and Daisy appears. Her last life experience has made her the perfect counterpart for Anthea. She has an understanding of pain and suffering in the human experience and will be perfect to assist others in their life reviews.

"Let's get started, my ward," Anthea says to Daisy, and they vanish.

"So am I being punished for my actions in that past lifetime?" Jack asks.

"Jack, the universe on all levels is not a place of punishment. It is one of balance. You were necessary to be here to achieve that balance. Destiny is a real thing, but free will is even greater. In that past lifetime, you made poor choices, and it rippled out and affected the lives of many more people than you know. You being here, has helped to put that in balance. It's time for you to move on as well."

The Director motions toward the darkness of the hallway. Jack feels its inexorable pull but continues to resist.

"No. Please don't send me into the Dark. You told me the light was where I needed to stay. I don't want to be sent to hell or whatever place you call it here," Jack pleads.

"Jack, what do you feel right now?" she asks.

"I feel relieved and isolated."

"What else?"

"I feel a ridiculous pull down that hallway toward that man who has been calling my name out."

"How does that make you feel?" she probes.

"Honestly, it makes me feel like I want to run that direction, but I don't want to go to the dark. I don't want to make bad choices again, I don't want to hurt anyone, ever again..." He looks into her eyes helplessly, seeking absolution.

"Take this, you're going to need it." TD hands something to Jack.

He looks down and looks quickly back up at her in astonishment. Moosey! "How did you get this?" he asks.

"Hello, son."

Jack turns quickly and sees his father standing there.

"Dad? Oh my God, *Dad*. I've been wanting to find you here."

"I thought you would be there, when I crossed. But instead, it was my mother and my father... all my aunts and uncles... but not you, son. Not you. Thank God I found you." Dr. Richman says, wrapping his arms around Jack.

"I don't belong here, Dad. I need to get back home. I'm not done yet!" Jack says desperately.

"I know, son. I know... I cannot help you with this. Just know I love you and will always love you. You were a better father to your children than I was to you. I am proud of you, and you are my boy... Always." Jack's dad embraces him.

"You'll need to say your goodbyes, now," TD says with a cool smile.

"Goodbyes? Why would I have to say my goodbyes?" The two Jacks look at each other...

The Director gives her final piece of information before she leaves her role and this job to move on.

"To quote your daughter Faye, every story has an ending. This story is one that Dad cannot be part of. Your next adventure will completely help you pay off all the karma of the previous lifetimes. It's time to move on."

Jack knows he is faced with a choice and a challenge—to stay in the hospital like Annie did for God knows how long, or to accept the challenge that was calling him down the darkness of the corridor. He holds Moosey close to his chest and says, "You asked me a question before that I didn't answer, and my response is, yes, I am ready to face that darkness."

"For what it's worth, Jack, in all my years doing this, this has been my favorite case," The Director says, with a wink.

Jack winks back at her. "I love you, Dad," he says, as he turns to walk down the corridor toward that dark energy. The lights keep flickering and dimming. They go completely black for a second, and in that second he hears his dad whisper, "Tell your mother she was the prettiest girl at the fair."

The lights come up and Jack finds himself in a part of a hospital that has tremendous activity. Yelling and screaming… beeping… Nothing like the tranquil place he was just in. He doesn't like the feeling he was having. This is a more dense place, a lower level of energy and existence in some way. Where the world had been light and airy now it is heavy, somehow more substantial. The people he is floating past seem not to notice him.

He is thrust into a room, and it is as if his perspective suddenly is from a darkened closet. He can't see anything but the crack of light. He reminds himself that it only takes a little bit of light to alleviate all the darkness, so he refuses to succumb to the fears he had as a child. Instead he holds on to Moosey. He pulls Moosey closer, the soft toy reminding him of his old life. One day, he would be reunited with that family as well…

"Mom? Can he hear us?"
POP!
Jack is standing at the foot of his bed. Brian and Kimberly stood on each side of him.

"He's in a coma, you idiot," Kimberly says. " People in comas can't hear you. Mrs. Literia said he was like a cucumber."

Jack is staring at how old he appears in the bed, not the etheric image he has been accustomed to. The perfect body is gone, and there he lies with all the miles of a typical thirty-something man.

"You moron," Brian taunts. "A vegetable. She compared him to a vegetable not a cucumber."

"A cucumber is a vegetable!"

"Guys... really?" Christina says. "Is this how we are going to spend our hour with him?"

Jack is dazed and stunned. Hour? He stares at this scene for what feels like an eternity. and then it all ends when he questions it.

Jack's world slowly melds with the reality of the earthly plane. He realizes that the weight of his physicality is returning, the pull of gravity on his body—which he has gotten used to being without. And one by one, as if switches are being turned on, his senses come back. He can hear the murmur of voices and smell the air in the room where he lies. First n his fingers, then his arms, then throughout his entire body, he feels what had once been normal but now seems a new and odd sensation of movement as blod flows within his veins. Had it stopped flowing when he was on the Other Side?

Now he is reclaiming his life and his physical being. Emotions flood through him even as he begins to understand that to those around him he is still "unconscious." What is *consciousness,* anyway? he muses.

"What is going on?" he asks softly. He is finally and fully back in his battered earthly body. His gratitude is immense. He is so overwhelmed to see his family, to feel their presence, to be with them again. He realizes what he needs to tell them.

"I love you. I love you all, so much," he whispers to them, realizing this is just the beginning of his journey.

The Council of Elders

The Director, now the *former* Director, faces the twelve Elders who meet her gaze directly, their thoughts focused as one with care, concern and gratitude.

"Your decision is not necessarily the one we would have recommended, but it was one option," the senior female Elder states—rather, communicates with her mind, touching the other's mind and soul. The words, though straightforward and somewhat critical, are filled with emotion.

The entire Council is listening intently, and the spirit in the chamber blankets the women standing before them.

"I understand," The Director says, with deep humility. "I am merely pursuing the truth as it has been made known to me."

"That is the essence of wisdom. I hope you can continue to find your way through the truth and to the truth—and that you may guide another in that direction, too. For the good of all."

"My hope also. When I first started as Director of the hospital, I never would have thought that something like Jack Richman's story could have happened in the way it did and in so short a time. There is something of a miracle happening here. Even I haven't absorbed it all yet."

Another Elder says, "We chose you in the first place because we felt you possess the vision needed in such a role and the strength of mind and character to do the difficult things that are required to restore balance and justice in such cases. No doubt, the task has depleted your energies, yet you wish to delve deeper and are willing to move to a lower level with your subject in order to achieve the best outcome for the subject, the one called Gregorios."

In the silence that follows, the former Director closes her eyes but opens her soul to receive the blessing of the Council. And in that moment she glimpses Jack Richman on Earth, restored to his family, his spirit healed, becoming attuned to a new phase of life—to the gift of *life*. She wonders what lies ahead for him and for those he loves.

"We never know at the beginning how a story is going to end, do we?"

No, the Council answers in a unanimous voice. *We depend on you to tell us. So, please stay in touch.*

CPSIA information can be obtained
at www.ICGtesting.com
Printed in the USA
LVHW081357251120
672668LV00036B/516